THE SILENT SCREAM

In total, the presentation probably only lasted fifteen minutes, but it seemed three or four times that long. It's hard to describe what I saw—body parts, blood, and these strange machines that looked straight out of a futuristic science fiction movie. It was horrifying yet strangely exhilarating at the same time.

The most amazing thing by far—and if I'd seen it anywhere else I'd have laughed and sworn it was faked— was a human head severed below the chin, with its spinal column still attached but openly exposed in a glass chamber filled with some milky amber-colored fluid. It was the head of a male, a dark haired man whose age was virtually impossible for me to even guess at. His eyes would open and close every four to five seconds, his nose twitched steadily, and once his mouth opened up wide in what appeared to be a soundless scream....

THE
JIGSAW
MAN

GORD ROLLO

LEISURE BOOKS NEW YORK CITY

A LEISURE BOOK®

August 2008

Published by

Dorchester Publishing Co., Inc.
200 Madison Avenue
New York, NY 10016

ISBN 10: 0-8439-6012-4
ISBN 13: 978-0-8439-6012-9

The name "Leisure Books" and the stylized "L" with design are trademarks of Dorchester Publishing Co., Inc.

Printed in the United States of America.

10 9 8 7 6 5 4 3 2 1

This novel is dedicated to my father, James Rollo, who gave me my love for reading and helped inspire my first steps toward becoming a writer. While this book might not exactly be his cup of tea, I think he'll get a kick out of it....

No book is ever truly written alone, so I'd be remiss if I didn't acknowledge some of the people who have helped make this happen: Gene O'Neill, Michael Laimo, J. F. Gonzalez, David Nordhaus, Brian Keene, Jimmy Z Johnston, Shane Staley, and Don D'Auria. I also want to give a shout-out to my brothers Tony, Brian, and Stuart, and a special thank-you to my wife Debbie for putting up with me.

THE
JIGSAW
MAN

PROLOGUE

The Reason

Drummond Brothers Rock and Bowl,
North Tonawanda, New York

Hell of a place, Drummond's, an old-fashioned, family-run bowling alley suffering from an identity crisis of late. The comfy wooden tables and chairs have been replaced with ugly black plastic stools with shiny chrome legs; the soft overhead fluorescent lighting with purple and red retina-destroying spotlights; the soothing background music with bass-heavy, blow-out-your-eardrums heavy alternative rock. People used to come here with family and friends to bowl, have some good clean fun, and the best damn cola floats in Western New York. Now the rowdy young crowds come to get drunk, fight, shot put the bowling balls at their buddy's head, and scream out obscenities and pickup lines over the horrendously loud music.

If old Mr. Drummond were still around to see what his sons had done to the family business, he'd have burned the place to the ground, his good-for-nothing prodigies still trapped inside. Still, the Rock and Bowl, with all its gaudiness and utter contempt for its humbler beginnings, was making money hand over fist—even the old man couldn't have argued with that.

Thursday night. A big crowd.

Two guys sitting at the end of the bar, a bit older than the usual early twenties crowd, three more friends standing at their backs cheering wildly as the seated pair raise their frosty mugs to their lips and start chugging.

The phone rings on the wall behind the bar, twice, three times, hard to hear over the pulsing hypnotic beat of Rob Zombie's "Living Dead Girl" blaring on the overhead speakers. Finally, the overweight bartender waddles over, answers it, cupping his free hand around the earpiece to hear what the caller wants. His face drains of color as he slowly turns to look at one of the beer drinkers.

He lays the phone down on the back counter, approaches the group of five men joking and arguing over who won the chug contest, and leans over the bar to interrupt them.

"It's the police," he tells the thin drunk sitting on the right. "Lookin' for you. You'd better come take this."

The man looks worried but is still trying to play it cool in front of his friends. He rises to his feet, almost trips over the chair, and stumbles and weaves his way toward the far end of the bar where it's open and he can walk around to grab the phone. Fear has him by the short hairs but he isn't sure why. For a moment, vertigo hits hard and the noisy room starts to spin. He grabs the counter to steady himself, closing his eyes tightly until the nauseous sensation passes. Then, the phone—

"Hello?"

"Michael Fox?" A cold voice. Irish accent.

"Uh-huh. Who's this?"

The inebriated man listens quietly for several minutes, swaying on his feet, threatening to go down at any minute. He remains upright, it's the phone that drops to the floor, already forgotten as the man screams and runs for the exit. Outside, it's raining hard. He's had far too much to drink tonight to be sprinting but that doesn't stop him from trying, the police officer's words still haunting him, urging him onward.

"I'm sorry, Mr. Fox, but there's been an accident. . . ."

PART ONE

THE BRIDGE

CHAPTER ONE

Asleep in the gutter, middle of the afternoon, the concrete curb not a very comfortable pillow. I don't actually remember waking up, but I know I lay there for several minutes in the grip of the dragon, shaking like I had Parkinson's, waiting for the pain in my bones to go away before even trying to open my eyes. When I did, it was a mistake, the sunlight burning into my head, setting my drug-saturated brain on fire. My skull felt like it was going to crack wide open. Part of me wished it would.

Why the fuck do I keep doing this to myself? How can I be so weak? So stupid?

Good questions. Not so easy to answer. Everyone on the street has their own dragon, their own personal demon that keeps them in check. Whatever it is, it'll make you feel good, sure, let you soar with the eagles for a while, but it's a hell of a fall back to ground level. Dreams were for regular people, not guys like me. Every time I got too cocky, started thinking I might make it out of here back to the real world, the dragon reared up and bit me on the ass again, making damn sure I knew my place.

To each his own, but my dragon's name was Sterno,

that stinky blue-flamed fuel people used to warm their hands on ski trips or to caramelize brandy inside those big glasses when they ordered dessert coffees in fancy restaurants. You can buy Sterno easily enough but it's expensive and to be honest, I didn't need to buy it. I broke into cars for mine. It's common knowledge for hardcore street folks, especially the people who've survived long enough to learn what's what up here in the colder climates, that the emergency kits people carry around in the glove box or under their front seat are mini gold mines. They held the kind of things we regularly needed: matches, Band-Aids, aspirins, needle and thread, chocolate, and—surprise—a little container of Sterno fuel, in case you broke down in the snow and needed a little heat to make it through a cold night until help arrived.

You strained it through a slice of bread, which got rid of most of the poisonous shit, then drank the alcohol base that was left. Don't try it; it's horrible tasting, a lot like wood alcohol, but man does it make your problems go away in a hurry.

So I finally dry-heaved my way into a sitting position, reminding myself that it had been a few days since my last meal. I was thirsty. Really thirsty, and like magic this bottle of water appeared in front of my eyes. There's a hand attached to the bottle, and my eyes followed the dark-skinned arm up, surprised to see the only real friend I had left in the world smiling down at me.

Blue J was an all right dude, once you got by his ever-increasing penchant for sniffing glue, and his rather nasty habit of vomiting on himself while sleeping it off.

His name had been Jason when I first met him, a real good-looking guy. Tall, dark piercing eyes, smooth black skin—looked a bit like Wesley Snipes, without the attitude. Unfortunately, life on the street had stolen his good looks. His pretty-boy ebony skin had turned pasty and discolored, for some strange reason turning a shade closer to blue than black. I didn't know if it was all the glue he sniffed or the cheap booze he guzzled, but that was why I changed his name. Whatever I called him, he was a decent guy, bad complexion and all.

"Hey, buddy," he said. "Wanna sip?"

Man, did I. I had this god-awful taste in my mouth, and I could just imagine the foul smell of my breath right now. I grabbed the water and drained the whole bottle in a greedy series of gulps. It wasn't until I was done and handing the bottle back that I noticed my friend wasn't alone. He had a woman with him. Well, more of a girl than a woman, but who was I to judge. She was pretty: dark hair, nice legs, and a big set of cans squeezed into a dress two sizes too small. She was a little dirty and rough-looking around the edges but hey, weren't we all?

"This here's my man, Mike," Blue J said to her.

She nodded, apparently satisfied. I might have asked what her name was but I had a good idea where this was leading so her name wasn't really important. I put a half smile on my face—the best I could do with my head still pounding—and went with the flow.

"What's up, J?" I asked, eyeing the girl's curvy body, quickly moving from one vice to the next as I climbed shakily to my feet.

"Well, unless you got 'portant places to go, this here fine lady say she wanna party with us. Dig?"

I dug.

Blue J wasn't the handsome man he'd once been, and Lord knows I wasn't anyone's definition of a lady-killer, but we still made out all right. Why? Simple: at the start of each month—for as long as they lasted—we had drugs. J received a monthly prescription of Valium, clonazepam, and Haldol as part of his Vets disability. He'd only spent five months over in Desert Storm, but he'd convinced some doctor at the VA hospital he was suffering from depression and combat dementia. He rarely took any of his own drugs, instead saving them to barter for food, booze, and, like today, the services of a young runaway.

Don't read too much into that. J and I weren't bad guys. This was just the way life worked on the street, a business deal for people who had nothing else to offer. Drugs for sex—where was the harm in that?

"I'm in," I said. "Lead the way."

Blue J winked at me, dug in his pocket to hand each of us a blue pill. The girl and I dry-swallowed the pills without even asking what they were, then she marched off down the sidewalk. J and I hurried to keep pace.

She took us several blocks uptown, then veered into an alleyway between a Chinese restaurant and a Bank of America. She was living beneath a rusty, metal staircase that led to the second floor of the restaurant. Somewhere she'd found a big green tarp and had strung it under the stairs to make a fairly effective roof. The tarp draped down near the ground, giving her shelter from the elements and, more importantly, us a small degree of privacy.

Inside, J and I went right to work, getting her out of her gear in a hurry. None of us were expecting romance, and foreplay just wasn't happening when three drugged-up losers were huddled inside a four-by-ten-foot shelter. I was getting ready to do my thing when J blew the whole deal.

"What's your name again, sugar doll?" he asked.

"Arlene," she smiled, her eyes already glassing over from whatever it was J had given her.

Oh shit.

. . . rain pouring down as I run, tears just as heavy flooding from my eyes, stumbling blind past the dark buildings and parked cars until I spot the flashing lights of the police cars and ambulance. I run harder, panic and desperation the only things keeping me on my feet. Then I'm there among the twisted metal, policemen pushing me around until I can stammer out who I am. Their attitude changes then, but all I notice is the upside-down car, and the diluted puddles of crimson staining the pavement below the driver-side door . . .

That was it for me. My hard-on did a nosedive, and I made a dash for the alleyway, throwing up my stomach-full of water with my jeans around my ankles. Blue J poked his head out of the tarp to see what was wrong but I waved him away, pulled up my pants, and bolted for the street.

Arlene was my daughter's name. *Is* her name, I should say. She survived the crash that killed my wife and son that awful night, but not her old man's stupidity in the months and years to come. Good thing my sister-in-law Gloria was good enough to take care of her when I couldn't. I haven't seen Arlene in nearly three years. I wanted to, of course, but by the time my head had straightened enough to know what was important in life, she refused to see me. Can't say I blame her.

Arlene'll be seventeen now, a young woman all set to head to college next fall. She's probably—

Probably a lot like the young girl you just left stoned on her back with Blue J. You're a real fuckin' hero, Mike. Father-of-the-year candidate, once again.

"Shut up!" I screamed out loud, causing several nearby pedestrians to take a wide path around me.

One thing crazy people in the city never had was a lack of elbow room. Was I crazy, though?

Truly crazy?

I dropped to my knees on the sidewalk, sobbing uncontrollably, on one hand ignoring the question, but then again, perhaps answering it all in the same motion. Who knows? Who cares?

I was so sick of living like this.

I just wanted to end the suffering. Mine, Arlene's . . . everybody's. From my knees I eyed up the traffic roaring by on the street beside me. It would be so easy to just get up and stumble out in front of—

Stop, I scolded myself. *You know that's not the way it should go down.*

True.

I had a better plan.

For months I've been thinking about it, setting things up, ironing out the kinks. Now all it took was having the balls to go through with it. I could do it, though. No worries there. It had nothing to do with me anyway. It was all for Arlene. I'd destroyed any chance of a life we might have had together, but if I could pull my shit together one last time, I could maybe give her a start on the life she deserved. The life I'd selfishly stolen away.

Do it then. No more bullshit. For once in your pitiful life do the right thing.

Climbing to my feet, tears dried up and long gone, I stood still, eyes closed, thinking about Arlene while I swayed to the music of the city. I was in no hurry and didn't give a shit if I was blocking people's way.

Tomorrow, I decided.

I still had a letter to write and a package to drop in the mail, but tomorrow afternoon would be perfect. I could have pulled it off tonight but screw it; tonight I was going out to get rip-roaring drunk.

Why the hell wouldn't I?

CHAPTER TWO

Trust me, I wasn't about to get all teary-eyed leaving my home and worldly belongings behind. Good riddance, as far as I was concerned. Everything I owned was crap anyway, someone else's tossed-out garbage. I wouldn't need them again, that was for sure. It was one of the few perks of planning to kill yourself—you didn't need to pack luggage.

I should introduce myself better. Sorry, my head wasn't screwed on quite right yesterday. My name's Michael Fox, Mike to my friends, but unfortunately most people just called me a bum. I was homeless, that much was true, but for the record I certainly wasn't a bum. I was a fairly regular-looking white boy, thirty-nine years old, five foot ten, one hundred and seventy pounds, with dark hair and a baby-stubble beard that steadfastly refused to grow more than a few downy curls. Sure, I begged for money and food, but I also worked here and there, whenever I could. Some of the money I earned I used to buy clothes, and I washed them regularly at the local Laundromat. Basically I tried to stay clean, to stay *human*, as best I could.

For the last year and a half, I'd lived in Buffalo, New York, not that it mattered much. The name of the city was sort of irrelevant. Where I actually *lived*, was in a blue metal Dumpster beneath the rusted-out Carver Street Railway Bridge. For whatever reason, the Dumpster wasn't used by the city anymore, so me, Blue J, and another street loser named Puckman had inherited it, flipped it on its side, crammed it full with our individual yet collectively useless junk, moved in, and called it home sweet home. Lovely.

It was always cold, always crowded, and it reeked of cheap booze, vomit, and layer after layer of filthy piss- and shit-stained clothing. The roof leaked so badly we were forced to huddle together at one end to avoid getting soaked, and that was if it was only a light sprinkle. If it was a downpour—forget it—we may as well stand outside. The Carver Street Bridge, about thirty feet above, helped shelter us a bit, but we had to put up with the rickety old freight trains thundering across it day and night, every twelve hours.

It was a terrible way to live. Degrading. We were like sewer rats—worse—at least the rats were too ignorant to realize how much life like this really sucked. The best thing I could say about our crummy little corner of the world was that being located beneath the bridge, at least I wouldn't have to walk very far to kill myself. Good thing, too, because I was exhausted, mentally and physically. So goddamned weary, I wasn't sure if I'd have enough energy to climb the muddy embankment in time to make the next train or not.

As quietly as I could, small brown package in hand, I stepped over the passed-out prone body of Blue J, sprawled in his usual late afternoon position blocking our makeshift plastic tarp doorway. Dropping my last forty cents—a quarter and three nickels—into his shirt pocket, I silently wished him luck and eased out the door without disturbing him.

Outside, Puckman was sitting on the ground, leaning

up against one of the rectangular concrete bridge abutments, about fifteen feet to my left. He was busy eating what looked like a large rat but might just as easily have been a small brown kitten. Normal society might frown on such a feast, but around here a meal was a meal. It had probably been hit by a car and left sticking to the road somewhere. Roadkill wasn't exactly one of the staples of any homeless person's well-balanced diet, but when times were tough you ate whatever was available. Nothing better than a half-burnt/half-raw hunk of unrecognizable meat with the tread marks from a truck tire still visible on it. It might be disgusting and make you want to puke—hell, sometimes it *did* make you puke—but you did whatever you had to do to survive on the street.

Anyway, Puckman was chewing away on *something*, when his beady little eyes turned and locked on mine. His face contorted into an angry grimace and, believe it or not, he actually started to growl. Obviously, he had no intention of sharing his meal with me. Not that he had to worry. I didn't want anything to do with the crazy bastard today.

Puckman wasn't my friend. Never had been, never would be. Blue J and I put up with him because he paid us rent, if you could call it that, to share our Dumpster. Sometimes he paid with money but more often he supplied us with food and clothing. He was good at begging and was an even better pickpocket and thief. Other than that, he was a no-good lousy bum. It was guys like him that gave the rest of us homeless people a bad name.

Puckman was a short fat Mexican with greasy black hair hanging halfway down his back. He didn't even know where he was most of the time, far too whacked-out on homemade Screech to realize he wasn't still pining away in sunny Acapulco, or wherever the hell it was he came from. He'd been brought up to Canada three summers ago on a temporary work visa, to pick tobacco. It was real hard work but they were treated well and the pay was excellent. The manual labor was too much for his fat lazy ass, though, and he'd made a dash for the U.S. border, swimming across the Niagara River near Fort Erie to illegally enter this home of the brave and land of the freeloader.

The name Puckman came from his annoying obsession with collecting hockey pucks. He'd gathered hundreds of them from all over the city and they were stashed away in dozens of white plastic bags in his corner of the Dumpster. There were so many of the damned things he was forced to sleep on top of them but he didn't seem to mind. He told me I'd understand if I'd ever lived in Canada where hockey was like a religion. Yeah, right. He'd spent three weeks in Canada, on a tobacco farm, in the hottest part of August, and somehow he'd become an authority on their favorite winter sport. What a crock of shit. Puckman wasn't an authority on anything; he was just a lunatic and definitely not someone I was sad to be leaving behind.

"Adios, asshole, see you in hell," I called over to him, then started walking away.

He growled at me again, smiling triumphantly, like he'd won some tough-guy macho battle because I hadn't asked for a nibble of his yummy supper. He wouldn't be smiling so much if he'd known I had one of his beloved hockey pucks stuffed in the pocket of my ragged jacket. When that freight train was screaming toward me, ready to bust my body into hundreds of pieces, my hope was that God would grant me one last wish. I wanted to look down from the bridge, hurl that stupid hard rubber disc at Puckman's big fat head, and bean him one right square in the kisser. Then I could die a happy man. It probably wouldn't pan out that way but I could always hope, right?

Without another glance, I began climbing the steep muddy embankment leading up to Carver Street. From there, I could walk straight out onto the bridge and wait for my ticket out of this shitty life. I slipped and stumbled on the way up but within a minute I was standing on the first railway tie, at the foot of the bridge.

The Carver Street Railway Bridge was a fine example of human stupidity at its best. As far as I knew, bridges were usually constructed to span the distance over the top of something: things like rivers, canyons, or other roads and train tracks. Not this bridge; it stretched a track across an expanse of about eighty feet over the top of—nothing. Well, Blue J and Puckman were down there, but I seriously doubted they were in the city planner's mind when the bridge was designed. Maybe at one time a road had been planned, but for whatever reason, hadn't been built? I have no idea. Doesn't matter.

I started out onto the bridge, only to remember the brown envelope under my arm. *Idiot.* How could I possibly forget something so important? It was vital I drop my package in the mail before going through with this. Luckily, that wouldn't take too long. There was a postal box only half a block south of Carver on Dupont Street.

The package was addressed to Gloria Churchill, the sister-in-law I mentioned. Inside were the last three things I would ever give to my daughter. There was an envelope of cash—only a hundred and thirty dollars from my last SI check—a letter, and an insurance policy I'd taken out on myself. The cash was meaningless, but it was all I had. The letter was short and sweet, telling Arlene things you don't have the need or the right to hear, but the insurance policy, *that* was the important thing. I'd been making the premiums through Gloria for well over a year now, and if anything was to happen to me, like say, being *accidentally* run over by a freight train, I'd set it up so Arlene would be the recipient of the death benefits. It wasn't a lot, just twenty-five thousand dollars, but that would be more than enough to get her first few years in college out of the way. Might even pay for it all. Either way, it would give her some breathing room to pursue whatever dreams she had for life.

I'll admit, I selfishly hoped she'd think nice things about me, maybe tear down the wall she'd built around her heart to keep me out, but in the end none of that would really matter. At least I'd finally be helping her out, finally be her dad, instead of the forgotten loser who always buggered things up.

At the mailbox, I checked and rechecked the address and made sure the postage stamps were stuck on securely. With a tear in my eye, I kissed the package good-bye and prayed to whatever gods were listening for the envelope to make it safely to Arlene's door. If my death could give her the key to a happy life, it would be worth it. I hoped she was old enough to understand that.

Hurrying back to the tracks, I paused to catch my breath, gazing out across the bridge's rusty rails to a spot on the horizon about three miles away. There, cutting a line across an elevated grassy knoll on the outskirts of the city, was another set of railway tracks. Twice a day, six days a week, a freight train out of Erie, Pennsylvania, would roll down that hill, snake through the bowels of the city, and then rocket across the Carver Street Bridge on its way to Rochester, New York. Twelve hours later, the same train—or more likely, one that just looked a lot like it—would rumble back across this bridge, reversing its route, heading home to Erie. After all the times this train had roared over my pathetic excuse for a home, I still had no idea what type of cargo it carried.

I guess I never would.

Almost as if my thinking about it caused it to happen, the train slowly chugged into view, temporarily reducing its speed as it descended into the city. I watched the train until it disappeared behind the tall buildings and then immediately began walking out onto the bridge. If the freight train didn't experience any unusual delays, I had approximately eight minutes left to live.

CHAPTER THREE

September in Buffalo was a great time of year. Beautiful. The trees were turning a million different colors, the temperature had finally dropped back into the sixties and seventies, and the stale city air felt clean again after a long summer filled with sweat and smog. Fall was by far my favorite time of year, but unfortunately clean air and pretty leaves just weren't enough to postpone today's plan.

There were many reasons why I wanted to kill myself, but other than the insurance policy, none of them were particularly important. I had the same sad sob story most homeless people tell. Had the good job, nice family, nice little house with the white picket fence, blah, blah, blah. None of it mattered. I lost it all; that's what counted. You know some of it already, and can probably guess the rest. My wife, Jackie, and my little boy, Daniel, were killed during a heavy rainstorm in an automobile accident. No other vehicles were involved. Jackie was driving, but it was a hundred percent my fault. A few buddies had talked me into going bowling of all damn things. We played a few games, hit the bar, and before long I was drunk out of my mind and called Jackie to come pick me up.

"It's only a few raindrops, honey, what could possibly happen?"

Famous last words.

Anyway, I lost everything important to me that day—my wife and son to death, my daughter to hatred—lost my job and the house about seven months later, moved into the whiskey bottle on a full-time basis, and ended up here on this bridge ready to say, Fuck it, I'm out of here. I don't need to explain myself. I don't need a reason to die. I'm doing it for Arlene, but to tell you the truth I'm also fed up with the rest of life's bullshit. Plain and simple—I've had enough.

I never heard the car pull up behind me, lost in my sorry-for-myself thoughts, but when I made it to the bridge's halfway mark and turned around, there it was. It was one of those big stretch limousines—sparkling white with golden trim and matching gold wire spoke rims. Christ, it looked about thirty feet long. A car like that stuck out almost as much as a dancing elephant would've, in this neighborhood. I was momentarily taken aback at the sight of it, but not because of how out of place this fancy car was. What surprised me most was how *familiar* it looked. I couldn't remember where or when, but I was positive I'd seen this limo before.

The rear driver's-side door suddenly opened and a tall muscular man in an expensive gray pinstripe suit stepped out onto Carver Street. He looked at me, bent down to say something to the driver, and then started walking out onto the bridge. He was white, bald-headed with a neatly trimmed goatee, stood maybe six foot four, and guessing, I'd say he weighed at least two hundred and sixty pounds. My surprise was quickly turning into shock because as he approached, I realized that he too looked familiar. Where the hell had I seen this guy and his car before? I tried, but just couldn't remember.

What does he want?

Now there was a good question. All kinds of nasty scenarios spun through my head. Did I owe somebody money and this monster had been sent to collect it? That would be just my luck—I'm out here ready to commit suicide, and some big ape was going to break my legs before I got the chance. I seriously considered running for the far side of the bridge but what he said stopped me dead in my tracks.

"Wait, Mr. Fox. I need to speak with you about something important. Really important."

How did he know my name? I was scared, but I didn't run. I waited until he came within fifteen feet.

"That's close enough," I said. "What do you want?"

"Nothin'. Just to talk for a minute. Trust me, it'll be worth your while."

I laughed at that one. If I had a nickel for every time someone on the street told me I could trust them, well, I guess I wouldn't be a homeless bum anymore. But I *was* homeless, and I wasn't falling for it.

"You may not believe this," I said, "but I think I've heard that line before. If my so-called friends screwed me, why should I trust a complete stranger like you?"

"Because I'm not really a stranger, am I? Don't you remember me, Mr. Fox? We met briefly last night. You were pretty out of it. Maybe you've forgotten?"

His words triggered a memory of me being punched in the face and tossed roughly to a threadbare green-carpeted floor. Not a very nice recollection and I'd heard enough. I decided to run from this mysterious man after all. Before I'd taken my first step, though, my jumbled memories of last night cleared and I did remember meeting him. It hadn't been him who'd hit me. It had been someone else. This man had tried to help.

Yeah, now I remembered. I wanted to go out with a bang, try one last time to fit into this crazy world before calling it a life. After leaving Blue J and the young woman behind, I picked out some new clothes at the local Catholic Church. They weren't anything fancy but they were clean, dry, and best of all, free. I cleaned myself up and went to one of the local bars to have a drink. It was a stupid mistake. I'd been drinking with Puckman before leaving the Dumpster—grape Kool-Aid and cheap gin—and had smuggled a flask of it into the bar. I was almost too drunk to stand up, but nobody seemed to care about that. It wasn't until the bartender caught me sipping out of the flask instead of buying my drinks that all hell broke loose. He sent a bouncer over to toss me, but I was too stupid to go quietly on my merry way. Not me. I picked a fight with this man-mountain and soon I'm eating his considerably large fist and picking myself up off the floor.

"You helped me, didn't you? That bouncer was ready to mop the floor with me and you stepped in to drag him away. Everybody started fighting, but I ducked out the side entrance and took off. Your car, your white limo there, it was parked outside by the curb. I knew I'd seen it before."

"That's right. Now let's get off this bridge and go have a drink. The train will be wandering by in about what, three, four minutes?"

"How . . . how—" I tried but he cut me off.

"We've been watching you. You've been timing the train all week but this is the first time you've wandered out onto the tracks. Suicide's not the answer, Mr. Fox."

Had I been that obvious? It terrified me that this muscle head had been following me around without me having the slightest clue, but it also pissed me off at the same time. What right did he have to talk to me like that? I'd kill myself if I damn well pleased—thank you very much. To hell with this clown if he didn't approve. Let him try to survive on the street like I had. Take away his fancy car and expensive clothes and he probably wouldn't last six months.

"Suicide's not the answer?" I asked sarcastically. "But I suppose you are, right?"

"Not me, Mr. Fox, the man I work for."

He walked over to me, removed his billfold from his pants pocket and pulled out two crisp hundred-dollar bills. He handed them over and started walking away toward the safety of Carver Street. I glanced down at the money in my hand—the most money I'd possessed at one time in three years—and had to ask.

"What's this for?"

Looking back over his shoulder, he paused to say, "Chump change, Mr. Fox. You get that for simply coming down off the bridge. There's two hundred more if you'll come into the limo and listen to my proposition. You're under no obligation to accept, but I'm pretty sure you'll like what you hear. We've been looking for a guy like you for weeks, and you're perfect for what we have in mind. It's simple really. Let's go have a drink and I'll tell you about it. There's more money where that came from, Fox, a hell of a lot more. Come get yourself some."

Without another glance, the muscular bald man quickly retraced his steps back to the limo and disappeared inside. He left the door to the car open, an obvious invitation for me to join him. Was I prepared to do that? Was I really that stupid? Sure, he'd helped me out in the bar and he'd given me two hundred bucks for nothing, but was that enough to risk trusting him? I had no idea who this guy was or who he worked for. I didn't have a clue what he wanted with me or what this offer was all about. This had all the makings of a big, big mistake.

What did I have to lose, though, really? The worst thing that could happen was it was all a sham and he was inside, the limo with a knife, waiting to slit open my throat when I entered. That might be a nasty way to die, but was getting run over by a freight train any better? Maybe he was queer, out trolling around for a date? No, if that was his game, he could buy it for a lot less than the four hundred he was offering me. He wouldn't have been following me around for days either.

My feet were walking before I'd even made a conscious decision to do so. I suppose they knew that when it came to the prospect of money, I was a weak-willed jellyfish at heart and would cave eventually, so why not get it over with. Maybe it was crazy, but to me at least, it was worth the risk. Besides, I could always catch the train again twelve hours from now if things didn't work out.

I was near the bottom of the bridge, maybe ten feet from street level, when the Erie freight rounded a corner, speeding into view. I had lots of time to hurry to the bottom and step out of harm's way, but for a second I hesitated, thinking maybe I should just stick to plan A and find out if things were any better in the afterlife. The thought of the additional two hundred bucks was something I just couldn't resist, though. To hell with it, it was stupid to die with all this money in my pocket, especially if there was a chance of—how had he put it—a hell of a lot more.

How much more?

I made it onto Carver Street in plenty of time and watched as the train rocketed by me like a huge metallic serpent snaking its way toward Rochester. When it was gone and there was nothing left to hear, save for the normal loud din of the chaotic city, I turned to find the limo door still open. It was too dark inside to make anything out, but I had the feeling the bald-headed man was watching me with a big icy smile on his face.

Come into my parlor, said the spider to the fly.

Two thoughts swirled through my head as I approached the fancy vehicle. The first was that if I got into the back of this car I'd probably be dead by midnight, and the second was that up on the bridge, I'd missed my chance to cream Puckman in the yap with the rubber hockey puck in my pocket. I must really be in a weird mood because the second thought upset me far more than the first.

"What the hell am I getting myself into?" I wondered aloud, but as the cliché goes, there was only one way to find out.

I climbed into the back seat.

PART TWO

THE OFFER

CHAPTER FOUR

While it's true we all have to choose our own paths in life, it's fair to say that other people we meet can heavily influence those choices.

And so can their snazzy cars.

The spacious interior of the white limo was, in a word, amazing. There was seating for ten on the softest, most comfortable leather I'd ever had the pleasure of touching. A fully stocked bar, complete with an ice-making refrigerator, sink, and hanging glass racks. A 14" color television, a DVD player, and a killer stereo unit with surround-sound speakers and a five-disc revolving CD tray.

To the average Joe, this beautiful car symbolized status, glamour, and delightful extravagance, but to me—considering the seedy places I'd been spending time lately—this excessive luxury was an assault on my senses. The odor of expensive leather mixing with the smell of brand-new plush carpet was incredible, almost intoxicating. I took deep breath after deep breath, savoring the sweet aroma like a rare treat, which to me it was.

It smelled truly wonderful, but what it smelled the most of was money. Cold hard cash. It was impossible to sit in this magnificent vehicle and not realize that its owner had to be not just rich, but rolling in the bucks. I felt weird sitting there, stunned. It was like a heavyweight's punch to my gut of all the things I had lost in this world but still secretly desired. Like I'd entered a forbidden fantasy place, a land as strange and foreign to me as a space shuttle trip to the surface of the moon.

Obviously I was impressed, but I was smart enough to realize these people wanted something from me and this show of obscene wealth was a part of their game plan. It was bait—dangle the money in front of the penniless bum's nose and see if he'd bite. Admittedly, it was working. I liked what I saw and wanted more of it. Not ready to swallow the hook quite yet, but getting mighty hungry.

My muscular host was the only other occupant in the back of the limo and he was seated across from me with his right ankle draped over his left knee, relaxing casually while talking softly on a tiny cellular phone. He pretended to ignore me, concerned only with his phone conversation, but I kept catching him sneaking a peek, observing me checking out the surroundings. I didn't hear much of his call as I'd come in near its completion, but I did hear him say "Yes, sir" a few times so he was presumably talking to the boss he'd referred to earlier. Probably assuring his employer how I'd be an easy mark, what with the way I was staring around with wide-eyed wonder like a kid on Christmas morning.

"Sorry about that," he said, clicking shut his phone and slipping it into the inside pocket of his suit jacket. "Had to check in with the office, so to speak. Anyway, let's get the introductions out of the way. I already know who you are: Michael Benjamin Fox. But I'm not sure what name you'd prefer I use?"

"Most people call me Mike. That'll work."

"Fine, Mike it is. I told you who I was last night in the bar but obviously you don't remember. No big deal. My name's Drake, Alexander Drake, but I prefer just using my last name. Fair enough? Good. Let's have that drink and we'll get into this."

Drake tapped twice on the smoked glass partition separating us from the driver and the car immediately started to roll. I had no idea where they were taking me but it really didn't matter. Anywhere was better than here. Without bothering to ask what I wanted, he poured us both three fingers of single malt scotch over ice and handed one to me. To someone used to drinking cheap gin or homemade Screech, the single malt went down like it was nectar of the gods. Realizing it made me look like the proverbial bum but not caring, I slurped the whole glass dry and held my hand out for more. Drake smiled knowingly and topped me up without saying a word. Managing to control myself this time, I only took one small sip before setting the glass into a built-in cup holder beside me. I settled back in the plush seat and tried to relax.

"So now that we've been introduced," I said, "what's this fabulous offer you have for me?"

Drake took a tiny sip of his scotch—barely wetting his lips—then set his glass aside and began his spiel.

"As I've already hinted, I'm employed by a very wealthy and important man. His name is Nathan Marshall, Dr. Nathan Marshall, to be more precise. He's one of this country's top neurosurgeons, the holder of twenty-seven medical patents for various surgical and research related innovations. The man's a genius, no doubt about it, Mike. His work on brain stem injuries and spinal column nerve regeneration is second to none.

"Dr. Marshall has made a fortune on his medical patents, not to mention the private and government grants that came pouring in after all his success, but he was filthy rich before his career even started. His family had money coming out of their wazoos from way back. He never needed a nickel right from day one, which is why, when he became furious with the medical community and fed up with their restrictive rules and regulations, he simply dropped completely out of the public eye to devote his time and vast wealth into his own private research.

"He's one of a kind, Mike, you'll like him, I know you will. What's not to like? He's got the four G's."

"The four G's?" I asked.

"Yeah, he's good-looking, he's a genius, he's generous with his money, and he's got gazillions of it to toss around. The four G's, man. He's Bill Gates, with a scalpel!"

It was obviously a line Drake used often, but he still managed to laugh at his own joke. Personally, I didn't find it very funny, but I chuckled anyway to play along. When Drake settled, I decided to get down to business.

"And what does this rich and famous doctor want with a broken-down bum like me?"

Drake's smile disappeared immediately, as if it had never existed, replaced with a condescending scowl.

"Now, Mike," wagging his finger in my face, "that's not a nice way to describe yourself, is it? You're forgetting I've been following you around and I know you better than you think. You're not a bum. I don't think so anyway, and I don't think you believe it either. You're a guy who's down on his luck, that's all. A guy who knows there's more to life than living in a Dumpster. Even though you were getting ready to kiss the front grille of that freight train, I think you still want to get back up on your feet and live again. Not this pointless existence you're so sick of, I mean *really* live. Am I right?"

Drake had no idea about my plan for helping out Arlene, but what the big brute said *did* stir me a little. Then again, words were cheap. It was way too early to answer his question and sometimes my mouth gets me in more trouble than I'd like to admit, so I decided to just shut up and listen to what my host had to say. He apparently took my silence as an affirmative and carried on.

"I knew it, I just knew you were the right guy, Mike. That's why I'm here today, to help you get back on your feet. On my recommendation, Dr. Marshall is prepared to offer you a great deal of money for helping him continue his research. What he wants you to do is perfectly legal and no one is going to get in trouble. Everything you've lost, you can get back, and more. Everything you've ever dreamed of or desired, you can have it. It's simple, Mike. If you're willing to give Dr. Marshall what he wants, he's willing to make you rich."

I didn't like the way this was starting to sound. No amount of money would get me my wife and son back, which is what I desired most, but this big steroid monkey would never understand that. Money was the only thing that mattered to guys like him. Speaking of money, they knew I was homeless and didn't have a nickel—making me rich probably meant forking over two or three thousand bucks. That wouldn't do me any good. Wouldn't do my daughter any good, either. Sure, I could live it up for a few months, but then it would be right back to where I was now. And what about that helping the doctor out with his research part? What the hell did that mean? Did they want to sign me on as a human guinea pig? Maybe inject my balls with radioactive soap bubbles to see how big testicles can swell before exploding? No, I didn't like the way this was shaping up one bit but I'd come this far. I may as well hear the rest.

"And what does Dr. Marshall want from me, exactly?"

Drake set his scotch down again and looked me straight in the eye. In a hushed tone, almost a whisper, he said, "He wants your right arm."

For a second, I thought he was joking again, but something in his eyes and the set of his shoulders and jaw tipped me off that he was indeed serious.

"He wants *WHAT*?" I screamed, suddenly angry with myself for getting involved in this nonsense. "Stop the car, Drake. I've heard enough of your bullshit. You can tell Dr. Bigbucks he can go straight to Hell. Just because I'm homeless, dirty, and sometimes eat out of trash cans, it doesn't make me an animal he can play with in his sick twisted little experiments. Fuck him, and for that matter, fuck you too. You come down to the slums in this fancy car looking for an easy mark. Well, start looking elsewhere because I'm out of here. Now stop the goddamned car!"

I wasn't in much of a position to be making threats and I was worried I'd gone too far. There was no doubt this huge man could easily snap my spine in two like a twig but screw it, I was mad. Fortunately, Drake remained perfectly calm throughout my little tirade, waiting patiently until I was finished before responding.

"Whatever, Mike. I told you from the start the choice was yours and you weren't under any obligation whatsoever."

He made the same tapping gesture on the glass divider as earlier and the limousine driver pulled over to the gravel shoulder and stopped the car. Drake reached over and opened the door for me, then sat back to allow me passage.

"You sure about this, Mike?" he asked. "You're tossing away a lot of money."

"I'm sure all right. He wants my *arm*? You've got to

be out of your mind! Where's the other two hundred bucks you promised me for listening to this crap?"

Drake gave me a coy little smirk, meaning either he was laughing at me or perhaps respecting my pathetic display of bravado. Either way, he reached for his bill-fold and peeled off two more hundreds. He crumpled them up in a ball like garbage—chump change he'd called it—and slapped them into my hand. Pocketing the money, I quickly shuffled across the seat, headed for the door.

I fully expected Drake to stop me before I made it out of the car. His large baseball mitt of a hand would roughly grab me by the shoulder and he'd yank me back-ward onto the floor. Hovering above me, he'd scream, "You're not going anywhere, mister. We want your arm and I damn well mean to take it right here, right now!" Drake would then put his shiny size-twelve dress shoes onto the center of my chest and rip my arm off with his bare hands.

None of that happened, of course, but I couldn't seem to shake the image of my blood spraying all over the nice new carpet until I was safely clear of the limo and stand-ing on the sidewalk. Having paid no attention to where the driver had taken us, I wasn't exactly sure where I was, but it was no big deal. I could just walk until I came to a main intersection, one I recognized, and then find my way back to Carver Street easy enough.

Already trying to put this nasty episode behind me, I started planning how Blue J and I could go out on the town tonight first class with the four big bills in my pocket. If all went well, I'd be wined, dined, and drunk out of my mind just in time to play chicken with my freight train returning from Rochester in about eleven and a half hours. My feet had just started heading for home when Drake stuck his massive head out of the limousine's door and said something that stopped me before I'd taken my fourth step.

"No hard feelings, Mike?" he said. "Believe it or not, I give you a lot of credit. It's not every day you meet a guy with enough balls to just get up and walk away from two million dollars."

CHAPTER FIVE

Two million dollars?

Two *MILLION* dollars?

Had I really heard Drake say that? No way, it had to be a mistake, or possibly another joke. Then again, Drake had said his employer was filthy rich. Maybe—

TWO, MILLION, DOLLARS?

The number was so staggeringly immense, when I tried to visualize it, all the zeroes kept ricocheting painfully back and forth through my brain like the metal spheres in an arcade pinball machine. I was rooted to the sidewalk, unable to resume walking, but deathly afraid to turn back around. Instinctively, I sensed that if I turned around to listen to any more of this madness, I'd be sunk for sure.

Just walk away Mike. Get out of here, I warned myself, but I couldn't do it. I just couldn't. How could I justify leaving behind that kind of money? Think of everything I could buy. The places I could visit and the things I could do with a stash like that—right arm or no right arm. Think about Arlene. Man, that twenty-five grand insurance policy was nothing compared to this. If I played my cards right, maybe I could get back together with her, actually be a part of her life again.

Easy fella. Don't get carried away. It'll never happen.

Still, it *could* happen. Couldn't it? What's that old saying? Damned if I do and damned if I don't. That pretty much summed up how I felt.

Eventually I did turn to face the limo again. If I was going to be damned, I may as well be rich, right? Drake was trying his best not to let his Cheshire-cat grin out of the bag, but tactfulness obviously wasn't one of his strong traits. He knew he had me right where he wanted, playing the fool, thinking about the money.

"You heard me right, Mike. Two million for your right arm. If you'll just listen for a second, it's nowhere near as sinister as it sounds. Nathan Marshall isn't some B-movie mad scientist performing, as you so colorfully put it, sick twisted little experiments. He's a highly respected physician for God's sake, a renowned medical researcher and neurosurgeon. What did you think he was going to do, chop off your arm with an axe while I held you down?"

As if from a great distance, I heard myself say, "I'm not sure—" but my brain felt detached from my mouth, drifting elsewhere in a vision of me lying comfortably in a lush green meadow, relaxing on a bed of two million one-dollar-bill blades of grass.

It felt strange, really weird, and so unlike me to daydream like this. Drake was speaking to me again.

"What?" I asked.

"I said, come on back into the limo and let me explain exactly how this deal would work. Come have another drink, listen to the *full* story, then make your decision. At the very least, we can give you a lift back home."

I didn't need a lift back home. What I needed was to run far away from here as fast as my legs could carry me, but damned if my feet didn't take a couple steps back toward the open car door.

Don't do it, Mike, my practical side silently scolded. *Don't be a fool. Take the money you've already pocketed and*

*head for the hills. Go out and live it up with Blue J like you'd
planned, and forget all about this crazy offer. He's talking
about cutting off your arm, your motherfucking arm, man!
Wake up and get out of here!*

But hey, Fox, think about all that money, the greedy
part of my conscience shot back. *Think of everything you
could have with that kind of dough, not the least of which is
your daughter maybe loving you again. The possibilities,
Fox, just think of the possibilities!*

And I was.

There was no use denying it. No matter how hard I
tried, and no matter how fucked up this whole scenario
was, I couldn't stop thinking about how much money
was at stake.

Visions of sprawling houses, cobalt blue pools, tennis
courts, luxury cars, vacations in Europe, and beautiful
long-legged women all flashed before my eyes. Before I
could stop myself, I was climbing into the backseat of
the limo for a second time and accepting another glass
of single malt scotch.

Drake tapped on the divider and the driver had us on
our way again. "Good man," he applauded me.

"Now let me explain this properly, so it's not so much
of a shock. It's true Dr. Marshall wants to remove your
right arm, but he won't just hack it off. Like I said earlier,
he's a world-class surgeon. He's working on damaged
nerve regeneration. Don't ask me to go into the specifics
because I haven't got a clue. Dr. Marshall will explain everything when you meet him. All I can say is that a long
time ago, he progressed as far as he could go in his research, using test animals and computer simulations. He
needs to test out his advanced theories using live human
subjects. The medical community would never allow this
type of thing, of course, which is precisely the reason Dr.
Marshall funds his own research. Although this might be
frowned upon, that doesn't make it illegal. You have every

right to donate your arm to medical science, just as he has every right to compensate you for your trouble. People do it all the time. All over the country people are selling part of their livers, or one of their kidneys, and they're getting compensated for it. Why shouldn't you?"

I sat rigid as a stone, not even sipping my expensive scotch. I'd heard the stories of people selling their kidneys for big bucks but hadn't really thought much about it. This wasn't that much different, was it? I wasn't completely convinced it was legal, but who really cared? Dr. Marshall wouldn't be calling the cops to report me; that was for sure. By the time anyone found out, if ever, Arlene and I'd be nestled away on some warm tropical island somewhere.

"Where and when would all this happen, if, and I do mean *if*, I decided to go through with it?"

"This weekend. You'll be brought to his private medical center about three hours from here, where you'll meet Dr. Marshall and his top-notch medical staff. You'll get a tour of the facility and have a chance to ask any and all questions you have before giving your final consent. The money will be wired into a bank account for you and you'll receive confirmation of its deposit before the operation begins. The operation itself I'm told is simple, a couple of hours, tops. You won't feel a thing.

"After it's over, you'll be cared for and pampered for as long as it takes your wound to properly heal. About the worst thing you have to worry about will be fevers and the risk of infection, but the doctors and nurses will be monitoring you closely. They won't release you from the hospital until you've been given a one hundred percent clean bill of health and you're free of pain. Hell, they'll even give you a rehabilitation course to help you cope with getting by using only one arm. Luckily you're left-handed, so that should make things—"

"How do you know that?" I interrupted him, more

than a little shocked that these strangers knew so much about me. I was in fact left-handed, as he'd said.

"What? Oh, well that's easy. You're holding your drink in your left hand."

I screwed up my face and started to protest but Drake immediately started laughing.

"I'm kidding, Mike. I'm a little more professional than that. I asked around, found out your name, and then anything and everything about you can be found. I checked all your records. You name it—financial, medical, educational. I checked them all.

"When are you going to realize this is the real deal here, Mike? We're not just fucking around, wasting time. Dr. Marshall is a very important man who's willing to make you rich if you'll help him. Obviously, losing a limb will be hard on you for a while, I know that, and he knows that. That's why he's willing to give you so much money. It's a huge sacrifice you'd be making. *Huge*, but I'm willing to bet within a year you'll be mighty happy you met me.

"Just say yes and show up. Meet Dr. Marshall and ask him anything you want. Spend a few months in the hospital and bang, you're a multimillionaire. It's up to you, Mike. What do you say?"

It was a good question. One I didn't have an answer for yet. To stall for time I started taking sip after sip of my drink, giving myself time to think. Drake sat back with his own scotch and left me alone.

Fact one: I hated my current lifestyle and earlier had been fully prepared and more than willing to kill myself to escape it.

Fact two: I didn't want to lose my right arm. Self-explanatory, what can I say? After thirty-nine years, I was rather attached to my limb—literally and figuratively.

Fact three: I believed everything Drake was telling me. I might be a fool, but that was my gut feeling.

Fact four: I badly wanted the money. It was absurd, but the four hundred in my pocket was already starting to feel like the chump change Drake described it as. Even if Arlene never loved me again, I could still set the both of us up for life.

I sat sipping my scotch, going over and over these points, trying my best to sort everything out. Maybe I should just flip a coin? Christ, I was confused. It was almost inconceivable that I was considering this ridiculous offer. I couldn't let someone cut off my arm, could I? No, when it came right down to it, probably not.

That's right, Mike, now you're thinking straight. I know the money's tempting, but just forget it. You've got the four hundred, enjoy it, but get out of this car, and don't look back. Stick to plan A.

Almost as if the limo driver had a direct link to my brain and could hear my thoughts, the car suddenly pulled to a stop. I looked out the window and was mildly surprised to see we were back to where we'd started. From my comfortable soft leather seat, I could easily see our rusty Dumpster beneath the Carver Street Railway Bridge and Puckman sitting outside of it still savagely biting red juicy chunks out of his disgusting supper.

I was free to make my escape, just open the door and walk away. Why wasn't I halfway out the door, then? After all, I'd already made up my mind, right? I couldn't go through with it, right? I took one more look at the life of poverty and humiliation waiting for me outside the window. Made up my mind? Yeah, I guess I had.

"Sign me up, Drake," I said. "I'm in."

CHAPTER SIX

Feeling like a dorky little kid waiting impatiently for the school bus, I stood on the side of Carver Street bundled up in my blue bomber jacket with my ratty suitcase in my hand, ready for Drake to come pick me up in the white limo. He'd told me to be ready by 7:30 A.M. but I don't own a watch, so I'd been standing here since just after sunrise to be sure I didn't miss my ride.

The last three days had swept past in a blùr. It's funny, I never noticed before how time slowed down to a crawl, becoming basically irrelevant when you're a homeless man. When there's absolutely no schedule to follow, no job to go to, no calls to make, no mail to open, no bills to pay, no appointments to keep, and no family to interact with, what did it matter what time it was? Or what day of the week, month, or year it was, for that matter? Every minute of every day was the same old static waste of life. Ever since agreeing to Drake's bizarre offer, though, time, or perhaps the lack of it, had suddenly become important to me again.

I couldn't stop thinking about my right arm, and how soon it would be gone. Every time I used that arm to pick something up, or drink a glass of water, or scratch my ass, I'd be thinking, *Hey, you're not gonna be able to do this anymore, Mike. Never, ever, again.*

I tried to stop thinking about it, but it was next to impossible. *What about shoes? You're not going to be able to wear shoes with lacés anymore because you won't be able to tie them by yourself.* The list of things I'd never be able to do again was endless. How was I going to manage?

Fortunately, two million dollars has a heck of a way of making a guy feel optimistic about almost anything and deep down I believed I'd get used to whatever hardships lay ahead. I'd still have my good arm—my left—to use, and if it was busy I could always hire someone to scratch my ass, right?

Gallows humor; it's good for the soul.

"Come on, Drake, hurry up before I change my mind."

I had no intention of doing any such thing, but saying it out loud helped channel my thoughts away from my arm.

The four hundred dollars Drake had given me was gone. Blue J and I went out on the town Wednesday, getting a suite in the swanky Four Seasons hotel uptown. We really lived it up too, compared to our usual standards anyway. Our room was huge, with separate areas for sitting and for sleeping. The sitting room came complete with leather couch, chairs, rolltop oak desk, and a complete home theater set up with stereo, surround-sound speakers and big-screen satellite television. The bedroom had a four-post king-size canopy bed with shiny satin sheets and a balcony overlooking nearby Lake Erie.

The best part was our bathroom, which had a four-person hot tub and enough free soaps, shampoos, and bubble baths to clean an army. Blue J and I ordered steak and wine, then later on, pizza, chicken wings, and beer, and spent almost the whole night partying in the tub. Unfortunately, four hundred bucks doesn't go very far in a high-class hotel, so first thing Thursday morning we were out on the street and back in our Dumpster again. Oh, well, it was fun while it lasted.

For some reason, I couldn't tell Blue J what I was about to do. I said the money for the hotel binge had come from my wife's sister, Gloria, who had tracked me down and invited me to visit her and Arlene for a couple months. Blue J believed me, and we sat talking about how I might be able to get back on my feet, start a new life with my family again. I hated lying to my only friend, but I just didn't feel right about telling him the truth. Maybe I thought he'd laugh and call me a fool, or maybe I thought he'd want to come along. I don't know. My plan was to come back and get him once I had my money. He deserved better than this. Puckman, on the other hand, I told nothing, not even good riddance. I wouldn't be coming back to his rescue. Fuck him.

The sound of an approaching car caught my attention and I looked to my right to see the white limo headed my way. A maroon-colored van followed closely behind it and I was surprised to see both vehicles pull over and stop near me. The passenger door at the back of the limousine opened and I walked around the car ready to climb in. Drake stepped out of the car, holding his hand out to stop me. He looked bigger than I remembered, meaner, and far more like the hired muscle he really was, wearing an all-black jogging suit with white running shoes.

"Whoa there, Mike," he growled. "Where do you think you're going?"

I was confused. "I'm coming with you, aren't I?"

"Not in the limo you're not. Why should you get special treatment? Get in the van. You can ride to Dr. Marshall's estate with the other guys."

Other guys?

I looked back at the maroon van parked ten feet away, but the windows were tinted dark enough I couldn't make out anyone inside. I looked back at Drake.

"What do you mean, ride with the other guys? *Other* people are selling their arms, too?"

"When did I say you were the only one?"

"I don't know? I guess I just pre—"

"Look, Mike, I don't have time to explain all this. We're already late, so get in the van. Dr. Marshall will explain everything when we get there, okay?"

Drake climbed back into the limo and slammed the door. I was about to re-open it and ask another question, but I heard the door locks engage, putting an end to that idea. I was still confused, but I didn't have much choice except walk to the van and do what I was told.

It was a fairly new Dodge Caravan, and the big sliding rear passenger door opened just as I was reaching for the handle. I took one last look at the Carver Street Bridge and the hovel of a place I'd called home sitting below, steeled my nerves then climbed into the van.

There were four other people inside: one driver and three nervous scruffy-looking dudes sitting in the back. The driver, a black man in a gray pinstripe suit and dark sunglasses, was probably employed by Nathan Marshall, which meant there would be four of us going under the knife. Looking at the guys in the back was like looking in the mirror: all white guys in their thirties dressed in clean but obviously hand-me-down clothes. Every one of them also had a little beat-up suitcase or knapsack sitting beside him. We all looked different of course; two guys had beards, but we were basically the same—bums. From just one glance I could tell they were also homeless, or, if not already out on the street, they weren't far from it. That made sense, though. It would have to be a guy down on his luck to accept such an offer.

"Come on, fella," the driver told me. "Grab a seat, the limo's already pulling away."

"Yeah, okay," I said, and since no one was sitting up front in the passenger seat, I dropped my suitcase and climbed up beside the driver. "Mind if I sit up here?"

"Don't mind at all. Hold onto your hat, though, 'cause it's my ass if I lose track of the limo."

That said, he floored the pedal and we rocketed off in pursuit of the rapidly fading limousine. He cranked on the stereo and really loud jazz blasted out of the speakers. The music was good, but way too loud for my tastes. Conversation would be almost impossible, but then again, that was probably a good thing and maybe the sole reason for it. The driver leaned over and practically had to scream in my ear.

"Relax, buddy, we've got a good three, three and a half hour drive ahead of us."

He gave me a little wink and then turned his full attention back on the road. Those were the only words I would hear for the entire trip, which only ended up taking two hours and fifty minutes according to the digital clock on the dash. God knows where we were. Somewhere south of Buffalo I guess, probably close to the southern border of Western New York. I'd seen a sign saying we were near Allegheny State Park and some small town named Millhaven, wherever that was. When the driver finally turned down the music to inform us we were almost "home," as he put it, I let out a nervous sigh of relief and stretched my legs and back like an awakening cat.

Sure enough, within minutes the big white limo pulled off onto a paved road marked PRIVATE and through the trees in the distance I could just make out a huge redbrick building. The road twisted and turned through the trees for perhaps a mile until breaking clear of the forest and giving me my first good look at Nathan Marshall's estate.

I was disappointed, to tell the truth. It was a dirty four-story rectangular building with what looked like a tower room on the front left corner. A U.S. flag flew on the peak of the tower, looking a bit tattered, like it hadn't been lowered in twenty years. The rest of the building was in disrepair also, looking more like a crumbling medieval castle than any state-of-the-art medical research center I'd ever seen. Mind you, I'd never seen a state-of-the-art medical research center so what did I know? I'm not sure what I'd been expecting, but this ugly building, this architectural monstrosity, sure wasn't it.

"Not very pretty, is it?" I said to the driver.

"You got that right, buddy, but don't let it fool you. Doc Marshall is a hell of a surgeon and this place is equipped with nothing but the best. You've heard that expression, you can't judge a book by its cover? Well, that fits this place. You'll see."

The limo pulled up to the huge double front doors and we stopped behind it.

"Everybody out," the driver said. "Oh, you two in the back just hold on a sec and I'll get your chairs." He gave me a slap on the arm and said, "Can you give me a hand with their wheelchairs?"

"Ah, sure, I guess."

We went to the back of the van, removed two rickety old chairs, and helped the two bearded guys into them. I was shocked to see that both were missing one of their legs, although not the same one. I hadn't noticed that when I'd climbed into the van. I had to ask.

"Jesus, guys, don't take this the wrong way, but both of you have already lost a leg. Don't you need both of your arms to get around?"

"Yeah," the red bearded guy missing his left leg answered. "What's that got to do with anything?"

"Well, everything. If you're already in a wheelchair,

how can you sell your arm? You won't be able to push yourself around. Not very easily anyway."

I had a brief image of a frustrated one-armed/one-legged man trying to cross a street in his wheelchair, going nowhere but around and around in circles.

"What are ya talking about, mister?" the brown-bearded man said. "I'm here to sell my left leg, not my arm. Like you said, I need my arms."

"Me too," Red Beard said. "Only I'm selling my right leg. I don't got no use for it anyway. May as well take the cash, right?"

Wait a minute, Mike. What's going on here?

I turned to the other man standing quietly over by the front door. "What about you? What are you selling?"

"My left arm. That's what I thought you guys were selling too. It doesn't matter though, as long as we all get our money."

I guess he was right. It didn't really matter. It just caught me off guard for a moment, that's all.

"I suppose. It's just a bit of a surprise," I said. "Two arms and two legs. I mean; I know this place *looks* like Frankenstein's castle but nobody told me we were here to supply the parts for Dr. Marshall to build a body."

It was an attempted joke but looking around at each other, this creepy place we were in, and thinking about what I'd just said, nobody laughed—nobody at all.

Jesus H. Christ!

What was I getting myself into?

PART THREE

THE CASTLE

CHAPTER SEVEN

Drake opened the massive door leading into the medical center, and hurried the four of us inside. I helped push Red Beard's chair, while the limo driver aided the other wheelchair-bound man. Once we were all inside the building and clear of the door, Drake told us to stay put while he checked to see if they were ready for us. The moment he walked around the corner, the limo driver hurriedly said good-bye and exited through the front door, leaving us alone.

There was nothing to do except stare at each other and wait for Drake to come back. The hallway we were in was made entirely of concrete, including the floor, with a set of stairs leading up to our left. The ceiling towered fifteen feet above our heads and even though sound would probably echo quite well in here, no one said a word and it was as quiet as a tomb. So quiet, it was making me nervous, so I took the initiative and introduced myself.

"The name's Smith," the other nondisabled man said—the man donating his left arm. "William Smith, but I'd rather you call me Bill."

"Hey, imagine that, I'm a Bill too," said the brown-bearded man missing his right leg. "Bill Tucker. Just so we don't get confused, most people back home called me Wheels, on account of this chair and all."

We all agreed Wheels would do just fine.

Red Beard's name was Sinclair Halderson. I think I preferred calling him Red Beard and when I jokingly mentioned this to him he smiled and said that was all right with him.

"Lot's of people call me Red. You can too, Mike, if you'd like."

"Sure," I said. "We're in this crazy adventure together, and who better to have on an adventure than a pirate, huh? Red Beard it is."

Together, we laughed and it seemed to break the tension a little. Everyone was uptight and nervous about what we were getting into, but at least we were approaching it properly, with a sense of humor. It felt good to laugh; we needed it. Soon we were kidding each other about what we should do with all the money once this was over. I also learned that I'd been right with my original assumption: all four of us *had* been living on the street before accepting Drake's offer.

Only for a moment did I pause to wonder how this Dr. Marshall could possibly be willing to shell out eight million dollars to us four misfits of society. Didn't that sound like a little *too* much money to just toss away?

Maybe—

My mind started to think things through, but then Drake reappeared and yelled at us to get a move on. I might have continued with my train of thought but when we followed him around the corner, what lay ahead made me gasp out loud and forget all about any lingering doubts I may have been harboring.

The featureless concrete hallway opened up into a lavishly decorated four-story, glass-roofed atrium. A highly polished emerald-green marble floor spread out across the grand expanse of a room measuring seventy-five feet across, and what had to be damn near sixty feet high. To our left was a long cherrywood reception desk, a stunning depiction of a flock of doves skillfully hand-carved along its length. Luxurious black-leather couches and chairs were artistically spaced out around the room, along with several glass display cases filled with statues, paintings, and other valuable treasures. My eye was particularly drawn to a display of jewel-encrusted swords lying on a carpet of ancient gold coins.

All the seating and displays faced the north wall, drawing my eyes to where a massive ten-foot-high fireplace was cut into the colorful fieldstone wall. On either side of the fireplace, twin fifty-foot-high tapestries were hung, both gloriously depicting the rising sun majestically suspended over the tips of two godlike outstretched hands.

I'd never been in a room quite like it. It was simply incredible—breathtaking in its beauty compared to the building's shabby, crumbling exterior. Earlier, I'd compared this place to a medieval castle rather than a medical center; seeing this immense fireplace and the exquisitely woven twin tapestries only intensified my initial impression.

What would all this extravagance cost? This doctor must be loaded!

This room alone would have cost a fortune. Maybe eight million for us losers wasn't as big a deal as I'd originally thought.

Drake led us through the atrium, past the reception desk, and into a smaller room, which at first glance I mistook for a movie theater. There were five rows of ten high-backed seats arranged in a semicircle sloping down toward a large white projection screen. Beside the screen, on the right-hand side, was a raised wooden pulpit with an attached silver microphone available for someone to address a crowd. This room was obviously a conference room of sorts, where meetings, media interviews, and video presentations could be held.

"Everyone grab a seat," Drake barked. "Dr. Marshall will be here in a minute to go over everything with you. If you have questions, this will be the time to ask them. There's room for the wheelchairs at the end of each row. You other two, sit anywhere you'd like."

I helped Red Beard get settled at the end of the third row of seats, then plopped down in the same row a couple of chairs in. Wheels rolled down the wheelchair ramp to the first row, while Bill Smith took a seat at the back on the far side of the aisle.

"Good enough," Drake said. He peeked out into the atrium, smiled, waved at somebody, then walked down the wheelchair ramp to the front of the room. "Well, no big fanfare or anything, 'cause I'm no good at speeches, but it's time you guys met the man responsible for bringing you here today. It's my pleasure to introduce you to the most brilliant man I've ever known. Treat him right or I'll break your heads. Anyway," he gestured to the doorway, "Dr. Nathan Marshall."

Drake was right; he certainly wasn't much of a speechmaker, but I suppose that introduction was as good as any. I turned, as did everyone, just as Nathan Marshall entered the room. I doubt I was the only one surprised to see a man sitting comfortably in a blue metal wheelchair with shiny chrome wheels, his legs concealed beneath a thin yellow wool blanket. Taking a quick glance at Bill, Red Beard, and Wheels, it was obvious none of us had known the good doctor was disabled. Not that it really mattered—it just wasn't how I'd pictured him in my mind.

He was just as handsome as Drake had alluded, with thick wavy black hair crowning his thin, regal-looking face. He had to be at least sixty years of age, but looked remarkably younger if you didn't study him too close. It was his eyes, I think—powerful, piercing blue eyes that glimmered with just a hint of green. His skin was quite pale but not from sickness; it was probably because he spent so much time indoors.

He was casually dressed in a dark blue pullover sweater with the sleeves bunched up around his elbows. The yellow blanket hid his legs, but below that he was wearing brand-new white Adidas runners. His legs appeared to be thin and somewhat wasted away, but his upper body was very well developed. Dr. Marshall obviously spent countless hours in the gym despite his disabilities. All eyes were on him as he slowly made his way down to the podium.

"Good morning, gentlemen," Dr. Marshall said when he finally positioned himself on the raised platform. He ignored the microphone and just spoke to us in a strong clear voice. "I'm so glad we can finally meet."

He had a slight accent when he spoke—European for sure, maybe German. It was slight but detectable, especially when he said *finally*, pronouncing the word with a *V* sound, rather than an *F*. His tone was friendly and he seemed genuinely happy to be meeting us. Right off the bat, just as Drake had predicted, I liked him. I couldn't help but feel a little in awe. I'd never accomplished anything in my whole worthless life and here was this courageous man who'd earned worldwide recognition and countless achievements all from the seat of that chair. He'd been dealt a bad hand in this world and had probably never complained half as much as I had. Made me feel like a first-class loser. I didn't deserve to sit in the same room as this guy.

Drake took care of the introductions for everyone.

"You'll have to excuse me if I don't get up to shake everyone's hand," Dr. Marshall said, and everyone chuckled, especially Red Beard and Wheels, who could appreciate the humor far more than Bill or I.

"First of all, I want to thank you for agreeing to come here today. I know how great your sacrifices will be and I want you to know I don't take them lightly. What you are about to do is a very special thing, not only for me, but also for medical science and all the future people who will surely benefit from our successes. I have a much more personal reason to be grateful to the four of you, but I'll get to that later."

Dr. Marshall paused to whisper something in Drake's ear. Drake, in return, nodded, stood up, and exited the room through a metal door off to our left. The door swung shut, cutting off my view of him, so I turned my attention back to the man on the podium.

"Okay," Dr. Marshall said. "We've got a lot to cover, so let's get started. As Mr. Drake has surely informed you, I'm a surgeon who left behind years of public service to concentrate my efforts on private research. My work here is basically no different than any average research scientist, except I fund all the projects myself without the need to grovel at the feet of the various bankers, government agencies, and private sector financial backers. You'd be amazed how much time is wasted by wonderfully talented people who have to delay their research to beg for further grants and loans. Trust me, delays and insufficient funding can destroy you in this game.

"Fortunately, money has never been an issue here. Consequently, my research tends to flow along much smoother and faster than most. If there's some new advancement or technology available that will help whatever I'm working on progress quicker, I go out and get it. Cost be damned. Money is rather insignificant. Knowledge is far more important to me than dollars and cents."

One thing was for sure. Dr. Marshall was a good

speaker. His compelling words and the conviction in his voice as he said them had everyone's rapt attention. The small conference room was silent while he spoke and when I glanced at my three companions, they were all nodding along with the good doctor's spiel, all of them obviously just as adamant in their thirst for knowledge over the lowly pursuit of cash.

What a crock of shit!

This man was a billionaire—he could afford to talk like that. We were all street bums, two or three missed meals away from starving to death. None of us wanted knowledge. We wanted cash. Two million bucks' worth to be exact, or why else would we be sitting here in this room? I personally wasn't here to give my arm away for the benefit of mankind—screw that—I was here for the benefit of Michael Fox.

Still, the doctor's words were sincere and moved me enough that I found myself bobbing my head at all the appropriate spots along with the other guys. Who was I to disagree with a billionaire, especially one who was about to make me rich? If Dr. Marshall said we were here for the benefit of our fellow man and to acquire knowledge—right on, dude—that's what we were here for.

"For over thirty years," Dr. Marshall continued, "I've concentrated the bulk of my studies on the human nervous system, or more precisely, the repairing and healing of these nerves when they are damaged or accidentally severed. Things like spinal column injuries, paralysis, and accidental amputations are my specialties. Someday I hope to tackle dreadful diseases such as Parkinson's, epilepsy, and multiple sclerosis, which are all ailments caused by genetically faulty or accidentally damaged nervous systems, but cures for them are still a pipe dream and a long way off in the future.

"When I started, people publicly called me a fool. No one wanted to mess with the nervous system because it was considered a losing battle. By losing, I mean there was no money in it. If you couldn't get positive results, you couldn't get the funds to further your research, so why bother? It was easier for scientists to choose other areas of specialization, where funding and results were more attainable. I disagreed, and by the time I went into private research, no one was calling me a fool anymore.

"Since then, there have been great strides made; not only by me, but by many dedicated scientists the world over. I just happen to have made more strides than most."

Drake casually reentered the room, gave his employer an affirmative nod of his head, and sat back down in the first row of seats. As if this was the signal he'd been waiting on, Dr. Marshall sat up straighter in his chair and started rubbing his hands together, his excitement clearly visible. When he spoke, his voice was louder than before and his slight accent even more pronounced.

"I could probably sit and talk for hours about medical advancements and breakthroughs, but it's doubtful you'd understand much of it. No disrespect, of course, but sometimes the details can be a bit dry and confusing. I'd much rather show you what we've accomplished so you can see for yourself how far we've come.

"We'll be taking a tour of the facility after lunch, but for now, I've taken the liberty of creating a video presentation of some of the highlights of our program. That's why we've met here in this cramped room, instead of somewhere more comfortable. Mr. Drake has assured me the video is ready to roll, so why don't we watch it and then discuss things after it's done. Fair enough?"

We all agreed that was fine—what else were we going to say? Drake waited for his employer's approval, then went over to the switch on the wall, ready to dim the lights.

"Oh, wait a minute, Mr. Drake," Dr. Marshall stalled. "Perhaps I should say a few words about what we'll be seeing on this video before we jump right in. It's just that the material you're about to see, well, it's a little *graphic* in nature. Probably more so than you're used to, I'm afraid. Medical science isn't pretty, to be bluntly honest. Sometimes it can be downright nasty, but that can't be helped. If the sight of blood makes you squeamish or nauseous, feel free to close your eyes or look away. I thought it would be easier for you to see it here first, on video, rather than simply marching you into the labs unprepared.

"This will certainly prepare you for our tour later, but the point of the video isn't to shock anyone; it's to prove what we are about to attempt here can and *is* being done. I truly believe we are going to succeed."

I wasn't sure about the rest of the guys, but I was sitting there wondering what he meant by that. What was it we were about to attempt? I considered asking the doctor but he was busy shuffling his chair off to the side so he wouldn't block anyone's view of the video.

"Anyway," the doctor continued, once he'd finished repositioning himself, "enough said. Mr. Drake, let's have a look, shall we?"

Drake immediately hit the lights, and a moment later the large white video screen blazed into life.

CHAPTER EIGHT

In total, the presentation probably only lasted fifteen minutes, but it seemed three or four times that long. It's hard to describe what I saw—body parts, blood, and these strange machines that looked straight out of some futuristic science-fiction movie. It was horrifying yet strangely exhilarating at the same time.

Dr. Marshall had obviously developed ways to keep organs and limbs *alive*, I guess was the best word. Somehow, he could take a severed leg, for instance, and hook it up to this machine that continually pumped blood through it, as if the leg were still attached to a body. Hundreds, maybe thousands, of these tiny wires were attached to the stump and they must have been transmitting electrical stimuli to the exposed nerve endings, causing the leg to move. The wires must have been pumping juice pretty good too, because in every example we were shown, the arm, leg, heart, or *whatever*, would be twitching and dancing to beat the band.

It was an unusual sight indeed to sit and watch a dis-embodied hand open and close, flutter its fingers, then flop around spastically on the top of a lab table. It scared the hell out of me at first—creepiest damn thing I'd ever seen—but the more I watched the steady stream of examples, it became more bizarre than creepy. Bizarre is probably too strong of a word. Strange, maybe? Yeah, I like that better. It was so damn *strange* to see a foot, cut off just above the ankle, rhythmically tapping its toes to some unheard beat.

The most amazing thing by far—and if I'd seen it anywhere else I'd have laughed and sworn it was faked—was a human head severed below the chin, with its spinal column still attached but openly exposed in a glass chamber filled with some milky amber-colored fluid. It was the head of a male, a dark-haired man whose age was virtually impossible for me to even guess at. His eyes would open and close every four or five seconds, his nose twitched steadily, and once during the thirty seconds the head was on film, his mouth opened up wide in what appeared to be a soundless scream.

Below the chin, where the neck should have been, several red and blue color-coded tubes disappeared up into the neck cavity, somehow connected to the poor man's brain to supply it with life-sustaining blood. Below, submerged in the glass tank, a vast network of wires and electrodes were connected along the length of the man's spinal column, causing it to thrash around in its watery home like the tail of a filleted fish that stubbornly refused to die.

When the video finally ended and Drake hit the lights, the conference room was bathed in an uncomfortable silence. No one seemed to have a clue what to do or say. I mean really, what *could* you say after seeing something like that? It would be different if you knew this was some cheesy horror flick made with ketchup and cheap special effects, but that wasn't the case. This was real—all of it—even the severed head.

Still, as shocking and grotesque as Dr. Marshall's experiments certainly were, in the aftermath of the video, I found myself far more amazed at the doctor's work than repulsed. What he'd accomplished was nothing short of miraculous, and sitting thinking about it left me speechless. I had a million questions I wanted to ask, but couldn't seem to find the words to start. Apparently my fellow body part donors had been similarly affected by what they'd seen. The looks on their faces clearly expressed the same mixed feelings of horror, disbelief, acceptance, curiosity, and fascination likely mirrored on my own face. It was Drake who eventually broke the silence.

"Do you still need me, sir?" he asked his boss.

"Err . . . no, Mr. Drake. You can run along if you'd like. Why don't you check and see how Cook is coming along with lunch. I'll just answer whatever questions our guests have, then we'll meet up with you in the dining room."

Drake nodded and flew out of the room without another word. Maybe my eyes were playing tricks on me, still getting used to the bright lights again, but I was fairly sure I'd seen the front of Drake's tracksuit pants bulging out as if he'd had an erection. Was that possible? I found it inconceivable anyone could find anything we'd been shown remotely arousing. Incredible, yes, but erotic—not a chance. Drake would have to be one totally sick fuck to be turned on by—

"Any questions, gentlemen?" Dr. Marshall asked, interrupting my dark thought. "Come now. Surely someone has something they'd like to ask?"

"Were those things *real*?" Wheels asked, absently scratching the stump of his missing leg.

"Things?" the doctor asked, being playfully coy. "The body parts? Of course they were real. I should apologize. I underestimated how shocking this all must look. I did warn you the video was a bit graphic."

I almost burst out laughing. That had to be the understatement of the year. It was like saying the Pacific Ocean was a *bit* wet.

"How on earth did you do it?" Red Beard wondered. "How do you keep them alive?"

"That's the million-dollar question, isn't it? That's always been the crux of the problem. For years, surgeons have been able to reattach severed limbs and other areas of massive nerve damage, but the problem has always been with the nerves dying and no longer being able to function. It's useless to sew someone's arm back on if the nerves are dead and it's just going to hang there uselessly. Things *are* getting better and sometimes the surgeons are getting lucky with eighty to ninety percent function return, but more times than not, the patient is only regaining about thirty to forty percent of their original dexterity.

"Is that adequate? I, for one, say no. My goal here is, and always has been, one hundred percent. My patients will achieve total use and control of their damaged limbs. That's a rather lofty, and some would say arrogant, claim, but I firmly believe it's realistic.

"The trick is stopping the nerves from dying, which is far easier said than done, but it isn't fantasy anymore. What you have to understand is that the human neurological system is made up of billions and billions of individual nerve cells, all lined up in rows like, say . . . a marching band. Not a great analogy but it works. When the bandleader, the brain in other words, wants the trumpet player to perform a certain tune, it tells the first nerve cell in the line. This first link in the chain then passes the request along to the next cell until the trumpet player gets the message and starts playing the song, or in human terms, the foot starts to walk, or the fingers start to wiggle, or whatever. Get it?

"Well, when one of the nerve cells is damaged or dead, the message from the brain can't be passed along properly, but we've come up with a way to fix that. There are a few factors that are vitally important in order to succeed, though. Time is one of those factors. The severed limb can't be allowed to just lie around. Blood is another. A steady and strong blood flow must be reestablished as soon as possible. The faster this can be done, the better.

"This is where most scientists and surgeons go wrong. In their haste to reestablish blood flow, they immediately reattach the severed limb back onto the patient's body. The blood flow is returned, but the nervous system is usually dead or dying and now there's no way to try repairing it. They just sit back and hope time and rest will eventually heal the damage.

"At this institute we've taken a radically different approach. Blood supply must be reestablished, of course, but nobody said we had to sew the limb back onto a body to accomplish that."

Wheels, in the front row closest to the doctor, let out a little gasp, drawing all of our attention. Slapping the armrest of his chair for emphasis, he finally made the connection I'd figured out earlier while watching the video. "It's those damn machines isn't it? They're what pump the blood. They're how you reestablish the blood supply without a body, right?"

"Exactly. It's relatively simple too. We just connect the tubes right into the existing main veins and arteries. If you've ever known anyone who's undergone a heart transplant, or more common still, heart bypass surgery, you'll know that the doctors stop the patient's heart so they can work on it. To do this, they hook the patient up to a machine called a cardiopulmonary bypass machine, or CBM for short. The surgeon redirects the flow of blood away from the heart into this CBM, which will perform the function of the human heart and lungs for as long as the operation takes.

"It's an amazing machine. Not only does it rhythmically pump blood throughout their bodies, it also warms the blood to maintain the patient's core temperature, and oxygenates the blood as well, acting as a set of healthy lungs.

"An interesting fact a lot of people don't know is that when a patient flatlines in ICU after bypass surgery, they bring him or her into the OR and hook them back up to the cardiopulmonary bypass machine. That way, the doctors can work on the patient's heart without the frantic pressure of the ticking clock working against them. Instead of minutes, their window of opportunity can be expanded, and they will often *resurrect* someone whose heart has been literally stopped for hours. I've always found that fascinating.

"Normal CBMs are quite bulky and heavy to move, but ours have been redesigned smaller, more efficient, and portable so they can be moved from operating rooms, to the labs, to anywhere they might be needed. We have a minor problem keeping up with our constant need for fresh blood, but besides that, the system works fabulously.

"In the medical community, the record for the longest a patient has been kept alive on one of these machines is twenty-eight days. Most people would agree that's an impressive number, but not around here it isn't. Using a specially modified version of this heart bypass machine, which I hold the patent on, some of the body parts shown on the video were kept alive for several months. Our personal record is one hundred and nineteen days . . . and counting. That's right, it's still alive. It's a left leg, and if you're up to it, we'll check on how it's doing when we tour the labs after lunch."

Everyone agreed they'd like to see the doctor's work with their own eyes. I put my hand up to ask a question but Bill Smith beat me to it.

"Hey, Doc? What about those wires running all over the place? I figured out they were what was making the body parts move, but can you tell us how?"

"Certainly, Mr. Smith, but the how is the easy part, it's just electrical stimuli. The real question is *why*? It's not just to freak you guys out. Far from it, in fact. The motion you witnessed is the most crucial part of our research here. Let me go back a bit and explain.

"Blood supply is obviously important, but what we've found is even more vital is electrically stimulating the multitude of exposed nerve endings. Remember we talked about how the nerve cells line up in a row? Well, the human nervous system is incredibly complex, but basically it's made up of the nerve cells, the synapses, or gap between the cells, the spine, which acts as the highway for the stimuli, and the brain itself, which runs the whole show. The brain is a type of huge battery source, which produces and sends an electrical impulse down the spine and along a certain nerve chain, cell by cell, to reach a specific spot. It's called electrotonus, which is the altered state of a nerve during the passage of an electric current through it. You understand this all happens almost instantaneously and it's far more complicated than I've gotten into, but not nearly as complex as we once thought.

"Take the hand you saw in the video. Normally, the brain would send the signal down the proper neuropathway to tell the hand to, let's say, flex its index finger. My fiber-optic network can do the exact same thing. The hand in the video has no idea that it isn't still attached to an arm and a body, as it once was. It's still receiving the electrical signal to move one of its fingers. It doesn't make any difference, as far as the hand is concerned, that the stimuli are being transmitted along a wire rather than a chain of nerve cells. The function of the brain in these experiments is performed by a highly sophisticated computer program, nowhere near as complex as an organic brain, but more than capable of carrying out the rudimentary tasks we're asking it to do."

The scientist paused long enough to see if we were managing to keep up with what he was saying. It was making some sense to me but a couple of the other guys were kind of shaking their heads in confusion. Rather than answering a ton of questions, Dr. Marshall held his hand up to quiet us down, and carried on with his explanation.

"Let me walk you through it. I hope it will make things clearer. Okay, when a limb suffers the kind of severe trauma associated with an accidental amputation, it's inevitable that many nerve cells will be too damaged to survive. There's nothing anyone, including me, can do about it. This is why it's wrong to try reattaching the limb to the patient's body right away. All you're doing is connecting two dead nerve cells together, effectively blocking the path the brain signals travel along.

"We've discovered that if we place tiny electrical receivers and transmitters into the exposed body tissue, the nerves below are still healthy and wondering what the hell is going on. Not on the surface tissue, where the nerve cells are mostly dead or far too damaged, but below that, into the next link in the chain, if you will. These nerves are still ready and waiting for the brain's next signal.

"Our mainframe computer tracks the transmitting signal it is sending out, and when it is received by a neuropath inside the limb, the computer locks on its location and continues to feed it electrical stimuli. It's a bit hit and miss, but we try and locate as many undamaged neuropathways as we can, then sit back and wait. If all goes as planned, the traumatized limb settles back down and starts to act as if nothing has happened. It's receiving a more than adequate blood supply and a constant transmission of brain-simulated electrical stimuli. I'm oversimplifying again, but basically those are the only two things the limb needs.

"Those spastic, jerky motions you noticed in the video are actually induced by us. The body parts don't really need that much stimulation to stay healthy, but we do it anyway just to keep the muscles from succumbing to atrophy.

"It's not a perfect system, by any means, and sometimes all our efforts still end up going for naught, but our success rate now stands at just over ninety-one percent. Not too shabby, huh?"

He stopped talking and once again the small conference room was silent, but this time it wasn't uncomfortable. Unlike the tension-filled silence that had succeeded the video presentation, this quiet was more of a pondering, absorbing all the facts kind of quiet. We'd been fed a lot of information, both visually and verbally, and we each needed a minute or two to chew it and digest it at our own speed. Realizing this, Dr. Marshall remained quiet, busying himself with straightening out and tucking in the blanket covering his legs. It didn't need straightening, but it gave us the time we needed to gather our thoughts.

My thoughts weren't particularly nice ones. In fact, they were downright nasty. I couldn't quite get the image of my own arm out of my head. I kept picturing it severed from my body and twitching on some lab table with thousands of those little colorful wires trailing out from its ragged bloody end. It wasn't a pretty image to sit and think about so I stood up to ask the doctor a question, just to derail my morbid thoughts.

"Doctor?" I asked. "Earlier, before you showed the video, you said the point wasn't to shock anyone but to prove what we were going to attempt here could be done. Maybe I'm missing something but with the obvious success you're having with this type of thing, isn't it becoming old hat for you? I mean, you've done this over and over with various body parts, and to me at least, you seem to have it down pat. What do you need us for? What are you planning to attempt with *our* limbs that's so special?"

Dr. Marshall seemed to deflate in his wheelchair and for a moment I thought I'd blown my chance at getting rich. I was sure he was about to get mad and have me tossed out on my ear. Instead, he rolled his chair closer to us and asked Bill and I to move down so he wouldn't have to shout anymore. I helped move Red Beard down beside Wheels and Bill and I grabbed chairs in the first row too.

"Much better," Dr. Marshall said with a smile, then took a deep breath. "I was going to save this until after lunch but what the heck, now's as good a time as any. Mr. Fox has brought up a very good point. There comes a time in any research project when simply repeating the experiment becomes redundant. What's the point of doing something again if you already know it can be done? It's a waste of time and resources.

"Our research, while miles ahead of the public sector, has basically slammed up against that proverbial redundant wall, so I've decided it's time to take the next step up the ladder. It's time we used the knowledge we've acquired not only to keep a severed limb alive and healthy but to go ahead and reattach it to a human host, fully functional and strong as ever. This is where you people come in. Yours will be the first limbs we ever try this with, which is why I felt it was important to have this talk today."

"Are you saying you're going to remove our different parts like we'd agreed, set them up on those machines to keep them healthy, then reattach them to us?" Bill Smith wondered aloud. "I'm actually going to walk out of here looking just like I do now?"

There was a glimmer of hope in his voice and my thoughts were racing too, but the look on Dr. Marshall's face made it clear our hopes were in vain.

"No, Mr. Smith," the doctor said. "I'm afraid that's not going to happen. I have *other* plans in place. I'm sorry, but I've already promised your limbs to someone else."

"Who?" all four of us asked, speaking in quadstereo.

Dr. Marshall seemed to shrink even further into his chair and with a heavy sigh, whispered, "If you remember, I mentioned that I had a personal reason for thanking you. Well, that personal reason is my son. I'm planning on giving your arms and legs to him."

CHAPTER NINE

"I'm going to attach your arms and legs onto the body of my son," Dr. Marshall repeated, but even though I'd heard him say it twice, I was still having trouble grasping what he was telling us.

"I don't understand," I said, my confusion obviously shared by my companions. "You can't be serious. Your son, he needs all four of our . . . I mean . . . he doesn't have *any* of his own . . ."

I couldn't even finish the sentence. Jesus! How could I ask this man if his kid was nothing but a torso? Maybe I had this situation all screwed up. His son might have both his arms and legs intact, but something was wrong and he just couldn't use them. That sounded more like it—for a minute there my imagination got away from me. I apologized to Dr. Marshall for my callousness, then decided to shut the hell up before I put my foot in my mouth again.

"No need, Mr. Fox," he said. "Actually, your assessment of my son's situation was right on the money. At least for the moment, he has no arms or legs. He's confined to one of my hospital beds upstairs."

The doctor was looking directly at me, seemingly expecting a response. His tone of voice had been light but the way he was looking at me was anything but friendly. Then again, I could be reading him wrong. I was trying to imagine what it must be like to lie in a bed day after day without being able to move, but I couldn't comprehend it. The doctor was still staring at me—really staring—and I felt a chill envelop me as I struggled to come up with something to say. Unable to come up with anything that might change the subject, but feeling like I should say *something*, I asked, "How did your son lose his limbs? Was it an accident?"

"No, no accident," he said. "I cut them off him myself, about three weeks ago."

For a moment, his eyes stayed locked on mine and I can honestly say I'd never seen such cold, penetrating eyes before. They were like dark marbles, almost reptilian in appearance, but then he laughed, and all traces of maliciousness were instantly gone. Might not have been any to begin with.

"That came out a little more sinister sounding than I'd intended." The surgeon smiled. "I did have to remove my son's arms and legs, but that was only in preparation for his operation in the near future. Let me explain.

"My son's name is Andrew, Andrew Nathan Marshall, and I love him with all my heart. He's had a fairly happy life but it's also been a difficult one. He's been severely disabled since birth and every pain-filled day he's endured has been my fault. It was me who caused his disabilities and I've never forgiven myself for it. Now I'm hoping to finally make it up to him.

"I was a young man back in the early 1960s, a promising doctor and surgeon who thought he knew it all. What I was, was a first-class fool. My wife, Julia, was pregnant with our first child and was having a terrible time with morning sickness. Me, being the brilliant doctor I thought I was, prescribed her the drug thalidomide, which in those days was being used during pregnancies to stop nausea in the first trimester. There were reports out that thalidomide was causing birth defects but I didn't pay attention to them. I thought I knew what was best for my wife and unborn child. I was wrong.

"Andrew was born in the summer of 1963, and was a perfect example of the classic thalidomide baby. His head and torso were completely normal-sized, his brain and spinal column fully developed and normal in every way, but something in the drug had stunted the development of his arms and legs. They formed, but not the way they should have. Basically he had small paddlelike flippers where his arms should have been, and his legs, although somewhat better formed, were still grotesquely underdeveloped and have never been able to hold his weight.

"I lost the use of my legs in a freak car accident, but I at least knew the joy of walking for my first forty-five years. Because of my stupidity, my son has never walked a day in his life. He's never played a game of baseball, never ridden a bike. He's never done any of the things a normal child would take for granted, but I vowed I'd never give up trying to help. That's why I chose this particular line of study. From day one, my only objective has been to help my son.

"Maybe now you can understand why I'm so grateful to you four gentlemen. It's too late to give Andrew back the things he missed in childhood, but with your help, it's not too late to give him the one thing he desires most, to stand on his own two feet and go outside for a walk."

A single tiny tear dribbled down the doctor's left cheek and he licked it away when it touched the corner of his mouth. To tell the truth, my eyes were getting a little damp, too. It was just such a beautiful story. This brilliant man had been pushing the boundaries of science for decades, not for the love of fame or money, but for the love of his invalid child. That child was a fully grown adult now, but Dr. Marshall had never faltered, never given up hope, in his quest to help him, and at that moment I admired the doctor more than any other man I could think of.

I was more than ready to help out. Although normally a cynical son of a bitch by nature, from what I'd already seen, I truly believed Dr. Marshall would be able to pull it off and deliver his promise to his poor son. Although it made no real difference in my life—I was going to be rich either way—somehow it made me feel a hell of a lot better about donating my arm knowing what I knew.

Not surprisingly, the other guys had been affected by the doctor's words, also. He'd been so open and honest with us, how could we not be? He didn't have to share this personal stuff with us. We wanted the money, sure, but I think we also really wanted to help.

We talked for a few more minutes, everyone quite comfortable with each other's company by this time. Dr. Marshall promised to introduce us to Andrew and talked about what we'd see on the tour we were going to take. Everyone was excited, including me.

For a second, I considered asking him about something in the video. It had bothered me when I watched it and it was bothering me even more now. I wanted to learn more about that severed head with the spine thrashing around in the glass tank. I mean, the arms and legs and hands and stuff I could understand, but not the head. Like ourselves, people could have donated those other body parts, but that man—whoever it had been—had died for that particular experiment. *Died*, for God's sake! Wasn't that taking things just a bit too far? No matter how noble and pure Dr. Marshall's intentions were, wasn't there a line that shouldn't be crossed?

Somehow this didn't seem like the time to get into it, though, so I bit my tongue. I'd ask him later if I got the chance. Who was I to spoil the friendly mood?

Drake poked his head into the room long enough to inform us that Cook had the food prepared if we were ready for it. He disappeared without waiting for an answer.

"Excellent!" Dr. Marshall said. "Is everyone up for a spot of lunch?"

After the graphic video presentation and everything else I'd seen and heard this morning, lunch didn't sound all that appealing to me, but when you've been on the street as long as I have, you learn never to pass up a free meal.

"Sure thing," I said, and followed the rest of the gang up the wheelchair ramp and out the door.

CHAPTER TEN

Seeing as my normal definition of fine dining included a WHOPPER® and fries from Burger King, when Dr. Marshall had mentioned "a spot of lunch," I'd been expecting a bowl of soup or maybe a peanut butter and jam sandwich. I couldn't believe my eyes when the waiter—a thin Asian man dressed in the whitest shirt, pants, and apron on the planet—kept bringing out tray after tray of gourmet delights.

To start with, we dug into crackers and cheese, deviled eggs, pickles, and jumbo shrimp cocktails. Then we moved on to fresh garden salads with our choice of two different kinds of thick, delicious soups. By this time I was already reasonably full, but there was no way I was going to miss out on the main course, which was honey-roasted ham with creamy scalloped potatoes and asparagus tips in melted butter. There was a dessert tray too, but I couldn't go anywhere near it without threatening to burst. If that was what they called lunch around here, I could hardly wait to see what supper would be like.

When Dr. Marshall finally managed to drag us wide-eyed slobs away from the feast, he delivered on his promise of the personally guided tour of his incredible medical facility. We learned that the entire building had been designed as wheelchair accessible, and not just for Dr. Marshall's benefit. Wheels and Red Beard were suitably impressed they wouldn't have to "sit out" certain areas of the tour like they normally might in a building this size.

The first floor we covered quickly, since we'd already seen the majority of it. Besides the lavish four-story reception atrium, there were three conference and video rooms, the dining hall, the kitchen, and a rather impressive medical library and computer research station.

The second floor was the real heart of the facility, where Dr. Marshall's laboratories and operating rooms were. Like the driver who'd delivered us here this morning had said, everything was state of the art. Not a penny had been spared; lab after lab was filled with the best surgical and research equipment money could buy. Some of the equipment here wasn't even available to scientists in the public sector. Dr. Marshall and his staff had developed, patented, then produced it strictly for their own benefit.

Being a layman in every sense of the word, I didn't have a clue what 99 percent of the gizmos and gadgets were for, but Dr. Marshall did his best to answer all of our questions and clue us in as best he could. We got to see all the experiments up close, which was kind of cool once you got over the queasy feeling of being in a room full of severed body parts. They were definitely grotesque, but for the most part I found them fascinating, almost like I had somehow walked into one of the science fiction movies I'd enjoyed so much as a kid.

The highlights for me included getting to see the leg that had miraculously survived for one hundred and nineteen record days and when I got to shake the hand of a severed woman's arm. I took hold of the hand as one of the medical lab assistants punched in a command on a nearby computer terminal. Almost instantly, the hand clenched comfortably around mine, scaring the shit out of me, and causing everyone else to laugh at my reaction. Freaky, man!

After checking out the three spacious and efficient-looking operating theaters, we headed up to tour the third floor. This floor was set up more like a posh hotel than a hospital ward, with thick luxurious carpet on the floor and beautiful paintings hanging on the walls. This was where the staff lived and also where our bedrooms were going to be for as long as our stay here lasted. I was anxious to explore my room but Dr. Marshall gestured for us to stop at room 301 near the end of the first hallway. He turned, and, when he talked to us, his voice was barely above a whisper.

"This is Andrew's room. Your rooms are around the corner at the far end of the building. You'll see your names on the doors. There really isn't much else to see. The fourth floor is just for storage and empty space for future expansion, but before you go get settled in, I thought you might like to meet my son."

"Of course," I said. Everyone agreed it would be nice to meet the guy we were here to help.

"Great. I'll just check in on him first and see if he's up for a visit. He's a little apprehensive about taking your arms and legs. He thinks you'll all hate him for it. Maybe you can set his mind at ease. It's the last thing he needs to be worried about right now. Just stay here a minute and keep the noise down. I'll be right back."

The surgeon disappeared quietly into room 301 and we waited patiently in the hall for five minutes. We were starting to get restless when Dr. Marshall opened the door and rejoined us.

"I'm afraid this isn't a good time for this. Andrew is sleeping comfortably and I don't want to wake him. He's on a lot of medication that tends to keep him pretty drowsy. I don't want him moving around too much before the operation. The nurse tells me that lately he's been sleeping during the day, and up watching television most of the night.

"I'm going to take you in to have a quick peek but you have to stay quiet. I want you to meet him more formally, of course, but that will have to wait for another day. I'm sure you'll have lots of chances to talk to each other over the next few months. Come on in."

We paraded into the room as quietly as possible and gathered just inside the door. Andrew's room was huge, his hospital bed easily thirty feet away from us, situated beside a large three-paned picture window so he could see the fields outside. Andrew was only a small lump under the sparkling white bed sheets. He was bandaged up worse than an Egyptian mummy, so much so that I'd have never been able to guess there was a man on the bed if I hadn't been told. An oxygen mask covered his face, obscuring our view of his only exposed skin. It was a sad, sobering sight, and at that moment I was glad he was asleep because I wouldn't have been able to think of a single thing to say to him.

The rest of the room was taken up with various monitoring equipment, medical supplies, and a mainframe computer system. Thousands of tiny wires trailed from the computer station over to Andrew's bed, where they split in four directions to connect into the bandaged areas where his arms and legs should have been. We only stayed for a minute, but it was long enough for us to realize this poor man needed our help badly.

"Pretty unsettling, isn't it?" Dr. Marshall grimaced, once we were all back in the hall. "Maybe now you can fully realize why I've been so driven to help him. He's my only son. I hope he won't have to live his life in that room much longer.

"I took you in there because I wanted you to see how

I've prepared his body to accept your donated limbs. You noticed the fiber-optic connections? The same principle we talked about to keep your limbs alive once they are surgically removed is applied to *his* body for the re-attachment procedure. I removed his deformed stumps and have attached the fiber-optic network to all the healthy nerve endings we could find. During surgery, I'll be hooking up these healthy nerves to your healthy nerves, and there should be a minimal amount of function loss from your body to his. Essentially, given time to heal of course, he should be able to get up and walk away almost as if your donated limbs had been his own right from birth."

We thanked Dr. Marshall for the tour and each rambled down the hall to find our rooms. We agreed to meet back downstairs for supper at 7:00 P.M. sharp. After the lunch we'd been treated to, I for one didn't plan on being late.

My room was number 332, halfway down the corridor. It was a lavish suite, which even surpassed the splendor of the Four Seasons, where Blue J and I had spent the night earlier this week. It was only half the size of Andrew's room but seeing as I was used to sleeping in a Dumpster, this room far exceeded anything that I'd ever need. I sprawled on the bed, flipped on the boob tube, and watched a little mindless television for a while, just trying to mellow out from all the excitement. With all the information swirling around in my head, I didn't think I'd be able to relax, but within minutes my eyelids were drooping. I didn't even try fighting it, drifting off for an afternoon nap.

When I woke up it was already 6:11 P.M., which surprised me but still left me more than enough time to have a nice hot bath before heading downstairs to the dining hall. I was the last guest to show. There were also twelve men and women I hadn't met yet, probably staff, but they were eating at another table on the far side of the room. Dr. Marshall and Drake both ate with us.

Supper was wonderful. We had seafood chowder, then our choice of pasta primavera with boneless chicken strips or pork chops with applesauce. Being a pig, I had both. I also drank the better part of a bottle of expensive red wine. Nobody seemed to care. Eat, drink, and be merry, I guess.

After the meal, Dr. Marshall raised his glass to make a toast.

"To my new friends," he said. "Together, we make history."

There was some laughter and a cheer from everyone at the table; then Dr. Marshall said something else that made us cheer even louder.

"We only have one more thing to do today. We have to sign a contract with each other. Anyone interested in getting rich? Yeah? Well, let's go make each of you millionaires. How does that sound?"

Pretty damn good to me.

I followed Drake and his boss out of the dining hall and back to the glass-domed atrium.

An older secretary with a wrinkled brow and her hair tied up in a tight bun passed out our contract forms, in triplicate, and we signed them after giving them the old once-over. Everything looked fine to me and, by this time, I suppose that I trusted the doctor.

Once the papers were collected and the secretary shuffled away with them, Drake had us sit with him one at a time in front of a fax machine. On the phone, he was talking to a representative of the First National Bank down in the Cayman Islands. Grand Cayman was a popular choice for anyone wishing to wire-deposit large amounts of cash into an offshore bank account. Their strict laws of nondisclosure made it virtually impossible for anyone—like say, the United States Internal Revenue Service—to stick their noses into the accounts and start asking questions. Dr. Marshall had previously set up these accounts and Drake was passing on the final information to activate them in our names. The fax machine started spewing out confirmation that I was now the holder of a bank account with an impressive balance of $2,000,000.00 in cold hard cash.

I held the document with shaking hands, reading it over four times to make sure it really had as many zeroes as I thought it did. I couldn't believe it. Yesterday I was a penniless, street loser—today, a multimillionaire.

After the last of us received our confirmation papers, we went back to the dining hall and had one hell of a party. Dr. Marshall and Drake left the four of us to it and soon we were sloshed out of our minds and whooping up a storm. If there's one thing homeless people can do best, it's party like there's no tomorrow, especially if someone else is picking up the tab for the booze.

When I left the party, the others were still hard at it and Red Beard had started to sing. Terribly, I might add. That's when I knew I'd had enough. It must have been around eleven o'clock when I stumbled upstairs to call it a night. It was a good thing they'd put my name on the door because damned if I could remember my room number. Anyway, I made it into bed, flicked off the light, and happily basked for a few minutes in the alcohol-induced glow.

"I'm a millionaire!" I rejoiced. "A goddamned millionaire. I can't bloody believe it. *Yaahooooo!*"

I laughed and laughed and could hardly get control of myself. This was one of the best nights of my entire life.

Unbe-fucking-lievable!

I curled into the wonderfully soft pillow and easily floated off to dreamland like a baby cuddled to its mother's bosom. I hadn't felt that comfortable and totally contented with life in a very long time.

CHAPTER ELEVEN

Comfortable and contented or not, I only managed to sleep until 4:07 A.M. I had to piss like a racehorse, and when I returned to bed I tried my best to get some more shuteye. Wasn't going to happen. I felt like crap from all the booze I'd guzzled and my head was throbbing like someone was beating on a bass drum stuck between my ears. Whether I liked it or not, I was wide-awake. Rather than lie around suffering, staring at the ceiling, I decided I might as well get dressed and go find myself a cup of coffee.

Fifteen minutes later, I was digging through the kitchen cupboards searching for some java. I'd easily found the coffeemaker sitting out on the gleaming stainless steel countertop, but I couldn't locate any coffee to put in it. On my second search, I found a jar of Nescafé instant, and boiled some water in a pot on the stove to make do. A big mug of double-strength with cream, and I was feeling more or less human again.

I wondered what time Red Beard and the others had finally called it quits. It was a safe bet their heads would be feeling a lot worse than mine, whenever they eventually crawled out of the sack. My guess, and believe me I'm speaking from experience, was the other donor boys wouldn't surface until lunchtime.

So where did that leave me? What was I supposed to do? It wasn't even five o'clock yet, and I was probably the only person in the entire medical center up and at it. Then again, maybe not. I was remembering how Dr. Marshall had informed us that his son slept most of the day, but was usually awake watching television throughout the night. Maybe this would be a good time to pop upstairs and introduce myself. Couldn't hurt. If Andrew was awake, I'm sure he'd appreciate the company. If he was asleep, I'd just tiptoe back out without bothering him.

Up the stairs I went, taking them two at a time. I was surprised to realize how excited I was to meet Andrew. Part of it was simple curiosity, wondering what it must be like to lie in that hospital bed all the time, but mostly I wanted to set this poor man's mind at ease about receiving our donated limbs. Yes, I wanted the money, but I felt a real need to explain to Andrew that I believed in his brilliant father and I was honestly thrilled to be able to help him. He'd probably think I was full of shit, but I could at least try.

As I entered the third-floor hallway, I caught a glimpse of a tall man heading around the corner ahead of me, walking away from the front of Andrew's room.

One of Andrew's doctors?

I considered calling out to the man, but I didn't want to unnecessarily wake anyone up. Hurrying to the corner, I was in time to see the tall man slipping into another room a few doors down the hall. I only saw the back of him, as he was halfway through the door, but what I saw sure didn't look like any doctor I'd ever seen. He was too big, almost Drake's size, and his hair was long, greasy, and wild.

Room 301 was unlocked, so I opened up the door and, without knocking, quietly walked in. Andrew was bundled up in his bed looking just as small and pathetic as he had yesterday; the computer terminals and video screens were still flickering their various electronic data, but I was taken aback there was no one else in the room monitoring the patient or the equipment. You'd think there ought to be *someone* in here with him. Maybe the tall man really had been Andrew's doctor? Or his nurse? Not that it mattered; I could see for myself the television was turned off and Andrew wasn't moving. He was asleep, so I might as well get out before I disturbed him.

Two steps away from the door, my curiosity got the better of me. I desperately wanted to get a closer look at Andrew, and at how his father had managed to attach all those rainbow-colored wires into his son's living flesh. In my heart, I realized I was being a first-rate asshole. Andrew wasn't some sideshow freak people paid a dollar to point fingers and laugh at—he was a sick, unfortunate man whose life had been a living hell since the day he'd been born. The least I could do was have the decency to let him sleep in peace, but damned if I didn't find myself slowly edging closer and closer to Andrew's bed.

I felt weird sneaking around, really weird, like a clumsy amateur burglar trying to build up his confidence before attempting to steal his first wallet from a bedside table. The best thing to do would be to cut the crap and just walk up to the bed and have a look. If Andrew woke up, so what? Hadn't I come up here to introduce myself anyway?

Get on with it, man.

Taking my own advice, I stopped inching around like a fool, and walked over to Andrew's bed. Dr. Marshall's son was nothing more than a small lump in the middle of the large hospital mattress, even his face hidden from me by the formfitting oxygen mask he was wearing. Now, I'm no doctor, and no one ever accused me of being a genius, but I could tell right away that something was wrong with this picture. It was dark, but enough moonlight filtered in through the nearby window for me to clearly see Andrew wasn't breathing. No matter how deeply a person is asleep—even people that are comatose—you can still count the number of times they're breathing by watching their chest rise and fall. Under the thin wool blanket covering him, Andrew's chest wasn't moving at all.

Oh my God . . . he's dead.

The first thought to race through my head, and I'll admit I'm not real proud of it, was: *Fuck. There goes my two million bucks down the drain. Dr. Marshall will never cough up the coin now. Not when there's no—*

Then I glanced behind me and noticed the video display screens over on the wall. Every last one of them showed Andrew's various life signs as bang-on normal. Heartbeat, blood pressure, body temperature, oxygen saturation levels; everything reading in the normal range. I turned my attention back to the man in bed, leaning over to really get a good look at his chest. Nothing. Nothing at all.

Grabbing a corner of the wool blanket, I slowly peeled back the covers to see if I could get to the bottom of this strange mystery. I immediately figured out the problem, but in doing so, received one of the biggest shocks of my life. The reason Andrew wasn't breathing was because Andrew didn't exist. Under the oxygen mask and tightly wrapped sheet, the man in the hospital bed was a plastic fake—a department store mannequin with its arms and legs removed.

"What the fuck is going on?" I whispered out loud, no longer worried about waking anyone up.

Looking around for answers, none were readily found. The video monitors still spewed forth their "everything's normal" nonsense. The uncountable number of colorful wires—supposedly attached to Andrew's nerve pathways—still snaked across the room only to end in four tangled knots hidden beneath the sheets. It was crazy. This entire setup was nothing more than an elaborate sham, a cleverly designed ruse, the reason for which I couldn't quite get my head around. Why would Dr. Marshall do this?

Before I could even guess, I heard the sound of a toilet flushing in a nearby room. Don't ask me how, but I instinctively knew it was the tall, greasy-haired man I'd caught a glimpse of a few minutes earlier. Not a doctor. Not a nurse. But one of Drake's security team, taking a break while guarding room 301 from any wandering eyes. He was supposed to be here, making sure no one tried to get in, but he'd wandered off to answer a call from Mother Nature or maybe have a smoke and stretch his legs. I'd just happened along at the right time. Dumb luck.

I might have been wrong, but I wasn't planning on sticking around long enough to find out. I trusted my instincts, better safe than sorry, and bolted for the door. I hit the hallway running, flashing by the washroom door just as it started to open. The security guard only caught a view of my backside, and I was halfway down the hall before he started screaming at me to stop. Yeah, right. I ran like the wind, pumping my arms and legs as if the hounds of Hell were nipping at my heels.

I could hear the guard—I was sure that was what he was, now—yelling frantic orders to someone else. Probably using a walkie-talkie to contact Drake, or someone else from security. I wasn't looking back to find out. Instead, I turned on the jets even more, flying around the corner leading to the guestrooms. I had a brief moment of panic trying to dig my room key out of my pocket on the run, but I managed to yank it out in time. I had just enough of a lead on the guard to safely make it into my room, lock the door behind me, and turn off the lights before I heard his heavy footfalls race by and continue on down the hall.

Phew! That was cutting it close.

As I undressed and climbed back into bed, I couldn't help but think about what I'd just seen, sorting through the events of the last hour trying to make some sense of them. I wasn't having much luck.

There was a knock at my door, and before my heart had a chance to leap into my throat, Drake came charging into my room without waiting to be invited. Obviously he had his own key. He was dressed in a dark green bathrobe and running shoes, and from the look on his face I could tell he was surprised to see me lying in bed. Right away, I knew he'd had me pegged as the culprit, but his tall, greasy henchman had probably informed him the suspect was still on the run. Barging into my room, planning to find it empty, had been Drake's way of confirming it was definitely me causing all this commotion. Now he wasn't sure what to think.

"Mr. Fox, are you . . . are you all right?" he said.

He was squirming and it looked good on the bastard. I wasn't about to let him off the hook. I wanted him thinking it had been someone else prowling the halls tonight. Let him chase his tail elsewhere, in other words.

"What's going on, Drake? Christ! You scared the crap out of me. What's the matter?"

"Nothin', Mike. We had a report of a fire on the third floor. I was just checking things out. False alarm, of course. Go back to sleep. Sorry I woke you."

And with that he was gone, more confused and angrier than ever. I could relate. I was pretty confused and angry myself. It simply didn't make sense. So there

I lay, staring at the same ceiling I'd been looking at less than six hours ago when I'd gone to bed a happy, contented man, with one question swirling around and around in the storm building within my head: If Dr. Marshall could lie to us about his supposedly invalid son, what else might he be lying about?

CHAPTER TWELVE

They say breakfast is the most important meal of the day. Maybe so, but it's also the most nerve-racking, sitting around trying to keep a poker face while your hosts know someone at the table knows far more than they are telling.

"And how did *you* sleep, Mike?" Dr. Marshall's tone of voice was light and jovial, but his eyes were dark and intense.

He's knows that last night's intruder had to be one of us, and he's smart enough to have it narrowed down to two people. The greasy-haired guard saw someone running away from room 301—running—and since Red Beard and Wheels are confined to their chairs, they're off the hook. That leaves either Bill Smith or me. He's sizing me up, testing the waters to see if I'll crack.

"Me? I slept fine. Why?" I answered.

"Oh, no reason. I'm just glad Mr. Drake didn't disturb you too much, that's all. Sorry about him barging in on you like that."

I nodded and shrugged my shoulders, reaching to grab another blueberry pancake from the silver platter in front of me. I wasn't hungry—I'd already eaten my fill—but I needed a minute to think, and filling my face was as good a way as any to avoid having to make conversation. Luckily, I wasn't alone at the table. Besides Dr. Marshall and Drake, all four donors were present. I'd been wrong when I figured the other three party animals would sleep the morning away. I should have known none of these bums would ever willingly miss a free feed, nasty hangover or not. Concentrating on pouring thick maple syrup over my pancake, I decided to let them do the talking for a while.

Maybe I should just confess it had been me in Andrew's room last night, confront the doctor about what I'd seen in room 301 right here in front of everyone. If Dr. Marshall had a valid reason for lying to us about his imaginary son, let's hear it.

I wouldn't do it, of course. I wasn't *that* stupid. The last thing I wanted to do was tip my hat and come clean with them. Why would I? They obviously weren't being honest with me, so why should I be with them? No, it would be far better—far smarter—to bite my tongue and sit in the bush for a while. I needed to figure out what game Dr. Marshall was playing, before I could make my next move.

If telling us the sob story about Andrew was a harmless ploy to make us feel better about donating our limbs, fine. I could live with that. But if something else was going on around here, something darker than the rosy picture currently being painted for us, then I planned on slipping out the back door as quiet as a mouse, disappearing before anyone caught wind I was on to them.

That was the real problem, wasn't it? Even seeing what I'd seen, and knowing what I knew, I still had no idea if things were on the up-and-up here. Had I walked into a lucky gold mine, or stumbled into a sinister trap? Should I stay here and take my chances, or sneak away and miss out on all that money? Tough call, but seeing as there was no way Dr. Marshall or Drake could know which one of us had been in Andrew's room—they could guess, but they couldn't be sure—it seemed safe enough to stick around for a while. Safe, as long as I kept my big mouth shut and my eyes and ears wide open.

Easier said than done, of course. When I looked up from my plate, Drake was staring at me hard enough to make me bruise. Our eyes locked, and I could tell he was trying to intimidate me, break me by staring me down. It was going to work, too. I found it terribly hard to maintain eye contact with this semicivilized Neanderthal, and I just knew if I looked away first, Drake would see the guilt in my eyes. So I quickly thought of something to say to him, hoping to deflect his attention elsewhere.

"So, did you manage to put out the fire?"

Without breaking eye contact, Drake replied, "There was no fire. I told you this morning it was a false alarm."

Now he was really staring down my throat, as was Dr. Marshall. Both of them were actually leaning forward in their chairs, hovering above me like birds of prey ready to tuck their wings and swoop in for the kill.

Fuck, Fuck, FUCK! Now what was I supposed to do?

"Fire? Hey, what are you guys talkin' about?"

It was Red Beard butting into the conversation, taking a break from cramming whole sausages into his cavernous mouth, unknowingly saving my ass with his question. He gave me an excuse to break eye contact with Drake and forced Dr. Marshall to answer him.

I was so relieved I could have kissed him. Instead, I reached for the pancakes and syrup again, staring back down at my plate while Dr. Marshall explained to the table how there'd been a minor electrical glitch this morning that had triggered a fire warning sensor on their security panel. Drake had investigated, naturally, but there'd been no cause for alarm. I risked a quick glance around, and only Red Beard and Wheels looked surprised by the news. Obviously only Bill's room and mine had been checked.

"Wow," Red Beard gasped. "Good thing it was only a false alarm. A fire in a joint like this could do millions of dollars' worth of damage. Trust me, when I was in the department, we used to see a lot of nasty ones. A fire here would put up a hell of a fight."

Red's admission that he used to be a fireman was enough of a revelation to everyone present, and the focus of the conversation was turned away from me and onto Red Beard, who thoroughly enjoyed the attention. He explained how he'd been a full-time firefighter in Niagara Falls, NY, for thirteen years before he'd lost his leg in a warehouse fire. The roof had collapsed, crushing his left leg beneath a steel girder and tons of flaming rubble.

"You weren't *really* a fireman, were you?" Drake asked, sounding positively shocked.

I almost burst out laughing, hearing the skepticism in the head of security's voice. He was making the same stupid prejudiced assumption nearly everyone makes about the homeless. Drake simply couldn't picture it in his thick head that Red had ever been anything other than the desperate loser sitting in front of him today. He thought—and trust me, he wasn't alone—all homeless people were lifelong drunks and fools. Sure, those types of bums were around, people so messed up on booze and drugs they'd paved their own way onto the street, but in my experience, those types of people were the minority. Most street folk, like Red Beard, Blue J, and I, were normal, ordinary, hard-working, productive members of society before our worlds crashed down on top of us. Don't get me wrong. We were far from innocent victims—we all make our own beds—but people like Drake would never understand that *people like us* were exactly the same as *people like him*.

"Sure I was," Red Beard shot back, his angry tone making it clear he was frustrated by the same tired prejudices I'd just been thinking about. "I can prove it, too. Here, take a look at this—"

Red pulled up his left sleeve and showed us a large colorful tattoo that was inked onto his bicep muscle. His arm was covered with tattoos but this particular one was of a bright red fireman's helmet, with a yellow ladder and an axe crisscrossing in front of it. The words N.F. STATION #5 were boldly written below.

"She's a beauty, huh, Drake?" Red Beard taunted, pride evident in his defiant voice. "Our whole shift went out, got right shit-faced, and decided to get these. Never regretted it for a minute."

Drake glared at the tattoo for a few seconds, then got up and left the table without saying a word. Contented smiles spread across all our faces, and Red Beard winked at me as if to say, That'll teach the bastard to have a little respect.

Right on, brother, I winked back. *Right on!*

The rest of the day was a breeze compared to the "under the microscope" treatment I'd suffered through at breakfast. Our surgeries were all scheduled for tomorrow morning—mine was penciled in for 10:00 A.M. in operating room #2—but before we could go under the knife, we had to pass our pre-op physicals. Records were made of our blood type, heart rate, blood pressure, and temperature. They collected blood, urine, and stool samples, checked our vision, took X-rays, and brought out another stack of forms that needed to be filled out in triplicate, again. They asked about allergies, childhood illnesses, sexual diseases, and any other relevant health issues—past or present—that Dr. Marshall needed to know about. It was all bullshit, really. They'd done their background checks on all four of us, and I was willing to bet they already knew the answer to every single question they asked before we'd even been approached. Still, I guess it didn't hurt to double check to make sure their records were up to date and correct.

All the running around managed to take up the entire morning, and we didn't sit down to lunch until 1:15 P.M. Thankfully, Drake and Dr. Marshall didn't join us so it was nice and peaceful. After we'd eaten, we had the rest of the afternoon to ourselves. The other guys took advantage of the break to catch up on a little shut-eye. Not wanting to look out of place, and still trying to avoid Drake, I also went to my room and hid until supper.

Even supper was rolling along without incident, everyone making small talk and stuffing their faces until Bill Smith silenced the room by asking, "So, any chance we can pop up and visit your son tonight, Doc?"

The surgeon froze in place with his fork halfway to his mouth, and Drake nearly swallowed his, he was so caught off guard. Wheels and Red Beard thought Bill's idea was marvelous, so I quickly chimed in my two cents' worth of approval, too. They were serious, but I just wanted to see how Dr. Marshall was going to get himself out of this predicament.

"There's a small problem, I'm afraid," he began. "Tonight's not a good night to visit Andrew. I was up seeing him earlier, and he isn't feeling very well. He might just be nervous about tomorrow, but let's give him the benefit of the doubt. Let's get through our surgeries, guys, and then you'll all have time to get to know Andrew. Fair enough?"

Small problem, my ass. Not a good night to visit him, on account he doesn't even exist!

Still, I had to admit that Dr. Marshall sounded sincere. He either believed what he was saying, or he was an incredible liar. No one at the table doubted his sincerity. Even I did a double take when I saw the pain on his face when he'd said Andrew wasn't feeling well. Maybe it was *me* that was crazy here. Maybe, somehow, I had this all twisted around and was mistaken about the doctor. Man, I was confused.

Then confront him. Do it now, Mike. Stop fucking around playing secret agent and just flat out ask him about what you saw.

I was tempted to do just that, and I think I would have if I hadn't noticed the way Dr. Marshall and Drake kept giving poor Bill Smith death stares. They'd glare over at him, then nod slightly to each other as if sharing some secret message. They thought they had their man. Bill had inadvertently asked about meeting Andrew and the chief of security was on him like a bloodhound on a fresh scent. To Drake, Bill's harmless remark was the slip of the tongue he'd been waiting for all day.

Dr. Marshall remained civil but Drake was practically drooling beside him, grinning like the village idiot, thinking he'd discovered the nighttime wanderer. Seeing that deranged look on his face was more than enough to make me thank my lucky stars I'd kept my big mouth shut.

CHAPTER THIRTEEN

We went to bed early, all of us needing to rest up for our operations in the morning. Unfortunately, resting was a luxury I couldn't afford. Sprawled on my too-comfortable bed, I tossed and turned until after midnight, trying to decide if I should bolt for home or not.

Something deep inside me was whispering I should run before it was too late, but thinking about that big chunk of cash kept giving me a reason to stay. Two million reasons, actually, and as weird as things seemed around here at times, I didn't really have any concrete evidence Dr. Marshall was up to anything nefarious. Truth be told, he'd treated me with nothing but kindness and respect since I'd arrived. Could I be overreacting?

It was a fair question, one I didn't have an answer for—and never would if I just lay here in bed doing nothing. Time was running out. They were going to cut my arm off in less than ten hours. I had to do *something*, for Christ's sake!

I shot out of bed and put my clothes back on. Reasonably sure the majority of people here at the medical center were in their beds, I was going out on the prowl again. I had no idea where to look, or even what I should look for, but one way or another I was determined to find out exactly what Dr. Marshall was up to.

Find his office, that's the place to start.

My hand was reaching for the doorknob when I heard a noise outside in the hallway. I froze. There it was again, and this time I recognized it for what it was—a cough. Not a big hacking cough, just someone clearing their throat, but it was enough to send a chill down my spine.

There wasn't one of those tiny glass peepholes in my door, so as quietly as I could, I knelt down on all fours and pressed the right side of my face against the floor. Sure enough, just on the other side of my door, I could see two thick black rubber soles, and a large shadow on the hall carpet.

That bastard!

Drake had placed a guard outside my room. I was sure he thought it had been Bill Smith messing around in room 301, but obviously he wasn't taking any chances. There would be a guard outside of Bill's room, too. Drake was making sure no one was going anywhere tonight. I had to give him credit. He was smarter than he looked. What was I going to do now?

The window?

It was the only other exit from the room, and although I knew I was on the third floor of the building, I walked over to check it anyway. The moon was out tonight, but most of it was hidden behind a bank of dark clouds. It was too dark for me to see much of anything beyond the glass, save for my shadowy reflection staring back at me, but I didn't need to see to know the ground was way too far below me to consider climbing or jumping down. I was trapped in this room, whether I liked it or not.

The window itself was made up of three separate pieces of glass, with the biggest pane in the center and two smaller sections on either side that could be cranked out to let in some air.

Feeling slightly claustrophobic all of a sudden, I did just that, spinning the little brass hand crank clockwise to open up the left-hand panel. I took several deep breaths of the cool night air to calm down, and was about to close the window when I spotted something clinging to the outside of the wall a few feet over to my left. I cranked the window fully open, quietly removed the bug screen, and stuck my head outside to get a better look.

A surge of adrenaline shot through me when I realized it was a trellis covered in thick green foliage. I might be able to use this to climb down to the ground, and make my escape. Or up, to climb onto the—

Roof, I'd been thinking, but my thought process was permanently interrupted when I tilted my head to gaze skyward. The side panel of the window in the room directly above my head was cranked open just as mine was. If I wanted to, I could climb the trellis, re-enter the medical center one floor up, and carry on with my plans to search around this castle of secrets.

What had Dr. Marshall said was on the fourth floor? *Nothing but storage space and room for future expansion.* That meant no one would be up there. I could hit any of the stairwells, search anywhere I wanted as long as I was quiet and extra careful, then retrace my steps back into my room, hopefully without anyone knowing I'd ever left.

Would the trellis hold me? I could picture myself reaching out, hearing it crack and break apart in my hands, then taking the slow-motion drop to land on my back on some sharp unseen rock far below. Not a nice thought. Maybe I should just go back to bed and get some sleep.

I reached through the ivy (or whatever the hell type

of plant it was), and gave the trellis a good strong tug. Nothing happened. It was made from some type of metal, cold and hard to the touch, and from the way it didn't even budge I could tell the trellis had been securely fastened into the brickwork of the building. It would hold my weight, no problem.

Maybe.

Before I had a chance to think too much, I swung my legs over the ledge, and grabbed for the metal framework with first one hand, then the other. Seconds later, I was successfully onto the trellis. I hung there for a minute as still as a display window mannequin, hardly daring to breathe as I waited to hear the wrenching noise of metal bolts breaking loose that would precede my fifty-foot drop to oblivion. Nothing happened, and if the gods that watch over lunatics had decided to smile on me tonight, I wasn't one to question their reasons. I just started up the makeshift ladder hand over hand, foot over foot, as quickly and quietly as I could manage.

No doubt, I should probably be heading the opposite direction, down the trellis to the ground and getting the heck out of here, but I was too stubborn to do that. Call me a fool, but I still wanted to get my hands (well, hand, if I went through with this) on the money I'd been promised. Until I had solid proof Dr. Marshall was pulling a scam here, I wasn't about to let my vivid imagination cheat me out of my chance at being rich.

Scaling the trellis was easy, and getting into the fourth-floor room proved even easier. I'd expected to have to wrestle with the bug screen, popping it off and trying to catch it while dangling from one hand. Thankfully there was no screen on this window, so I just reached over and stepped right in.

Inside, it was too dark for me to risk blindly stumbling around, so I stood my ground and waited for my eyes to re-accustom to the gloom. Soon, I could make out enough details to guess I was in some sort of large storage room. There were several large bulky items arranged along both outside walls, but the center of the room was free of debris. Straight ahead, about forty feet away, I could just make out the rectangular-shaped outline of what had to be the exit into the hallway. I started walking in that direction, intending to find the nearest stairwell, but I stopped dead in my tracks before I'd taken my second step.

One of the bulky shapes against the wall to my right began to move. Then my eyes caught another movement somewhere over to my left. I remained calm, relatively speaking, anyway, until I heard a sound that sent my heart straight up into my throat. In that dark, supposedly empty storage room, someone began to snore.

Oh fuck!

I wasn't alone in this room. Someone was in here with me, still sleeping, obviously, but for how long? As my night vision improved, it became evident things were even worse than that. The bulky items I'd seen lining the walls were all beds, and nearly every one of them was being slept in. I counted ten, no, eleven people sleeping around me.

My first thought was I'd walked into a room full of security guards, slumbering in a barracks-type room until their shift in the morning. Something wasn't right about the way the people looked, though. The bodies looked weird somehow, far too small to be a group of fully grown men.

The moon chose that moment to emerge from behind the clouds, bathing the room in a soft white glow through the window behind me. I nearly screamed when I realized what was wrong with the people lying in the beds. They were fully grown men after all, but every last one of them had had their arms and legs removed. Clear plastic intravenous tubes were stuck in some of their shoulder stumps, chests, or in the side of their heads, and a dark fluid ran into several of the mutilated men from small machines sitting on the floor beside some of the beds.

What happened to these poor people?

I noticed the industrial-sized refrigerator with the sliding glass doors on the front of it, and the stacks of small liquid-filled bags separated into sections with labels like *A NEG* or *O POS*. Then I grasped the true horror of what was happening here in this secret room. The machines on the floor and the IV tubes weren't *giving* the limbless men the dark fluids—they were *taking* it.

My ears were ringing, vividly recalling how Dr. Marshall had said they had a problem keeping up with the constant need for fresh blood for his experiments.

Sweet mother of God!

This awful room was the solution to the surgeon's ongoing supply problem. They were his Bleeders: men kept alive for the sole purpose of being continually tapped and re-tapped for that most precious of humanity's resources. This wasn't a room full of sick men—it was Dr. Marshall's blood bank.

CHAPTER FOURTEEN

I couldn't move. I tried, but I couldn't. My feet felt like they were nailed to the floor. I'd seen a lot of weird things in my life, and I knew humans were capable of committing copious amounts of cruel and vicious acts, but I'd never seen anything as nasty as this. This was cruelty so extreme my mind was short-circuiting, overloaded trying to somehow justify what I was seeing. I couldn't do it. This wasn't something that could be rationalized. The only explanation for this was madness.

Taking a few deep breaths, I forced myself to calm down. I needed to think, decide what this meant in regards to my situation, and then figure out what my next move should be. I was just getting focused, when a strong, clear, man's voice said, "Hey, mister, you're not a guard, are you?"

For a second time I nearly screamed, the booming voice startling me badly, but at least breaking me out of reverie. Not having a clue who the voice belonged to, or where this man was, I darted my head left, then right, panic swelling inside me because I couldn't find him.

"Stop flapping your head around, boy, and get over here. Behind you, second bed from the door."

I turned and finally saw him. A tiny little bump of

meat hidden under a blanket with his seemingly large shaven head turned on its side watching me. He looked wide-awake, alert, and a little tense. Probably had been watching me for a while, maybe scared at first, wondering who I was, and why I was sneaking around in the middle of the night. Judging from his rough, gravelly voice—and from the way he'd addressed me as "boy"—I figured he was an older man, maybe sixty, but from what was left of his ravaged body, that was only a guess.

"Who the hell are you?" he asked, once I'd walked over to the foot of his bed.

He was talking too loud, so I hurried to answer him, more to shut him up than because I wanted to chat. "My name's Michael Fox," I whispered, "and no, I'm not a guard. I'm just a guest, and I'm not here to hurt you, sir, so quiet down a little, okay?"

"Quiet down?" he spoke in the same loud tone. "Why? For these veggies, you mean?" sweeping his eyes around the room. "You don't have to worry about bothering any of these fellas. Trust me. Their cabooses are still here, but the rest of the trains left the station a long time ago, if you catch my drift. The only one who's somewhat with it is Charlie, the guy snoring his head off over there, but he fades in and out. The rest, well, they're in a better place, I hope."

Quieting down a little regardless, perhaps for my sake, he said, "You can call me Lucas, Mr. Fox. Okay if I call you Michael?"

"Sure. Make it Mike."

"Fine. Now that we've been introduced, just what in blazes are you doing here?"

"Well, I couldn't get my room door to open," I lied, stumbling to find an explanation that wasn't totally idiotic. "It must be jammed, or the lock might be broken. It's the middle of the night, and I didn't want to bother anyone, so I tried my window and noticed—"

"No, no," he interrupted. "I don't give a damn why you're here in this room. Why are you *here*, in this godforsaken hell house?"

Hell house?

"Oh, I'm here to help Dr. Marshall with, ah, one of his experiments. He's paying me—"

"Let me guess?" Lucas interrupted again. "A million dollars, right?"

"Two million, actually. Already been wired into a bank account in the Cayman Islands. What do you know about it?"

"*Two* million? Wow. The stakes sure are going up. And you can forget the Caymans. You might have thought all that malarkey with the secretary and fax machines was real, but it was bullshit, Mike. They play that game with everyone. When I arrived, must be nearly two years ago, I was stupid enough to agree to six hundred thousand. Mind you, that was only for my right hand. Charlie, he was the one who said he'd signed for a million. I think that was for one of his legs, but I can't remember for sure now.

"Doesn't matter. Neither does the money. Doesn't matter what body part you agree to donate, or for how much. Hell, Doc Marshall could've promised you two *billion* dollars for your toenail, Mike, you won't see a dime."

My ears were hearing the words this partial man was speaking, but I was having a hard time making sense of them. After building up my hopes and dreams for a better life for my daughter and me, it was difficult letting myself believe what my heart had been trying to tell me all along. It was a lie. All of it. Dr. Marshall never had any intention of paying me for my arm. I had all the proof I needed lying all around me.

This revelation, although I'd had my suspicions and this was exactly the evidence I'd gone searching for, still hit me like a ton of bricks. A major part of me had desperately wanted this to work out, for something to finally go my way, just once. I should have known better. I bowed my head, stunned into silence.

"What are you supposed to be giving up?" Lucas asked.

"My right arm. I'm left-handed, and I figured, I just figured . . . ah fuck! I don't know what I figured."

"Listen to me, boy. Listen good. Dr. Marshall will take your right arm, but he won't stop there. He's been trying this shit for years, and it never works. Not the way he wants it to, anyway. The donor parts don't last, or they don't function right after a few weeks. He probably told you he's setting all these records for keeping body parts alive, but he's bullshitting you. He replaces the parts with new donors, and pretends it's the same one. He's crazy, man.

"He's not even a real doctor. Not anymore. From what I hear he was once a damn good one, but he lost his mind around the same time he lost the use of his legs. Something snapped and he ended up losing his license because he was caught doing unethical research. They nailed his ass to the wall, but he had family money to fall back on. Eventually he opened this place and hires all the failed surgeons and discredited nurses he can round up. Think about it. Who else would work for a bastard like him?"

I had no idea. My mind was spinning too fast to think straight. What a nightmare. Maybe I—

"Don't do it, Mike. Don't you give that crazy man anything, you hear me? He'll cut you to pieces, boy, just like he done me. First your arms, then your legs, then one day when you're of no further use to him, you'll end up in this room with me. Run away, right now. Run as far from here as you can, and never come back. Never!"

Nodding my understanding to the old man, I knew it

was time to leave. I'd seen and heard enough. Dr. Marshall might be a brilliant surgeon, and an incredibly smart man, but somewhere along the line his obsessions had pushed him over the edge. He wasn't bug-eyed crazy, just psychotic, a man driven to succeed at any and all costs. No sane man could justify the crimes he was committing inside this room. There was no way I was going through with the operation now. This roomful of Bleeders was more than enough to convince me it was time to pull out of Dodge, get as far away from this crazy place as I could.

And I'm taking my arm with me.

Turning on my heel, I started back toward the open window, intending to climb down to my room long enough to quietly gather my stuff, then use the trellis again to head for the ground and make good my escape.

"Wait," the old man cried out, sounding panicked that I was leaving. "You can't leave me here. Not like *this!*"

"I'm sorry Lucas, but there's no way I can take you with me. I'll be lucky if I make it on my own, never mind trying to carry—"

"I don't wanna go with you," he whispered, and when I saw the pleading look in his eyes, I finally understood what he wanted me to do.

"Oh no! No way, Lucas. I can't do that."

"Sure you can. Use my pillow, it'll only take a minute. Look, I know you don't know me, or know nothing about me, but I used to be a proud man, Mike. That bastard Marshall stole more than my limbs, he stole my life, my humanity, my soul. I can't live like this anymore. You're my only way out. Please Mike, I'm begging you."

Son of a bitch. How did I get myself into this mess?

The sad part was, I agreed with him. No man should

have to live like that, existing just to supplement a crazy man's depraved obsessions. I couldn't imagine what Lucas's life must be like, having his life fluids drained on a continuous basis, with no hope of relief until his body was spent, or his mind snapped like his companions. He didn't deserve this cruel fate, and I felt a need to help him. I just wasn't sure I had the strength to go through with it. Regardless of whether he was giving me his blessing, mercy-killing this poor man would still be murder. Wouldn't it?

I walked to the side of Lucas's bed and slowly wiggled his pillow out from under his shaven head. In doing so, an IV line that had been cruelly inserted into a vein above his left ear popped out, spilling fresh blood onto the white bedsheets. The blood, which appeared black in the moonlight, startled me but it wasn't gushing out—merely dripping—so I ignored it, not even bothering to mention it to Lucas. Why bother?

"You sure about this, Lucas?" I asked, hoping with all my heart he'd changed his mind.

"I've never been so sure of anything in my whole life. Bless you, Mike. I'm ready."

There were tears in his eyes as I lowered the pillow down onto his face, but he was smiling and nodding his head the whole time. I felt like a total bastard, but, at the same time, I knew I was doing the right thing, giving him the peace he deserved. He'd suffered enough.

Never having done anything like this, I wasn't sure how much pressure I should apply to the pillow. I wanted to get this over with as quickly and painlessly as possible. Trusting my instincts, I pressed down until Lucas's torso began to shake. He was struggling for air, but without any limbs he wasn't able to put up much of a fight. I turned my head away, hoping it would be over soon, unable to watch as his body continued to fight beneath me.

With everything going on, I failed to realize the snoring coming from the other side of the room had stopped. It wasn't until the man Lucas had identified as Charlie began screaming at the top of his lungs that I clued in someone was watching everything I was doing.

"Get off him," Charlie screamed, his frightened voice as high-pitched and ear-shattering as a young girl's. "Leave Lucas alone you cocksucker. He's my only friend."

I tried to talk to him, tried to reason that I wasn't hurting Lucas and this was what he'd wanted, but Charlie was having none of it. His mind wasn't altogether there anymore, and all he could see was a man hurting the only companion he had left in this world. He kept screaming, "Leave him alone, leave him alone," beating his head against his pillow every time he said it.

"Calm down," I yelled, but then I saw the red light flash on above his bed and understood immediately that Charlie wasn't as out of it as I'd thought. He hadn't been thrashing his head against the pillow; he'd been trying to activate the call button strapped to his bed, desperate to get help for his friend. Unaware he'd already succeeded, he continued to pound his head in cadence with his screams until the flashing red light went solid and a deep angry-sounding voice came through a small speaker mounted above his bed.

"What's going on in there? Charlie, is that you? What the hell do you want at this time of night?"

"You gotta help us. Someone's trying to kill Lucas. Get in here, quick!" Charlie wailed, his voice shrill, hitching with sobs, borderline hysterical.

Whoever was listening on the other end didn't bother replying to Charlie's rant. All I heard was someone curse as he fumbled for his walkie-talkie, keying the mike four or five times before shouting, "Carl? Are you there, Carl? Get your ass up to—"

The red light above Charlie's bed blinked out, disconnecting me from hearing the rest of the message. I had no trouble imagining every walkie-talkie in the medical complex beginning to squawk, and every guard running as fast as they could to get to this room.

Oh shit! This is trouble, Mike. Big, big trouble. Get the hell out, fast.

I lifted the pillow from Lucas' face, hoping he'd passed on, but it wasn't meant to be. He was unconscious, possibly near death's door, but I could clearly see his chest still rising and falling as his defiant body labored to breathe. Not knowing how much time I had before this room filled with angry guards, I couldn't risk taking the time to try smothering him again.

"Sorry, Lucas," I whispered in his ear, then quickly headed for the open window.

Stopping at my room to pick up my stuff was out of the question now. I'd just take the trellis right to the ground and make a run for the surrounding woods. Hopefully I'd be able to outrun anyone they sent after me, or at least find a hiding spot to lay low until they went away.

I was just about to step out onto the metal trellis, when a noise below nearly caused me to fall off the ledge. One floor down, a guard with blond hair and glasses stuck his head out the open window of my room and spotted me right away.

"I see him," the guard calmly spoke into his radio. "He's still on level four. Repeat . . . suspect is still on four."

This must have been the guy standing outside my door earlier. When the shit had hit the fan the first thing he'd have done was check on me, and found nothing but an open window. After reporting my current position, he tucked his radio away in his jacket and started climbing up the trellis toward me. My escape route effectively gone, I had no choice but to step back into the Bleeders' room and lock the window behind me.

Within seconds, the guard's face pressed up against the glass inches away from me, and he tried his best to talk me into opening the window.

"Unlock it, Mr. Fox. You're in enough trouble as it is. Don't make it worse. Open up."

Screw you, buddy.

Instead, I pulled the curtains closed, hoping he'd shut up so I could think for a minute. Unfortunately, I didn't have that long. The door to the Bleeders' room burst open, the overhead lights blazed on, and four large bodies walked into the room. All of them had a gun pointed at me.

"Hold it, right there," the man closest to the light switch said. "Take it easy, and nobody gets hurt."

The guard beside him lifted his walkie-talkie to his mouth and said, "No worries, Drake. We've got him."

"Good," Drake's smug voice filled the air. "Just hold him there. I'm on my way."

Guards in front of me and a guard behind, and the chief screw approaching fast. Things weren't looking good. I didn't like my chances. I was starting to look around for some sort of weapon to defend myself with, when my eyes spotted a possible way out. Directly to my left, between two of the beds, was a white metal plate with hinges on the top, fastening it four feet up on the wall. Written on the rectangular plate were the words: WASTE DISPOSAL CHUTE.

My mind started to spin. Could I dive into this garbage chute, ride it to the bottom, then still make a run for it? It couldn't be that easy. The opening looked more than big enough for me to fit inside, but what scared me was not knowing where the chute went. Was it an angled slide, or a straight drop? Seeing as I was standing on the fourth floor, the chute likely went all the way to the first floor, or even down to the basement. That meant I'd have at least a four-story drop, maybe five. If the Dumpster at the bottom was full of garbage, I might be okay—sort of like a movie stuntman landing on one of those airbag thingies—but if it was empty—

While I contemplated and weighed the pros and cons of my possible suicidal plunge, Drake finally appeared at the doorway, huffing and puffing and looking larger and more dangerous than I'd ever seen him. He was mad as hell. His eyes had that "I'm gonna lay a world of hurt on you" look to them that scared me more than the guns the men flanking him had. I decided there was no way I was letting that psycho muscle head get his hands on me, so as soon as he took his first menacing stride in my direction, I threw caution to the wind and ran for the garbage chute.

Drake was fast, but not fast enough. By the time the chief of security realized what I was going to do, it was too late. Like an Olympic diver, I thrust my hands together in front of me, tucked my head down in between them, and launched myself through the hinged gate. My marks for style wouldn't have been too impressive, but I made it into the chute nonetheless.

And immediately started dropping like a rock.

"*Oh shhhhiiiiiiiit!*" I screamed, terrified of the dark unknown void below me, but still enjoying the adrenaline rush of my crafty James Bond-ish escape from Drake and his goons' clutches.

It was too dark to see anything, but I could sense I was picking up too much speed. If I hit bottom going this fast, my head would splatter like a rotten mush melon run over by a truck. The chute was only a little larger than my body width, so I tried spreading my arms and legs against the smooth metal sides and pressed out with all my strength, hoping that would do the trick. It definitely slowed me down, but not a lot. Not nearly enough to save me if the Dumpster below wasn't full of nice soft garbage bags. I closed my eyes and prepared to die.

Just before I hit bottom, the chute must have angled or tilted off in another direction because I found myself not free-falling anymore, but rather sliding on my stomach. When I hit, I hit hard, but someone in heaven must like me because whatever I landed and rolled on, it was soft and spongy. It hurt like hell, knocking the wind out of me and nearly breaking my left wrist, but when my head cleared and I finally got my breath back, I was still alive and relatively intact.

When I stood up, my back was hurting pretty badly too, up near my shoulders, but I didn't have time to worry about my aches and pains. There'd be plenty of time for that, once I was far away from here. With that end in mind, I started searching for the lid to this Dumpster, the horrible stench just starting to register in my brain.

I hadn't expected it to be so dark. I couldn't see anything, so I was forced to grope around using my hands. No matter where I searched, high or low, I couldn't locate the exit. There were several entrance chutes like the one I'd fallen through, but no doors or hatches anywhere. I was confused and getting worried. It didn't help I kept stepping in and tripping over waist-deep piles of stinking goo.

God, what a stink!

I'd lived in and around trash for years, but I'd never smelled such an overpowering odor before. It was making me seriously nauseous. If I didn't get out of here soon, I was going to puke. Worse still, the clock was ticking. I didn't have time to be fucking around like this.

Outside, I heard the heavy clamor of men approaching on the run. With a sinking feeling in my gut, I cursed myself for taking so long. The opportunity I'd had to escape was gone. I'd senselessly risked my life and I was still trapped, no better off than I'd been in the Bleeders' room upstairs. I couldn't see the guards closing in on me, but I easily recognized Drake's booming voice as he started yelling something. No, wait, Drake wasn't yelling, he was laughing. Loud, gut-churning laughter, that for some reason chilled me to the bone. What could possibly be so funny?

"Hey Mike?" Drake said, still laughing. "You're priceless! Really, I enjoyed that little show. Pretty stupid thing to do, but damn brave."

"Yeah, real funny. Open the goddamned door and let me out. It stinks like Hell in here."

This comment made Drake and the guards with him laugh even harder. "Oh really?" he said. "And why do you think that is? Let me ask you something, Mike. Before you decided to dive into that chute, did you ever consider that WASTE DISPOSAL might not mean GARBAGE?"

I'll admit that sometimes I can be a bit slow, and I wasn't *completely* sure what Drake was talking about, but by the time I heard a lock removed and a sliding gate opened up on the ceiling of this chamber, I was starting to get the drift. Even before Drake's grinning face appeared in the rectangular opening and shone a super-bright halogen lamp down onto me, I knew what I was going to see.

Human body parts.

Under the intense light of the lamp, the inside of this chamber was still dark—mainly because every square inch of its walls were coated in blood so old and congealed it had long since turned black. Covering the entire floor and creeping halfway up the walls in the spots directly below several disposal chutes, mounds of soggy red meat and pasty-yellow bones lay heaped in various stages of decay. Arms, legs, feet, hands, torsos and even a few bloated heads lay scattered around my feet. The level of carnage was astonishing, almost indescribable. It was as if someone had detonated a bomb inside a room crowded with people, and then just walked away.

"Getting rid of the failed experiments used to be risky," Drake explained. "Obviously we can't just put this stuff into the trash, so Dr. Marshall had this incinerator custom built. The chutes deliver the waste from different areas in the facility: the labs, operating rooms, and upstairs on the fourth floor, of course.

"We usually burn it up at the end of each week, every couple of weeks, max, but it looks to me like we've been slacking off a little. This crud has probably been stewing for at least a month. I'd better make sure it gets cleaned up soon. Maybe tomorrow, huh?"

Why was he wasting time telling me this? Why didn't he just toss me down a rope or slide in a ladder?

"Get me out of here, Drake. Please." I hated the thought of begging to this lousy bastard, but I was getting desperate. I couldn't stand to stay in this human abattoir another second longer.

Drake smile vanished from his face as he briefly considered my request. "No, I don't think so. This is a good place for you, Mike. Somewhere I know you won't be sneaking away from anytime soon. Gives me piece of mind, you know?"

"You can't leave me in here," I shrieked.

"Watch me," he said, withdrawing the halogen lamp and slowly sliding the metal gate shut again.

I never did hear Drake replacing the lock on the gate, or him and the other guards laughing as they walked away. I probably would have, except at the moment I was far too busy screaming.

CHAPTER FIFTEEN

Someone much smarter than me once said, "what doesn't kill us only makes us stronger." I wish I could find that person and punch them right in the mouth. What the hell did they know? Force them to spend a night sleeping in a pile of rotting human waste and see if they're still singing the same tune. I highly doubt it.

Long after Drake and his boys were gone and I'd somehow managed to stop screaming, the smell of the dead flesh became too much for me. Ignorance had helped calm my stomach earlier, but once I knew exactly what I was breathing in, there was no way to plug the volcano. And man, did I erupt. I puked, and I puked, and then I puked some more—the smell of my own waste almost sweet compared with the unbearable stink around me.

When my stomach had nothing left to give, I blocked everything from my mind and started stacking whatever was within reach to build a high enough mound in the center of the incinerator so I could climb atop it and reach the sliding exit hatch. I was extremely thankful I was in the dark again, and was unable to see whatever it was I was grabbing. I doubt I'd have been able to touch anything, had the lights been on.

It ended up being a stupid waste of time. The hatch was locked of course, as I'd known it would be, and all I'd managed to accomplish was thoroughly coating myself in sticky black blood. Not a total waste, I guess. At least trying to do *something* had helped organize my thoughts, redirecting them onto something constructive rather than continuing to wallow in misery. I spent a little more time trying to find another way out, but soon realized I wasn't going anywhere until Drake came back.

I did eventually sleep, off and on, but I wouldn't say I got any rest. Just a number of exhaustion-fueled stress-induced power naps, with me curled in a tight fetal ball trying not to touch anything soft and squishy. It was a horrible, horrible night. I honestly don't know how I managed to make it through with my sanity intact.

But I did.

Fuck Drake and fuck Nathan Marshall—I wasn't letting them break me this easily. In the morning, when I awoke hearing the clatter of feet approaching, I jumped to my feet and made sure I was standing tall when Drake stuck his big ugly head through the sliding door again. If he even noticed my pathetic little show of defiance, he certainly didn't show it.

"Good sleep?" he asked.

"Screw you!" I hissed back, venom practically dripping from my mouth, but all Drake did was laugh.

"In a bad mood, Mike? Maybe I should come back tomorrow? See how you feel then."

Drake started to slide shut the hatch, and damned if I didn't fall for it. "No! Wait!" I squealed, my bravado evaporating under the threat of spending an entire day in this nightmarish place. The gate slid back open again immediately, and from the grin on Drake's face I could see he'd had no intention of leaving me down here. He'd just wanted to put me back in my place, make me understand it was him calling the shots here.

He lowered a twelve-foot aluminum ladder down to me, with only half of it needing to come through the opening before it came to rest on the mound of flesh and bones I'd stacked up during the night.

"Take those clothes off and leave them where they drop. Everything, Mike. You're not coming out of there with those filthy stinking rags on."

Fair enough.

They were ruined anyway. Anything to get out of here.

Drake watched me as I literally had to peel my gore-saturated T-shirt, pants, socks, and undies off, then stepped back as I climbed up and out of the incinerator. I hesitated at the top of the ladder, not at all comfortable with my nakedness. I wanted out of the chamber in the worst way, but now that I was standing fully exposed in the open air my self-conscious nature was kicking back in. Unfortunately there was nothing I could do about it. I had nothing to cover myself with and I sure as hell wasn't going back into the incinerator.

Wrinkling his nose in disgust, Drake pointed to another ladder propped against the side of the tank.

"You first. Move."

Before climbing to floor level, I took a moment to notice my surroundings, comprehending I was now beneath the medical center proper. The basement, with its cobweb-shrouded ceiling and poured concrete floor, was being used as a vast storage room. Natural light filtering in through small dirt-streaked windows on the foundation walls illuminated the area just enough that I could see the available floor space was cluttered with boxes and crates of all shapes and sizes.

There were also two other large containers similar to the incinerator I stood upon, but they were more globule-shaped, standing together over on the far side of the room. A myriad number of pipes, all painted white, rose from the spheres, branching out across the ceiling before snaking their way up into the medical center through holes drilled in the floor. For the life of me, I couldn't fathom what their purpose was.

Drake gave me a whack on the back of my head and told me to get a move on. Not wanting another, I did what he said, moving over to the ladder and starting down. Six guards waited at floor level, making me feel more vunerable and uncomfortable than ever, but they backed away when they got a good whiff of me descending. One guard—the same blond-haired guy with glasses I'd locked outside on the trellis last night— reluctantly moved forward and clamped a handcuff around my left wrist. Holding his breath, he half-walked, half-dragged me toward a wooden door not far away on our left. Instead of leading me through the doorway as I'd expected, he grabbed the other end of the handcuffs and attached me to the door's large brass handle.

What the hell?

Why would he chain me to the door? I tried yanking on the handcuffs, but they were on securely. I tried opening the door, but found it locked. It wasn't until I turned around to face Drake, and saw two of the other guards unrolling a length of fire hose that I started to get the picture.

"We're not taking you to see Dr. Marshall smelling like that," Drake said, tossing me a fresh bar of Irish Spring soap. "Turn on the shower, boys."

I started to protest, but an icy spray of water hitting me full force in the chest shut me up in a hurry. It felt like a million needles being repeatedly jabbed into me, almost stripping the flesh from my bones wherever the water touched me. Christ, it hurt. I tried to cover up, ducking and spinning and even curling into a ball, but there was no place I could hide, no position I could stand which didn't leave some area of my body exposed.

Suddenly the water was shut off and I thought the torture was over. Wrong. Drake wasn't finished with me yet.

"Get scrubbing, Mike. We haven't got all day."

Having no real choice in the matter, I began rubbing the bar of soap all over myself, making a half-decent effort to get myself cleaned up. It was great to smell the fresh pine-scented fragrance slowly replacing the rotten odor of congealed blood, but hampering my enjoyment was the certain knowledge that after I'd finished lathering up, Drake was going to order them to rinse me off.

Sure enough, I'd barely had time to run the soap through my tangled, sticky hair, when the jet spray of frigid water pounded into me again, unannounced. The merciless force of the water hurt even worse this time, battering and bruising my body until I could no longer stand. Only then did Drake order the water hose turned off.

"Get up," the chief of security ordered without a trace of compassion in his steely voice.

Drake walked closer, tossing a towel in my face and stood watching me as I dried off. He was standing too close, leering at me in a way that made me uncomfortable.

"You clean up pretty good," Drake leaned closer, whispering in my ear. "Not bad at all."

Is Drake gay, or just crazy?

"Can I have something to wear?" I asked, looking away from my muscular captor's lustful eyes.

"Shy, Mike?" Drake smiled.

Ever so slowly, he reaching behind me and I shuddered, thinking he was going to grab my ass. Fortunately, all he was doing was unlocking the handcuff attached to the door. Once free, he nodded to one of the guards to bring over my clothes. I thought they were only giving me a white dress shirt to wear, but once I unfolded the garment I noticed it was way too long, extending down past my knees, and that the opening was intended for the back instead of the front. Why were they giving me a hospital gown?

"What's this?" I asked.

"Have you forgotten already? You signed a contract with Dr. Marshall, my friend, and I'm here to make sure you keep up your end of the bargain." After consulting his wristwatch, he said, "It's just past nine o'clock, Mike. Your surgery is in fifty-six minutes. Dr. Marshall will be expecting you shortly, so let's get moving."

My arm! They're gonna take my arm!

Panic swelled within me, this primal emotion becoming almost a physical entity, wrapping its greasy fingers around my heart, squeezing fear out of every pore. Acting on instinct alone, with no destination in mind, I tossed the hospital gown in Drake's grinning face and ran like the devil himself was chasing me. Realistically, there was no place for me to go, but I ran anyway, the need to escape my appointed fate completely taking over my body.

Everyone started screaming, and of course gave chase, but a desperate man can be faster than greased lightning, given the proper motivation. With the threat of losing my arm hanging above my head like Damocles's proverbial sword, I was more than fast—I was *flying*! Unfortunately, it's impossible to outrun bullets, so when I became lost in the jumble of boxes, dashing between two large crates to find myself staring down the barrel of a big black gun, I knew enough not to try anything stupid.

The guard with the minicannon, a pimply-faced redhead who looked about nineteen years old, started shouting to Drake that he had me, while backing me up until my back was against a hard metal surface. I had nowhere left to run. Within seconds, other guards had found us and Drake was rounding the corner of the storage crate too.

"Let me plug him, Drake," the overzealous young redhead shouted. "He's more trouble than he's worth."

He's gonna do it. I watched his finger starting to tighten on the trigger. *He's gonna kill me!*

I closed my eyes as tight as I could, not wanting to see the bullet heading my way. At any second, I expected to hear the loud *BOOM* and feel my head begin to vaporize, but what I heard was Drake screaming a long, drawn out, "*NOOOOOOOOOOO!*" I opened my eyes just in time to see Drake run up and knock the gun out of his young recruit's hand.

"What kind of an idiot are you?" Drake screamed. "For Christ's sake, Brad, take a look where you are. Where *he* is. You'll kill us all."

The young guard looked confused, uncertain what his boss was angry about, but then his eyes opened wide, and I saw realization wash over him like a splash of ice water. The look on his face made me wonder what the guards knew that I didn't. All it took was for me to turn around, and I understood right away. I was leaning against one of the two huge spherical-shaped tanks I'd spotted from atop the incinerator. From this close, I could see the word OXYGEN painted in bright red letters with the unnecessary warning, DANGER: EXTREMELY FLAMABLE below it.

So that's what they were . . . oxygen tanks.

That explained the network of small pipes rising up through dozens of spots in the ceiling. The pipes supplied the various laboratories and operating rooms throughout the entire medical center. Drake had been right. If the guard had fired his gun, we'd all be dead by now.

Well, at least I won't be getting shot today.

I clung to the base of the oxygen tank like a capsized sailor might grasp a life preserver in the middle of the Pacific. With the threat of death by explosion taken out of the mix, Drake quickly regained control of the situation. He ordered two of his men to grab me, threatening to break their scrawny necks if they let me get away again. Then he marched right up to me until we were actually touching nose to nose and said, "I'm done fucking around, Mike. You're coming with me whether you like it or not. We can do this one of two ways: the hard way, or the *really* hard way. What's it gonna be?"

Neither sounded particularly good, so I just kept my mouth shut. I knew anything I said would end up earning me a fist in the face, or worse, so I quietly waited for whatever would come next. Had I known Drake was hiding a large hypodermic syringe behind his back, I might have struggled more than I did, but as it was, the chief of security grabbed me by the throat and ruthlessly jabbed the needle into my right shoulder before I knew what hit me.

Whatever drug he injected into me, it packed a hell of a wallop, because before I even had the chance to call Drake a sneaky bastard, my vision began to dim. The image of Drake's toothy grin froze in my mind, and began swirling around and around in my head, spinning faster and faster until someone finally pulled the plug, letting my dizzy consciousness drain down into the black sewer of oblivion.

CHAPTER SIXTEEN

When I woke up, I had a throbbing headache, so bad it felt like someone had backed over my skull with a tractor. My eyes were crusted shut, but I blinked a few times and managed to get them open. Bad mistake. The bright light on the tiled ceiling above me practically blinded me, sending daggers of shooting pain through my brain, making my poor head hurt even more. Refusing to make the same mistake twice, I kept my eyes closed as I tried to gather my senses and get my bearings.

Gotta stay away from that damn Sterno. I need a drink of water . . . bad.

Thinking about water made me remember the fire hose shower I'd recently been given. Once my mind started along that memory path it didn't take long to remember where I was, Drake giving me the knockout drug, and his promise to deliver me to Dr. Marshall for my scheduled surgery.

Oh God, no!

Had Drake already done that? Had Dr. Marshall already taken me to his operating room and removed my right arm? I was too frightened to open my eyes and check. Other than my head I wasn't in a whole lot of pain, but I was still woozy and half out of it so I might be pumped full of happy drugs for all I knew.

Almost as if on cue, my right arm started to itch. I felt it first near my elbow, and then slowly it began tickling its way up toward my neck. That should have been a good sign, assured me I was still in one piece, but I wasn't at all convinced the itch was real. I'd heard all sorts of strange stories of people feeling phantom sensations in limbs that had been amputated—even ones removed years earlier—so I wasn't getting my hopes up.

Open your eyes, Mike. You gotta know for sure. Do it, man. Do it now. Maybe it's not too late?

That was true. Maybe I hadn't been unconscious for as long as I thought. The surgery might not have started yet, and I might be lying in one of the waiting rooms. I might still be able to get up and sneak out of here. One way or the other, I had to find out.

Steeling myself against what I might see, I said a quick prayer, opened my eyes, and reluctantly let them slowly drift down the length of my body.

My right arm was gone, severed clean at the shoulder. And so was my left.

CHAPTER SEVENTEEN

Dr. Marshall kept me heavily medicated with a morphine drip for the next two weeks, then slowly began weaning me off the highly addictive painkiller. It was a hell of a lot easier dealing with my double amputation when I'd been high as a kite than when I started to crash back down to earth. Call me crazy, but I much preferred a drug-induced fantasyland where I still had both my arms to the cold sterile world of my disfigured reality.

Healing was a slow and painful experience, made worse by my murderously foul mood and combative attitude. The doctors and nurses who attended to me were professional and somewhat sympathetic to my plight, but whether they were just doing their job or not, they were part of the enemy camp and I hated them for it.

Not once, in the entire three weeks I lay recuperating, did Dr. Marshall come to see me. I liked thinking maybe he was a little scared of me, but it was more likely he just didn't give a damn, labeling me as so unimportant I didn't merit the wasting of his precious time. I was nothing but a commodity to him, flesh and blood spare parts kept in cold storage in case he had further need of me.

Drake popped in and out all the time, unfortunately, laughing at my pain and taunting me in childish ways like tossing me a tennis ball and saying, "Here, Mike, *catch*." He'd shriek like a loon when the ball would whack me in the face, or thud painfully against my bandaged shoulders. He enjoyed pissing me off, and loved hurting me even more. As helpless as I was, I vowed to someday pay that muscle-headed sadistic asshole back in spades.

The first day the doctors let me get out of bed was the day my mind turned away from revenge and started thinking seriously about escaping. The minute my feet hit the floor, I was already planning and scheming, keeping my eyes and ears open for a chance to bolt. Ironically, it was Drake—the big cheese of security around here—who gave me the opportunity I'd been waiting for.

He strutted into my room with his chest puffed out, cocky as usual, and ordered the two nurses who'd just finished changing my dressings to get out and stay out.

"Dr. Marshall's on his way to see you, Mike."

"What's he want?" I asked, curious, but more than a little nervous to hear the answer.

"I think he needs your legs," Drake smiled, clearly happy to be the bearer of such shocking news.

He pulled an apple out of his coat pocket, leaned against a filing cabinet by the door, and silently enjoyed his snack while relishing the terrifying effect his words were having on me.

God no, not my legs! Not my fucking legs!

I had a vivid picture of me carved down to nothing, lying upstairs in a bed beside Lucas and Charlie while three nurses began sticking the IV tubes into my head, neck, and torso to begin draining my first of countless donations of blood. The vision was so powerful, so *real*, I found myself unable to stand on my own power. Disoriented as I was, I tried grabbing hold of my dresser drawer to support myself, but I had no arms to clutch onto anything with, so I ended up sprawled out on the floor near Drake's feet.

Drake found my spill comical, naturally, nearly choking on the last bite of his apple he was laughing so hard. "Oh man, I've got to get out of here. You're killing me Mike, *killing* me!" Tossing his apple core toward the garbage can, he headed out the door, pausing only long enough to look back and say, "Dr. Marshall will be along soon, so be nice. I'll see you later on, back in rehab."

Then he was gone, the heavy metal door swinging behind him so that he assumed he'd left me alone in a locked room. That was his mistake. Although the door was automatically set to lock, as always, the chief of security had failed to notice that his gnawed apple core hadn't fallen into the trash can as he'd intended. Instead, it had bounced off the top rim and rebounded to the floor, coming to rest between the closing door and its jamb. Wedged between the two, the locking device couldn't engage, leaving the door open about an inch.

Lying where I'd fallen, I held my breath, waiting to see if the weight of the door would compress the apple core enough that the latch would click, but it never happened. Hope surged through me like a charge of lightning, burning away my ghastly thoughts of the Bleeders' room upstairs, and fueling my weakened body into action. I was back on my feet in seconds, rushing over to the door. Getting out of this room didn't guarantee me freedom, but it sure as hell was a good start.

How was I supposed to open the door? The knob was way too big to try grabbing with my teeth, and if I tried to nudge it open using my hip, I might just as easily push the door shut, locking myself in. I ended up using my toes, turning my left foot sideways, pushing them through the gap, and prying the door open enough that I could get my head and neck around to shove it open.

Drake was nowhere in sight, the hallway in both directions blessedly empty. Outside my room for the first time in almost a month, I felt great, almost giddy with excitement, thinking maybe this time luck would be on my side and I'd be able to just stroll on out of here unnoticed and unchallenged. I should have known better. I hadn't made it more than a few steps when Dr. Marshall wheeled around the corner, obviously on his way to my room. He was dressed in a blue sweatshirt and faded jeans, looking quite comfortable until the shock of seeing me out wandering in the hall spread across his face.

"How did you get out of your room?" he asked, a trace of alarm creeping into his normally confident voice. "Where's Drake?"

"Right behind you," I answered, and as soon as he spun his wheelchair around to look, I turned tail and took off at full speed the opposite way.

Glancing over my shoulder, I saw Dr. Marshall pull a long-bladed knife from under the cushion he was sitting upon, clamp it in his teeth so he could push with both arms, and race after me. I was out in front, but the small lead I'd bluffed for myself wasn't enough to stay in front for long. With every push of his powerful arms, Dr. Marshall was making up ground, closing in on me at an alarming rate.

It was hard to run fast with my arms no longer there to pump back and forth. I felt constantly off balance, and was having a heck of a time trying to run in a straight line down the hall without veering off to one side or the other. This wasn't going to work. I had to find someplace to run where Dr. Marshall wouldn't be able to follow me. Where, though? Where could I go, that a wheelchair couldn't?

The stairs. He can't follow me on the staircases.

I'm not the greatest with directions, but I'd been around this building a time or two since arriving, and I was reasonably sure I was heading toward the front of the medical center. Running past several lab rooms on both sides of the corridor, I now knew that the surgical recovery room I'd been kept in was located on the second floor of the complex. There should be a stairwell not too far ahead on my right. It would lead down to the short concrete hallway that served as an entrance to the four-story glass-roofed atrium I'd stood in when we first arrived. The front door to the parking lot would be there as well.

Sure enough, the door to the stairs came into view, and when I made my cut to the right, bashing through into the stairwell, Dr. Marshall had been so close to me he couldn't turn the corner in time. He took a wild swipe at me with the knife as his chair rocketed past the open doorway like a Roman chariot, but his aim was way off.

Not wanting to stand around and give him a second chance, I started down the winding staircase, but screeched to a stop. I could hear voices below me around the bend in the stairs, male voices, two of them, maybe three. I couldn't see them or tell if they were guards, doctors, lab technicians, or Darth Vader's Imperial Stormtroopers, but whoever they were, they were coming up toward me and I didn't want to run right into their arms. To avoid them, my only choice was to turn and head *up* the stairs instead of down. Maybe I could hide out for a few minutes on the third or fourth floor, just until the men approaching from below made it to wherever they were headed. Once the coast was clear, I could shoot back down the stairs and try making it to the front door.

Up I climbed, panic at being caught pushing me along like a strong hand on my back. When I rounded the curve to the level area where the door to the third floor opened, I started to realize I was in more trouble than I'd thought. All the doors in this stairwell opened inwardly from the various hallways, and in my panic to evade Dr. Marshall I hadn't stopped to consider exactly what that meant.

I'd had no trouble using my body to push down the latch-releasing bar to ram my way into here, but from this side to open the doors a person had to grab a little handle and depress a small thumb lever as they pulled backward. With no hands to grab the handle—and obviously no thumbs to depress the lever—there was no way to open any of these doors and get back into the hallways. I was trapped, with no other option than keep climbing stairs until I ran out of them. If the men below were headed all the way to the fourth floor, I was screwed.

I got lucky, for once. I'd just started heading up from the third-floor landing, when I heard the door below on the second being pulled opened, and the mysterious voices of my unseen pursuers fade to nothing as they moved off into the carpeted hall. I paused, halting my ascension, straining to hear if all the men had exited onto the second floor, or if maybe one or two were still climbing up. I heard a long, drawn-out squeak that had to be the door swinging closed again, but once the latch clicked, everything was quiet. No voices. No footsteps. Nothing.

Pheeeew. Thank God!

That could have gotten ugly, but I was still okay. Now with the staircase all to myself, all I had to do was make it down to the first floor, and hope I could find some way to get to the front door of this creepy place. I cautiously started back down the winding stairs, fully expecting to hear one of the doors bang open at any second. When nothing happened, my hope was renewed. I might make it out of here, after all.

That was when I rounded the corner leading to the second-floor landing and saw Dr. Marshall sitting contentedly in his chair, waiting for me, effectively blocking my path with not only his body, but with the large serrated knife he held casually in his lap. My feet grew roots quickly, stopping me midstair. I shouldn't have been surprised, but I was. Had I thought he'd just let me walk away?

Idiot!

When he saw me, a huge feral grin spread across the mad doctor's face, and in that second our eyes met, I understood he knew I was trapped in this staircase, and the only way out was through him. To tease me, he began playing with his large knife, picking imaginary dirt from under his fingernails with it. He was putting on a show, trying to scare me, but I tried not to let him know it was working.

"Get the hell out of my way, asshole, or I'll give you and your wheelchair a ride you'll never forget."

I half meant it too, considering charging into him and trying to knock him backward off the level landing area. I could imagine the satisfying scene of his arms pinwheeling for balance as the wheels of his chair tipped over the edge of the first stair, the overly smug look on his face replaced by sheer terror at the knowledge he was in for a painful, potentially fatal spill.

Dr. Marshall just laughed at me, my threat having no effect on his confidence. That was when I should have charged, should have caught him when he wasn't prepared, but I didn't. I might have—probably *would* have— but he asked me something so odd and began doing something that seemed so strangely out of place considering our situation, it knocked me completely off guard.

"Tell me, Mr. Fox," Dr. Marshall began, taking his knife and jabbing it into the blue denim material of his pants near his left hip, and starting to cut down toward his knee. "Have you ever stopped to think about my legs?"

"Your legs?" I muttered, trying to figure out why Dr. Marshall was in the process of cutting his pant leg off before my bewildered eyes.

"You should have," he smiled, calmly starting to cut into the fabric of his right pant leg now. "When we first met, I told you I lost the use of them in an accident, remember?"

I did, but I didn't bother answering. I was a little freaked out as to why we were having this calm friendly discussion in the first place. It was too surreal, Dr. Marshall's thin smile a little forced, and I didn't want to say anything that might trigger his murderous rage.

Why the hell is he cutting off his pants?

"I was only forty-five when it happened. That's a long time to live without legs, Mike. Too long, don't you think? Especially if you happen to have the skills, courage, and the means to do something about it. Understand what I'm getting at?"

Dr. Marshall began to rise out of his wheelchair, the shredded denim of his jeans falling to the floor as he stood, the jagged pink scars encircling his upper thighs clearly showing me where he'd grafted the new set of legs onto his still-healing body.

Mother of God! He experimented on himself!

"It took three attempts, three pain-filled failures, before I figured it out. I'd rushed into it, you see, too anxious and nowhere near ready. I learned from my mistakes, though, waiting patiently this time until I worked out the kinks, until I was sure it would work. My most trusted surgeon did the operation for me and I've been healing for about five months, working hard in physiotherapy before you even arrived here. It's working, Mike. This time it's working. This time I can stand up. I can walk." Then, holding up the long bladed knife toward me, "And I can even climb stairs."

CHAPTER EIGHTEEN

It wasn't until Dr. Marshall took his first tentative step toward me that the full impact of what he'd just said hit me.

He can climb stairs.

If I'd been thinking clearly, I might have still decided to charge the doctor, knock him flying while he was getting his balance, but I was scared, more than a little confused, and instead of charging I fled up the stairs, away from the doctor. Big mistake. Running away wasn't going to help me. Where was I going to go? I was trapped in the stairwell, nowhere to go now but up, while Dr. Marshall closed in on me from below. At some point, we'd both end up at the top of the stairs, and using only my legs I would have to fight off a knife-wielding madman.

Up the stairs I went, desperately trying to think of some way to get out of this death trap I'd snared myself in. Luckily, Dr. Marshall was having difficulties with the stairs, his legs not quite healed enough to move as quick as he wanted. I could hear him cursing below, as he slowly inched up the stairs at a snail's pace, a determined killer on feeble, fledgling legs. This would buy me time, a reprieve at best, but not the full pardon I was looking for.

Think, man. Think!

And I was, but thinking about various nasty scenarios all ending with me being stabbed to death wasn't much help, so I concentrated on climbing the stairs, deciding to put as much distance between me, my pursuer, and my morbid thoughts as I could.

I rounded the third-floor landing, wistfully eyeing the door leading to the hallway, but it may as well have been a solid brick wall, for all the good it did me. Gritting my teeth in panic and frustration, I continued on up the stairs. When the fourth-floor landing started to come into view, I fully expected to see the inevitable dead end that would seal my fate. There would be the last of the stairs, the closed steel door, and then the concrete wall where I'd have to make my stand.

What the hell?

Something wasn't right.

The stairs were there, and the steel door too, just as I'd thought, but there was no wall. No dead end. Instead, there was another flight of winding stairs disappearing around yet another corner. Had I miscalculated what floor I was on? No, I was sure of that. This was the fourth—and final—floor all right.

Then where do these stairs go? The roof? Heaven?

Did it matter? Up I went, but slower now, not sure how there could be a fifth-story staircase in a four-story building. Halfway round the bend the answer hit me.

The Tower Room.

The room on the front corner of the building with the tattered flag flying on its roof that I'd spotted on the day I'd arrived. That had to be it. My mind started whirling, wondering if maybe this presented me with any new options for survival, or if it just delayed the inevitable. Up I went.

As I rounded the corner where the next landing would normally be, the staircase opened up into a large room. There was a low humming noise coming from somewhere, just barely audible, but loud enough that I quietly crept up the final few stairs, pausing to peek over the floor level stair to check out my surroundings before I went any further. The tower room wasn't as large as I'd pictured it from the ground, maybe twenty feet by twenty, with a twelve-foot-high ceiling. It was oval shaped, with two large stained glass windows set into the wall farthest from the stairs. The room was spotlessly clean, but filled to the point of being cluttered with furniture, clothes, an expensive-looking stereo system, a computer terminal, lots of medical supplies, free-standing oxygen tanks, and a brass-railed bed. There was other stuff jammed in the room, too, but once I spotted the bed—or rather, who was lying on the bed—nothing else in the room mattered.

No way. I can't be that unlucky.

Sure I could. Fourteen feet from me, Drake was sprawled out, lying naked on top of the sheets, preparing to have a nap. Just my luck, but this junk-filled tower room was apparently his private apartment.

Now what was I going to do? With Dr. Marshall slowly gaining on me from below, and Drake the Neanderthal waiting above, my chances of getting out of this mess were close to nil.

Fuck!

Looking back over my shoulder, Dr. Marshall was still nowhere to be seen, but I knew he was coming—I could hear his slow, lurching progress echoing up the stairwell. At any second, I expected to see him round the corner, a vicious grin plastered on his face.

A noise above me brought my attention back to Drake. The head of security was sitting up now, his back toward me, facing the front windows. He stood up, yawning loudly as he stretched. It wasn't until he walked over to a nearby table that I noticed he was sporting a woody—his large penis fully erect, pointing at the roof, slapping his belly with every step.

Just what I need to see.

There was something set in the middle of the table he was standing beside, something large covered up with a white blanket. Drake carefully started removing the blanket. When he did, I had to bite my lip not to shriek.

Oh my God!

Concealed beneath the blanket was a severed head perched atop a glass, milky liquid-filled tank. Hundreds of colorful wires ran from within the ragged neckline of the head, down into the tank where they connected along the length of barely visible spine. Wires also ran away from the head, connecting into a circuit box beside a computer terminal. Several large crimson-filled tubes ran to and from the neck, over to one of the same machines I'd been shown in the video we watched our first day here. It was this machine that was making the low humming noise I'd noticed a few minutes ago.

Blood supply.

That thought made me realize what I was seeing. This wasn't just any severed head, this was *the* severed head—the same guy I'd seen in the video. I recognized the poor man's face. I could remember how it had given me the creeps back then, when I still thought everything was on the level here. Seeing it now with my own eyes, it was even more horrifying. How could someone do this to another human being? It was viciously cruel. Hell, it was diabolical!

Unfortunately, not nearly as diabolical as what Drake was doing. The sick pervert was rubbing his throbbing cock on the side of the glass tank, slowly working it up closer and closer to the head above. The defenseless man's eyes were wide open in fear, his entire head and spine thrashing about in a futile attempt to get away.

My mind flashed back to the day I arrived here, and

how I'd thought Drake had left the video show with an erection hidden in his tracksuit. I hadn't been sure at the time, wondering what he could possibly find erotic in Dr. Marshall's body parts presentation, but now I knew.

Drake crawled right up onto the table, and was trying to put his engorged dick into the disembodied man's tightly closed mouth, who was resisting the only way he could. Drake laughed at his defiance, and started to threaten him with a knife held to one of his eyes.

"Open up sweetie, or you lose your eyes," Drake whispered, his voice dripping with lust.

Stop it, you sick perverted fuck!

I wanted to scream that out loud, and almost did, but a shimmer of motion in the corner of my eye caught my attention. Dr. Marshall, covered in sweat from his exertions, was standing four feet away from me, the large serrated knife raised above his head, preparing to stab me in the back.

I did scream then, long and loud, my reasons for stealth now gone. I bolted up the remaining stairs, ran right past Drake, and didn't stop until I had my back pressed against the far wall. Drake looked shocked for a moment, but regained his cool, climbing down from the table to help Dr. Marshall up the last few stairs while at the same time keeping an eye on me. Not that he needed to—both he and Dr. Marshall wielded sharp knives and I was an armless man with nowhere left to run.

"What the hell's going on?" Drake asked his employer.

"Rather obvious," the doctor said. "Our boy, Michael, is trying to escape. Not doing so well, though. What's that saying, Mr. Drake . . . out of the frying pan, into the fire?"

Drake started to laugh, neither he nor Dr. Marshall seeming the least bit troubled by his nakedness.

"What are you going to do to me?" I asked, unable to keep the fear and dread out of my voice.

Dr. Marshall smiled at me, a cold, evil smile, then said, "Whatever I want to, Mike. Whatever I want."

My mouth went dry. I was so scared I couldn't have spoken a word even if I'd known what to say. We stared at each other in silence for a minute, then Dr. Marshall continued.

"I'm not the monster you're convinced I am, Mr. Fox. I haven't lied as much as you think. About the money, yes, but not everything. I told you all I've ever wanted was to help my poor unfortunate son. Remember?"

Of course I did. Lying bastard. "You're forgetting something, Marshall. I was in your supposed son's room. I saw the plastic body and the fake wires. That was nothing but a sob story to get us all on your side. Nothing but bullshit, so save your breath."

"Bullshit was it? You sure about that?" he asked.

Dr. Marshall limped over to the table supporting the severed head and spine. He lovingly stroked the matted hair of the man, then carefully repositioned the glass tank so it was exactly in the center of the table. I couldn't see the man's eyes from where I stood, but from the way his head and spine were thrashing around, the man seemed even more terrified now than while being molested by Drake.

"Easy now," the doctor said, his voice as soft and as soothing as he could manage. "Everything's gonna be fine."

The tremors in the head gradually faded away, then Dr. Marshall returned his attention to me, spinning the glass tank 180 degrees so I was looking directly into the haunted eyes of the bodiless man.

"Mike, I'd like you to meet Andrew Nathan Marshall. My son. Andrew, this silly man here is Michael Fox."

CHAPTER NINETEEN

The silence in the room was deafening. That phrase always seemed so cliché and ridiculous to me, until that very moment. The quiet in the tower room was a tangible thing, the tension in the air so thick I was almost choking on it, my mind spinning around trying to comprehend what I'd just heard.

His son?

He really does exist?

How could Dr. Marshall do this to his own son?

Why?

So many questions I wanted to ask, but I didn't. I just stood there, temporarily forgetting my own dilemma, forgetting everything as I stared into the bulging frightened eyes of the pitiable man before me I'd been stupid enough to sign a contract to try to help.

How does he cope, being forced to live life this way?

What must Andrew be thinking of all this?

What's he thinking about right now?

"Want me to take him out?" Drake asked his boss, finally breaking the dead calm and shaking me out of my stupor. "He's more trouble than he's worth."

"I'll be the judge of that," Dr. Marshall said. "He's still full of good spare parts. No sense wasting them."

"I suppose."

They were talking about me as if I wasn't even there, as if my opinion about the outcome of my life really didn't matter. And I suppose it didn't—to them at least—but it sure as hell did to me. There had to be a way out of this. I couldn't just stand here waiting for Drake to—

Drake!

An idea blazed through my head. Might not work, but it was worth a try. What did I have to lose?

"Hey Doc," I shouted, interrupting their casual conversation about whether or not I should be killed outright, or simply cut up for spare parts. "Do you have any idea what Drake likes to do to your beloved son when he's all alone with him? He forces Andrew to suck his cock at knifepoint. I saw him myself just a few minutes ago. Look at the big fuckin' pervert. Why do you think he's naked?"

It wasn't a great plan, but I hoped if I told Dr. Marshall how Drake was molesting his son, maybe I could turn the insane surgeon's rage toward Drake, away from me. Even if I could just get them arguing enough that I got a chance to bolt for the staircase. Give me a three-second window of opportunity, and I'd be off like a rocket, heading for the front door.

Instead of rage, as I'd hoped, Dr. Marshall started laughing. Drake apparently found my comments hilarious as well, and was soon laughing along with his boss.

"Trying to make me jealous, are we, Mike?" Dr. Marshall asked. "Nice try, but let's just say there's plenty of Mr. Drake to go around for everyone."

What the hell does that mean?

I wondered if it was possible Dr. Marshall was so insane, so far gone, he didn't even care that Drake was sexually abusing his son. Nah. Nobody could be *that* heartless. Could they? Then I watched as Drake walked over beside Dr. Marshall and his son, putting his arms around both of them. Dr. Marshall smiled, winked at me, then kissed Drake passionately on the lips. With his free hand, he softly caressed Drake's semiswollen member, starting to bring it back to attention.

Sweet mother of Jesus!

They were lovers. I couldn't believe it. How much more fucked up could this strange little family get? I mean really, a brilliant but thoroughly insane neurosurgeon kissing his steroid-filled chief of security boyfriend above the trembling head of his life-supported, disembodied son. Not a pretty picture. Certainly not Norman Rockwell-inspired family material; that was for sure.

This was too much for me. I couldn't take any more. I just wanted out of here, away from all this craziness and perversion and back to my smelly little Dumpster underneath the Carver Street Bridge.

Get real. You wouldn't survive a day on the streets. You've got no fucking arms, moron!

My conscience was right, of course. There was no going back for me. Only a fool would think otherwise. I should never have let Drake talk me down off those railway tracks the day he'd shown up in the limo. Should have stuck to plan A and never even listened to his crazy offer. Then again, maybe it wasn't too late.

Dr. Marshall and Drake were never going to let me leave here—alive anyway. Why not save myself the suffering and grief and spoil whatever nasty little plans they had in mind for me. Call me crazy, but I'd much rather go out on my own terms than theirs. I knew just how to do it, too.

"Hey freaks," I said to my captors, disturbing their little petting session.

Dr. Marshall licked his lips, anticipating violence, and said, "Watch your mouth, little man, or you just might lose that quick tongue of yours."

Drake took a step toward me, holding up his knife for me to see. "It's time you learned some manners, Mr. Fox."

I took a deep breath and prepared for what was coming. "Screw you, Drake. You two psychos deserve each other, but I'm not sticking around and watching any more of this bullshit. I'm out of here!"

I could tell my outburst confused them. "You're *what*?" Drake asked.

"You heard me. I'm leaving."

Once the initial shock wore off, both Drake and Dr. Marshall started laughing again.

"You're a funny guy, Mike, but I'm afraid you're not going anywhere," Dr. Marshall said, "except back to my operating room. You see . . . I need your legs."

Ten minutes ago, that statement would have terrified me, but not now. I'd moved past my fears, made peace with myself, and was ready to take care of business. Without another word, I made my move, running full out toward one of the large stained glass windows. If Dr. Marshall wanted my legs, he could send Drake to scrape them off the front driveway five stories below, along with the rest of me. Taking a nosedive onto the pavement from this height—which had to be sixty feet what with the high ceilings around this joint—and with no arms to cushion my fall, my head would explode like an overripe tomato being struck with a sledgehammer.

Perfect.

"Stop, you fool," Dr. Marshall shouted once it became obvious what my plans were. "Grab him, Drake. Hurry!"

Drake came after me, but I knew I had the angle on him. He knew it, too, but kept coming anyway. With a yell of pure triumph, I launched myself into the air, easily shattering the lead-framed stained glass window and was ready to fly free as a bird into the bright blue yonder. Fly for a second or two, at least.

Wasn't gonna happen.

I hit the glass hard, breaking through it easily enough, but my flight to freedom only lasted for another three inches. That was when I hit face-first into the wire mesh window screen bolted to the outside brickwork. It was heavy-gauge mesh probably installed on these expensive windows to protect them and it stopped my forward progress pronto, my nose painfully reduced to a red pulpy mess upon impact, the rest of my face and body a patchwork of cuts and puncture wounds from all the exploding glass. So much for my great escape.

Bounced back into the tower room, I landed with a heavy thump at Drake's feet, where he found the sight of my bloodied face and body tremendously amusing. He was laughing so hard, in fact, that Dr. Marshall was the one who came over and held me down so I wouldn't try running away again.

"Get the needle," Dr. Marshall said to Drake.

"What's the hurry? Why don't we let him have a run at the other window? I'd love to watch that again."

"Just get the needle, we've wasted enough time with this loser. I'm late for surgery."

"All right, it was just a thought," Drake said, still delighted by my suffering.

I watched him walk over to a rolltop desk and remove a large hypodermic needle from one of the drawers. He filled it with a clear yellow fluid—probably the same stuff he'd drugged me with down in the cellar—then walked over and handed the needle to his boss.

Part of me knew I should be flailing about, screaming like a banshee, and desperately trying to get away, but I just didn't have it in me. I was battered, bruised, and bleeding, and every inch of my body hurt like hell. Worse still, the impact with the metal screen had re-opened my right shoulder wound, and with the amount of blood I was leaking all over the floor, I was getting light-headed, feeling numb, stunned, and more than a little lethargic.

I'm sure I would have passed out on my own if they'd given me another thirty seconds, but Dr. Marshall wasn't taking any chances. He viciously plunged the hypodermic needle into my thigh, but I don't remember feeling any pain. I never even screamed. Within seconds, everything went black.

CHAPTER TWENTY

Speaking from the experience of someone who has drank several hundred gallons of cheap, often home-made booze, then eventually progressing to stolen Sterno, I knew what it was like to wake up with a head-ache. I was an authority on them, actually. I've had more hangovers than I care to remember, but none of those self-induced headaches hurt half as bad as the way I felt when I finally woke up and slowly stirred back to life.

My head was pounding, driving a six-inch spike of agony through my brain with every blood-pulsing beat of my heart. I didn't dare open my eyes. Heaven forbid. Instead, I lay perfectly still, just concentrated on tak-ing short, shallow breaths, and tried to ride out the storm.

Must have been a hell of a party last night. Blue J and I must have really—

Then, through all the pain and the hazy memories filtering out of my drug-saturated brain, I remem-bered where I was and what had happened to me up in the castle's tower room. I tried to fight it, deny my memories, because accepting the truth would lead me in a direction I simply wasn't ready to go. No way.

Maybe Puckman brewed up another batch of that awful Screech, and I drank so much I don't—

I gave up halfway through my pitiful attempt at avoiding reality. What was the point? I knew perfectly well where I was and why I had such a bad headache. All the lies and wishful thinking in the world weren't going to help my situation or make me feel any better. Why bother?

Because the truth scared me too much, that's why.

Obviously the reason I had a headache was because I'd been whacked out on drugs. Why had I been drugged? Because Drake was taking me to the operating room for surgery. Why was I headed to surgery? Because Dr. Marshall said—

He said he needed my legs.

Oh God, please. Not that. Not my legs.

Not my fucking legs!

My thoughts seemed to freeze up. I wouldn't allow—couldn't allow—myself to keep thinking about this. I wanted to die, right then and there. Die, before I found out if anything had happened to me.

I opened my eyes.

Then I started screaming.

I didn't have proof yet that my legs were gone—I hadn't looked down or anything—but I didn't need to. Lying six feet away from me, strapped in his own bed and looking straight at me was Lucas, the older man who'd begged me to end his suffering in the blood bank room. He was shaking his head and looking at me with a sad expression on his face.

"Welcome to Hell," Lucas whispered, then turned his face away from me.

This can't be happening.

But it was. There was only one reason I'd be lying next to Lucas. Dr. Marshall had made good on his threat to take my legs from me, and even worse, he'd decided to put me up in his special room on the fourth floor. He'd carved me up, and turned me into one of his Bleeders.

CHAPTER TWENTY-ONE

I must have passed out again, because it was nighttime when next I opened my eyes, the Bleeders' room deathly quiet and in darkness. The only light came from the window, the moonlight filtering in through a foot-wide gap left in the heavy curtains. It was still too dark for me to see much of anything, which was a little unnerving, but at least my headache was a lot better.

I tried to sit up a few inches, trying to peer through the gloom to get a look around, and that was when I learned I was strapped to the mattress. So I didn't fall out of bed, I suppose. With no arms or legs, it was probably a good idea, but it pissed me off. I started twisting and turning, trying to get myself free. I thrashed and pulled and lashed my body around in a senseless fit of pure adrenaline-fueled anger. Truth be told, my rage didn't really have anything to do with the straps, they were just the last straw after I'd been so violated body and soul lately. Eventually, exhaustion and pain calmed me down, and I lay panting for air in the dark with tears running down both cheeks.

"You okay, Mike?" a voice said on my right.

It was a familiar voice, but I couldn't quite place it. It didn't sound like Lucas, but that's who'd been beside me earlier, hadn't it? I turned my head and could make out a big lump on the bed next to me, but that was about it.

"Who's there?" I asked. "That you, Lucas?"

"No. Lucas is in the bed on your left. It's Red Beard, Mike, remember me?"

"Course I do. How you doing?"

Stupid question, but it was out of my mouth before I thought about it.

"Same as you," Red said, "Cut down to nothing by that filthy bastard surgeon, and wishing I was dead."

I looked around the room again, trying to see how many other beds were filled.

"I can hardly see, Red, are Bill Smith and Wheels here too?

"Nope. Just us. Wheels was for a while but he died in his sleep. I think they took too much blood out of him. Lucky bugger. Haven't a clue what happened to Bill Smith, though. Never saw him again."

"Maybe Bill made a run for it and got out of here. I tried that myself."

"Me too," Red Beard said. "That's how I ended up in here. Piss Dr. Marshall off and this is where he sticks you, I think. Oh, and don't worry about your vision. Your eyes will get better accustomed to seeing in the dark once you've been here a while longer. You've only been here for about three weeks. Give it some time."

Three weeks?

"What are you talking about?" I asked. "This is my first day, isn't it?"

Red laughed at that. "No, 'fraid not, my friend. They brought you in at least two weeks ago, but I think it was closer to three. They keep the new arrivals pretty drugged, to keep the pain down and let your wounds heal without you moving around. You were probably in a recovery room for a few days too."

Son of a bitch.

I guess that explained the killer headache—they'd had me out like a light for weeks. It dawned on me then that I had no idea what the date was, or how long I'd been here at the castle. I didn't even know what month it was.

"What's the date, Red? Any idea?"

"Does it matter?" he asked. "None of that makes a difference anymore, so forget about it. Around here there are only two days of the week you need to worry about. Bad days, when they drain our blood, and good days, when they leave us the fuck alone. That's it, good or bad. Nothing else matters."

We lay in silence for a long time, and I felt myself starting to nod off again. I was sleepy but I had to ask.

"Hey, Red?"

"Yeah?" he answered, sounding tired as well.

"What day is tomorrow?"

I heard him take a deep breath; then in a soft whisper said, "Bad. Get some sleep."

CHAPTER TWENTY-TWO

Apparently I slept in. I woke up at the crack of dawn, the sunlight just starting to chase the darkness away, but everyone in the room whose mind was still intact was already wide-awake and starting to get nervous. The nurses and the orderlies would be coming through the door soon.

"It can't be that bad, can it?" I turned to ask Red Beard, but it was old Lucas, on my left, who answered.

"You ever donated blood before?" Lucas asked.

"Sure," I said. "Lots of times. It was never that big of a deal."

"Yeah, I agree with ya. Where did they take it from?"

"What?"

"The blood. Where did they take it out of you?"

"Oh, my arm."

"Right. Which arm do you want them to take it out of today? Oh, that's right, you don't have any *friggin'* arms, just like the rest of us, ya damn fool. They'll be takin' it out of your head, for Christ's sake. Ever had a big needle jabbed into your head, Mike?"

Lucas was obviously hot under the collar, but I wasn't sure if he was genuinely mad at me for not killing him when I'd had the chance, or if he was just on edge, nervous about what was about to happen. Probably a bit of both, so I bit my tongue and didn't say anything back.

"Relax, Lucas," Red Beard jumped to my defense. "He's new, it's not his fault he doesn't know what's happening."

"I know," Lucas sighed. "It was just such a stupid question, and I feel like crap today. I just want it all to end, Red. I can't take much more of this, I really can't."

"I know, Lucas," Red commiserated. "We all want it to end."

I felt a bit like a spectator at a tennis match, turning to my left, then right, as my roommates talked back and forth. When they lapsed into silence for a moment, I jumped into their conversation.

"First of all, Lucas, I'm really sorry I didn't finish the job, back when you wanted my help. You don't need to forgive me, but understand something. I wanted to help, I tried to help, but I fucked up. I got scared and ran to save my own ass. Not that it did me much good."

"Ah shit, Mike," Lucas said. "I don't hold it against ya. I'd have done the same. It's just this awful place. It drives ya crazy. They torture us again and again, and there's nothin' we can do about it. Wears a man down after a while. Wears him until he snaps. Remember Charlie, the guy who started screaming and brought the guards running that night?"

"Yeah, I remember," I said, thinking about how I couldn't get him to quiet down and shut up.

"Well, he finally snapped. His body's still over there, third bed on the right, but his mind has shut down and gone bye-bye. God, how I envy him!"

"Don't say that, Lucas. You gotta keep fighting. We're not dead yet."

He just glared at me with that sad look on his face

again, as if he pitied my optimism, then turned his head the other way and refused to talk anymore. I tried a few times, but Red Beard told me to save my breath.

"Forget it, Mike," Red said. "He can get like this before we get hooked up. He'll be fine in a while. It's always better once things are underway. You'll see."

"So tell me what to expect." I asked. "What are they gonna do to us?"

"Okay. Here's the deal. Dr. Marshall goes through a shitload of blood around here, keeping all his experiments going. He gets some of it shipped in from a few legal blood banks, but most of the blood comes from right here in this room.

"Take a look around, Mike. Counting you, we have fourteen warm bodies strapped in tight and waiting for the nurses. *Fourteen!* That's it to fill the demand for all Dr. Marshall's experiments. You do the math."

"You can't be serious?" I asked. "He'd have to take a bathtub of blood out of each of us."

Lucas chose this moment to decide he was in a talkative mood again. "Exactly! They damn near drain us dry."

Red Beard quickly added, "Well, not exactly. It just feels that way. They take way more than they should, that's for sure. I heard one of the nurses say the average human body contains around ten to twelve pints of blood, depending on their weight. Something like that, anyway. Lose half your blood and you can kiss your ass good-bye. Trouble is, with our limbs removed, we must have less blood than an average human, right? Say seven or eight pints, tops. They take two and a half pints out of each of us, sometimes a bit more."

"Leaves you completely drained of energy and feeling like a sack of shit," Lucas said. "You'll be so tired, you'll sleep the whole day away. Then they'll let us rest tomorrow, so we can build up a new supply for them to do it all over again."

I remembered something from the last time I'd been in this room. "Why were some of you hooked up during the night, then? I remember seeing more than one of you with the drain needles still in your head."

"Don't remind me," Lucas said, shuddering at the thought. "We were working *overtime*. Getting punished. It happens every now and then. Dr. Marshall accuses us of holding out, as if we could, and he'll put us on the slow drip all night long. The needles hurt like hell, and it's just his way of abusing us and keeping us scared of him."

A few minutes later, two nurses and two large, muscular orderlies stormed into the room. They were all business and went straight to work. The nurses set the needles, and the orderlies hooked up the auto-siphon machines beside the bed and were also available to beat a little cooperation into any of us that dared to scream, cry, or turn our heads away from the needle.

None of them looked into any of our eyes or said a single word of encouragement or commiseration. You'd think they'd have at least some pity for us, but I never witnessed even a trace of compassion as they went about their cold methodical business.

How can these people be so cruel?

I don't know how much Dr. Marshall was paying them, but it must have been bundles. There's no other way anyone would be able to stomach doing this job every second day. Unless—were they just as fanatical about the doctor's work as he was? Nah, had to be the money.

Surprisingly, the long needle inserted into a vein running along the left side of my face didn't hurt as much as I'd been expecting it to. Going in, at least. It wasn't until the orderly turned on the siphon machine that things started getting bad.

Really bad.

All the previous times I'd donated blood in the outside world, I can't say I remember ever feeling the blood coming out. You just lay down on a bed, or sat on a chair, waiting for the little bag to fill so you could head for the dessert tray to claim your snack. Sometimes it might take half an hour to complete your donation.

That wasn't the case for us Bleeders. They turned up the juice on the machines, actually sucking the blood from our veins instead of waiting around for Mother Nature and gravity to do the job. With every pull of the machine, I felt like I was going to pass out, the blood surging within me as it was forced out the clear plastic tube attached to my head.

Within minutes, it started to hurt. Hurt like a bastard, in fact, the pain steadily growing with every throb of the machine. It might have been my nerves, or my imagination, but it felt like it was pulling blood from me harder and harder. I had this strange thought that the next time the machine pulled, it was going to suck my brain right from my skull out the tube like a big scrambled lump of pureed jelly. It didn't happen, but man did I get a splitting headache. Just as bad as the drug-induced pain I'd experienced after waking from my last surgery.

Headache or not, they kept sucking my life fluid out of me, taking more and more until I was sure they intended to bleed me to death.

Just like Wheels. Probably how they deal with all the troublemakers, sucking the life out of us with a big straw.

I started to become delirious, screaming for someone to help me, to stop them killing me like this. I thrashed around in bed, fighting against the thick straps that held me down, panicking, covered in sweat, and three-quarters out of my mind from having lost so much blood.

My screams brought the orderlies running and one of them mercilessly ripped the needle from my head to end my first session as Dr. Marshall's new blood donor. When he yanked it out, the needle scratched against my skull just above my ear. That set fireworks of agony flashing down the entire left side of my body, tiny pinpoints of light dancing in my glassy, unfocused eyes.

A nurse stepped forward and bandaged me up, but by this point I was so out of it, I barely knew what was going on. I couldn't figure out who these people were, or why they were standing around looking at me. Before I could attempt to ask, the lights went out again and I was plunged into a deep, dark, semidead sleep.

CHAPTER TWENTY-THREE

I was running down the center of the street, rain soaking me from above, plastering my hair to my head as I willed my legs to move faster and faster. I was dreaming, of course, and fully aware of where it was my dream legs were taking me, but I had no way of waking up or changing my destination even if I wanted to. Finding the dead bodies of my wife and son and the badly injured body of my daughter certainly wasn't a pleasant experience but at least I would see them again and that counted for something.

My dream was always a bit fuzzy at the start, but usually it started with the phone call. I was halfway through my beer, thinking how wonderful it was I was ahead and sure to win the silly chug game when the phone rang. I know now that it's for me, but back then it was just a distraction that made me slow down enough that my buddy beat me. We had a dollar on the line—which seemed pretty important at the time—so I was asking for a rematch when the bartender, Ronnie, tapped me on the shoulder with a pallid, blank expression on his face that made me think he'd seen a ghost.

"It's the police," Ronnie said. "Lookin' for you. You'd better come take this."

"Hello?" I asked, reminding myself to keep my sentences short so I wouldn't slur my words.

Sometimes the dream played out in full; me swaying on my feet as I tried to understand what the police officer was telling me. Jackie, Arlene, and Daniel had been in a car accident, a bad one, and things weren't looking good. There was an ambulance on the way and Jackie had told the cops where to find me before passing out; the last words she'd ever say, and I wasn't there to hear them.

Sometimes I got lucky, like tonight, and the dream skipped ahead a few minutes to my mad dash in the rain-drenched street toward the twisted piece of metal and plastic that had once been our family's silver Honda Civic. The car was upside down, the entire front end gone, wrapped around a wooden telephone pole on the soft shoulder of the road.

As I ran closer, I could see the windows were all smashed out and it's right here I usually want to wake up because I know from experience that in a few more strides I'll be able to see Daniel's body still trapped in the backseat, his blood-covered little arm waving in the air for help. I'll run even harder to get to the car, but by the time I make it there I'm always too late. Daniel is still alive and looking at me, but the light is fading in his beautiful blue eyes and he dies before we can say a word to each other. I don't even get to touch his offered hand before he goes, and I'll hate myself forever for not being able to run faster.

Something was screwy with tonight's dream, though, something different, because when I ran up to the car Daniel wasn't in the backseat. He wasn't in the car at all, and neither was his mother, who by all rights should be slumped over the wheel, partially impaled on the broken steering column, as I'd actually found her. Arlene was there in the passenger seat, but she wasn't covered in blood and screaming the way I remember. No, she was just sitting there, quiet as a mouse, staring at me with black empty eyes filled with hatred and accusation.

There was a cop standing near me, and I turned to him and asked, "What's going on? Where's Jackie and Daniel? They're supposed to be here, waiting for me in the car like all the other times."

The policeman looked at me kind of funny, but said, "The ambulance arrived about ten minutes ago. They've taken your wife and son to the closest medical facility."

This was news to me. It certainly never happened like that with the real accident so I wasn't sure how to react or what to do.

"Are they dead?" I asked. Of course they were, but I had to say something.

"No, sir. From what I understand, they're both busted up pretty badly but the paramedic treating them said they should make it if they get to the hospital in time."

"Which hospital?" I asked, feeling like a jackass for getting my hopes up. I know I'm dreaming and they both died years ago but none of that mattered right now. If they're still alive, even just in this crazy dream, then I had a chance to see them one last time. See them, hold them, talk to them, tell both of them how much I loved them and how I was sorry I made Jackie drag our family out on a stormy night like this just because I was too drunk to drive home myself. None of my words could change the past or make anything better, but I had to at least try.

"It's not far from here," the policeman said. "Get in the cruiser, I'll take you there."

Arlene got out of the car and walked over toward us. I held the police cruiser door open for her, thinking and hoping she was coming with me, but she walked off into the dark stormy night without another glance in my direction.

She's walking out of my life, forever, I thought. At least I had that part right.

Shaking my head to clear the rain and tears from my eyes, I jumped in the cruiser and waved for the cop to get moving. On the ride over, I was praying I wouldn't wake up. I wouldn't even speak to the police officer, thinking that any change of thought or focus and my dream might veer off in some other unwanted direction. This was the closest I'd come to seeing my wife and son in nearly four years and I knew it was too good to be true. It wouldn't last, couldn't last, but if I could just stay asleep for five more minutes, to kiss Jackie one more time, to hold little Daniel in my arms for just one minute, that was all I wanted. Was that asking too much?

My panic alarm started to go off as we left the city limits, the police cruiser taking a left onto a paved road that wound its way through a forest of tall sturdy trees. There wasn't a hospital outside of the city. Was there? Why hadn't they taken Jackie and Daniel to Buffalo General. Surely it was closer to the accident scene than this.

"Where are we?" I asked, looking at the policeman for the first time since getting into his cruiser.

"We're at the medical center," he said. "Don't you recognize the place?"

I looked back out the front window just as the car exited the woods and saw that we had entered the parking lot of Nathan Marshall's ugly red-bricked medical center. There was an ambulance parked near the front entrance, lights still flashing.

God, no! Not here!

"Why did they bring my family here? They need to go to a *real* hospital. This place is evil."

"Evil? Listen, man, I don't know what to tell you, but

if you want to see your wife and kid, this is where they are. If you'd rather I take you back into town—"

"No!" I screamed, a bit louder than intended. "Just hurry up, okay?" By the time we'd pulled to a stop beside the ambulance, the policeman looked relieved to see me get out of his car.

"Good luck, my friend."

I didn't bother answering or thanking him for the ride. I took off running again. I couldn't bear the thought of Dr. Marshall getting his hands on my family and every second might count. No one was inside the ambulance so I headed for the front doors, only to find both securely locked. I glanced back at the police cruiser, ready to scream for help, but the words died in my throat when I saw that it was Drake standing beside the car, dressed in policeman blue and grinning at me from under the brim of his rain-soaked hat. He pointed at the door, then held up his big meaty fist and made a knocking gesture in the air beside his head.

I didn't want to turn my back on Drake, but I was more concerned for my family at the moment, so I started pounding on the front door of the castle, screaming for someone to let me in. The heavy door swung open and Dr. Marshall's bitchy old secretary ushered me in out of the rain.

"Where are they?" I asked, my fear barometer steadily climbing, my patience gone.

"Relax, Mr. Fox. You'll find your family is quite well. Dr. Marshall has taken care of them and they're both resting comfortably up on the fourth floor. You can see them anytime you'd like. I think you know the way."

With that, the secretary spun on her heels and walked away into the high-domed atrium without a glance back to see what I intended to do. Not that I had any options.

The fourth floor—

Why would they have been taken to the fourth floor? None of the patient rooms were up there. The only thing on that floor was—

No. Please, no!

I headed for the stairs, bolting up them two at a time, moving as fast as I could. No matter how fast I moved, though, I had a sinking feeling where this dream was heading and there was no outrunning the shadow of dread that followed, nipping at my heels. I burst into the fourth-floor hallway and made a beeline for the Bleeders' room halfway down the hall. It was the only place up here my wife and son could possibly be.

At the door, I forced myself to walk inside. If I stopped to catch my breath I might never work up the nerve to go through with this. Jackie and Daniel were in the first two beds on the right-hand side of the room, and with one glance my worst fears were confirmed. Dr. Marshall had cut their arms and legs off and turned them both into Bleeders.

I ran to the foot of their beds, crying my eyes out and wanting so desperately to tell them how sorry I was this had happened, but I never got the chance. Jackie took one look at me and turned her head away in shame and disgust. Daniel, my pride and joy, didn't turn away. No, he looked right into my eyes and said, "Look what you've done to us, Dad. I'll hate you forever for this."

I woke up screaming, my sheets soaked with so much sweat it was as if I'd really been in the rainstorm of my dream. I cried for hours, huge racking sobs, but no one came to comfort me or see if I was okay. No one did anything; not even the other Bleeders in the room with me. Maybe they were used to hearing people scream, or maybe they were lost within their own nightmares tonight, and had no time to console me for mine. Either that, or perhaps there was just no one left on earth that gave a damn about me.

I closed my eyes and waited to die.

What else could I do?

CHAPTER TWENTY-FOUR

Lucas was right—this terrible place destroyed a man after a while.

Wears him until he snaps.

I hadn't really understood the truth in what he'd said at the time, and I hadn't been here even close to as long as him, but as the days slowly turned to weeks, I had no more doubts. As strong-willed and stubborn as I'd always prided myself in being, I knew this place was going to get the better of me. It was just a matter of time.

The days when they drained our blood were a total write-off—nothing but pain and suffering and, eventually, the welcome embrace of unconsciousness. On the off days, when they left us alone, all we did was sleep and hope the world would come to an end. As nighttime approached, the tension in the air would crank up a notch or two, everyone's thoughts—mine included—turning to what awaited with the rising of the sun. Exhaustion, anxiety, then full-blown fear were familiar emotions, a never-ending cycle interrupted only by sleep and the inevitable arrival of the nurses with their new batch of needles.

I wanted to die. So did all of the rest of the Bleeders—the ones still coherent enough to know what was being done to them, anyway. Kill us quickly, and get it over with. This slow torturous death we'd been condemned to was inhuman and unbearable. There was no end in sight, though, and nothing we could do about it.

At least things couldn't possibly get any worse.

Wrong.

"Why haven't they come yet?" I asked Lucas. "Have they ever forgotten before?"

It was a bad day today, but the nurses and orderlies hadn't shown up to hook us up to the machines. The clock on the wall indicated that it was almost noon, and so far, at least, not a soul had entered our room.

"Never," Lucas replied, fear evident in his hushed voice. "Very strange. Something must be up."

The words were barely out of his mouth, when the door burst open and in walked Dr. Marshall and Alexander Drake. An audible gasp was heard around the room, but then you could have heard a syringe needle drop on the floor, everyone deathly silent wondering what was about to happen.

Uh-oh. This can't be good.

Dr. Marshall and Drake never came up to the fourth floor to see us. Never. I highly doubted this was a friendly social call.

Lucas was right. Something's going on. But what?

They walked from one end of the room to the other, creepily pausing to check each of us out closely, before moving on to the next bed. Dr. Marshall had apparently discarded his wheelchair, and was now using a sturdy cane to help him maneuver around. He limped, but it was hardly noticeable. Quite a remarkable recovery, especially considering those weren't even his legs. Made me wonder whose legs they *were*, and what they had done to the poor bastard they took them off. Was he lying here beside me, somewhere in this room, or had his usefulness wore out, and he'd already made the trip down the WASTE DISPOSAL chute to the incinerator down in the basement?

Dr. Marshall and Drake whispered over by the window, turning to point to one bed or another, then slowly started making their way back to the door. My heart began to pound when they stopped at the foot of my bed and turned to look straight at me.

"You sure?" Dr. Marshall asked his sidekick.

Drake looked at me with eyes as cold, black, and unfeeling as those of a great white shark staring down his prey. Then he took a step closer, a feral grin on his face that made the resemblance to the shark even more chilling.

"Oh absolutely. He's the one," Drake said.

The one what?

Ashamed of myself, I was uncontrollably shaking with fear in the presence of these two madmen. A few months ago, I would have shot back a smart-ass comment, or at least told them to go fuck themselves, but most of my courage must have been cut away with my arms and legs, because I stayed silent, not daring to speak.

"Fair enough," Dr. Marshall said. "Bring him down as quickly as possible, Drake. We've wasted too much time already. I'll go and see that things are ready."

"Yes, sir. Right away."

Dr. Marshall left without another glance back, the other men strapped in their beds totally insignificant to him, now that his decision was made. No sooner was he out the door when a tall lanky orderly pushed a padded leather-covered gurney into the room and made his way over to stand beside Drake.

"Let's go for a ride, Mike," Drake said, loving every second of this. Then to the orderly, he whispered, "Get him out of here."

"Where you taking me?" I asked the orderly, as he unstrapped me from my bed and roughly heaved me over onto the bedside gurney.

He ignored my question, not even making eye contact with me, so I shouted at Drake, "What's going on, Drake? Leave me alone, damn it!"

He just grinned and turned away, motioning with his hand for the orderly to follow. Within seconds, I was restrained on the gurney and being pushed toward the door. I managed to get a quick look at Lucas and Red Beard. Both of them were trembling as badly as I was, their faces paler than Arctic ghosts. I might never see them again, and I wanted to say something to calm their fears and tell them not to worry about me, but I never got the chance. I was out the door and heading down the hallway before I could think of a single thing to say.

CHAPTER TWENTY-FIVE

It was a terrifying and disorienting ride on the gurney, having no idea where I was headed and being strapped flat on my back, seeing nothing but fluorescent lights flashing by on the ceiling as we hurried to catch up with Drake. He was waiting in the elevator, holding the door as we entered, still grinning at me like an evil clown with a dirty secret. I knew better than to ask him anything, so when the doors closed, the three of us rode down a couple of floors in silence.

Another mad dash down the hallway, once again racing to follow the chief of security (*Was this the second floor, or the first?*) until Drake finally stopped at a double set of solid wooden doors, putting his hand on a wall-mounted scanner and waiting for clearance.

"I'll take him from here, Steve," Drake said to the orderly, shooing him away and guiding the gurney himself through the open doorway.

Once inside, with the door securely locked, Drake wheeled me to the center of the room and flicked a switch on my gurney that enabled him to stand me almost upright, so I could see things easier. Not that there was much to see. It was quiet inside the room; the temperature cool and the air heavy with moisture, reminding me of the saltwater aquariums my father had taken me to at Marineland in Niagara Falls when I was a kid. When I craned my head around, I couldn't see any water, nothing but a big empty room with Drake and I as the only occupants.

"That you, Drake?" a familiar voice asked.

It was Dr. Marshall's voice, but I still couldn't see him, or tell where it was coming from.

"Yes, sir," Drake responded. "Ready when you are."

Dr. Marshall appeared out of nowhere, seemingly walking through a brick wall, until I noticed the heavy dark curtain flopping back into place and realized there was more to this room than I was seeing. He walked over to us and stopped right in front of me.

"Morning, Mr. Fox," Dr. Marshall started, his tone light and jovial, which immediately made my skin crawl. "Consider yourself lucky, my friend. You've been chosen to take part in something incredible. Something, dare I say, *miraculous*!"

I actually started to laugh. I didn't mean to, but I couldn't help it. Perhaps my brain was a bit fried and I was getting close to losing it, but the thought of me being considered "lucky" was so far beyond ludicrous, I couldn't help but chuckle.

"What's so amusing?" Dr. Marshall asked, the friendly smile sliding off his face.

I knew better than to piss this psycho off further, but I just didn't care anymore. Screw him!

"You are," I shot back. "What's wrong with you? You've cut me to shreds and turned me into something that's not even human anymore, and I'm supposed to feel *lucky*? Oh, for sure! Thanks *so* much, sir. God you're pathetic. You're so freakin' out of your mind it's comical, man. Just kill me and get it the fuck over with."

The room was quiet after my little tirade—really quiet—nobody making a sound. Dr. Marshall stared at me, his body shaking with tension, hatred clearly shining in his eyes, but he took a full minute to compose himself before speaking.

"Show him, Drake. Open the curtain."

Drake hurried over to the area where the surgeon had appeared from a few minutes earlier, and found the split in the center of the cloth. He opened the right-hand half of the curtains, dragging the heavy drapes over and securing them to the wall with a matching cloth tieback bolted in place.

Beyond the curtain, the rest of the room was in darkness. I could make out a large glass container of some sort, but with the way the meager light from this side of the room was casting shadows, I couldn't make out what I was supposed to be seeing.

Then Drake turned on the lights, and the breath was literally sucked from my lungs as I stared in disbelief at what was inside the glass tank.

It was the naked body of a well-conditioned man—or what *used* to be a man, at any rate—but the head was missing and there was a massive cut on the body's back, from the neck to just above the buttocks, where the man's spine had also been surgically removed. It wasn't dead, though. Not even close. What looked like millions of tiny colorful wires and electrodes trailed down into the grievous neck and back wounds, presumably attaching into the body's complex central nervous system because the body was twitching and dancing within the liquid-filled tank like a drunken vaudevillian actor.

"What on earth is that thing?" I worked up the courage to ask, my curiosity getting the better of my fear for the moment.

Drake laughed, walking over to whisper in my ear, "That *thing*, Mike, is what we're calling a flesh suit. Basically, it's a body in waiting. It's what's left of your buddy, Bill Smith. Should have been you actually, now that I think of it."

Bill?

"What do you mean?" I asked.

"We thought it was Mr. Smith who'd snuck into room 301 during your first night here. We thought he was the guy who discovered Andrew's room was a fake, so we grabbed him the very next night. It should have been you."

"But why?" I wanted to know. "Why would you do something like this to him, or to anyone?"

Dr. Marshall answered this time. "Two reasons. To shut him up, for one. We didn't want him telling the rest of you what we thought he'd seen in Andrew's room. We soon found out we'd made a mistake, but by then it was too late to turn back. More importantly, I needed his body for the most important experiment of all, the final step in my plan to free Andrew from his long life of misery."

Dr. Marshall bent over and stuck his face inches away from mine then continued, saying, "You can call me insane all you want, Mr. Fox, and this might strike you as comical and seem like nothing but a big joke, but this is serious to me, you worthless little piece of shit . . . deadly serious, and whether you like it or not, you're going to help me. Understand? Andrew *is* going to walk."

Now I was making the connections, putting it all together as far as Andrew was concerned, but where did I fit into all this madness?

"What are you gonna do to me?" I asked.

Dr. Marshall backed up a few steps and started smiling again, his friendly demeanor back in place.

"Simple really," he said. "I'm going to do to you exactly what I plan on putting Andrew through. He's in a very unstable condition, and time is of the essence, but

I don't want to rush ahead and screw up. He's only got one more chance, and I have to make sure all the kinks are out of my procedure. That's where you come in. You're going to be my final test, Mike. I'm going to try the entire procedure on you first to make sure it works. Then I'll be ready to heal Andrew."

I couldn't think of a single thing to say. I was shocked, and it must have registered on my face because Dr. Marshall started reassuring me things would be okay.

"Don't worry, Mr. Fox. Everything will turn out great. Glorious, in fact. You've seen my experiments, so you know I can do this. You should be grateful, really. I'm going to give you back arms and legs, Mike. Think about it. I'm going to make you walk again. You and Andrew both!"

There was part of me buying into the doctor's crazy spiel—a large part of me, actually. I had no doubts the doctor could successfully do what he was planning, and I desperately wanted to have my arms and legs back and be able to stand on my own two feet, rather than being strapped to this stupid gurney. Technically they wouldn't be *my* arms and legs, but in the half-bonkers state of mind I was in, that was starting to sound better than nothing.

But then I took another look at Bill's electronically animated body dancing in its tank in front of me and realized that to put me inside that body, Dr. Marshall would have to cut me down even further—down to my head and spine just like Andrew—and that was something I just couldn't handle. Another surgery would surely drive me insane and I didn't want any part of it.

"Please don't do this," I pleaded. "I didn't know him all that well, but I don't wanna wear Bill's body. I couldn't live with myself. I'm begging you. Just kill me now and let it be done with, okay?"

"Bill's body?" Dr. Marshall questioned. Drake and

he started to laugh. "Don't worry, you won't be wearing Bill's body. Are you crazy?"

I didn't understand what I had said that was so funny. I was tired and very confused. Had I missed something or heard the doctor wrong?

"You're not going to put my head on that body? But you just said—"

"Of course not, you fool," Dr. Marshall interrupted. "You think I'd waste a specimen like this on you? Bill Smith's flesh suit is perfect. It's fit as a fiddle and blemish free. It's the ideal new body for Andrew."

He nodded to Drake, who happily walked over to the left-hand curtains still drawn across to the middle of the room. With a wink, Drake slowly shoved this half of the heavy drapes to the side wall, revealing a second glass tank and a second flesh suit dancing in its own watery grave.

Sweet mother of Jesus!

The glass tanks and the myriad color-coded wires were virtually identical, but that was where the similarities ended. Bill Smith's body might have looked strange, suspended without a head, but at least it still looked relatively human. What was in the other tank could only be described as grotesque—a flesh suit made with bits and pieces from several different bodies (torso, hands, feet, arms, legs, fingers, toes), the parts all sewn and grafted together to make a hideous parody of a human being.

"*This* is your flesh suit, Michael," Dr. Marshall said. "I pieced it together from the various experiment parts I had lying around. It's an amazing accomplishment in itself, really, with more than twelve different body donors being used in all. Add your head and spine into the mix, and we'll have used thirteen. A nice baker's dozen. I know it's not quite as attractive as the suit Andrew will be getting, but beggars can't be choosers. What do you think?"

My mind froze on me again. My thought processes ground to a halt. Looking at the monstrous body that might soon be my own, I couldn't think or say anything that might help get me out of this craziness. Partly fascinated, partly curious, but mostly horrified, I just stared up at the headless dancing Frankenstein and prayed to die before Dr. Marshall could do to me what I knew he had planned.

God wasn't listening.

"Mr. Drake," Dr. Marshall said. "Take Michael down the hall, will you? Operating room three is prepped and ready for us."

"Be a pleasure, sir," Drake said. "A real pleasure."

CHAPTER TWENTY-SIX

The mirror had to have been Drake's inspiration. His sick twisted idea of humor to torture my fragile mind even further. Instead of breaking me completely, as I'm sure he'd hoped, if anything, it made me stronger. It replaced my fear and anxiety with good ol' red-blooded American bitterness and hatred, and I needed that intense level of anger to sustain me through the senseless indignities I was being forced to endure. Rage became my companion, my ally, my savior.

When I'd first opened my eyes, I thought they'd put me into a room with Andrew, put us so close together I was looking right into his haunted bloodshot eyes, and seeing his ragged neckline with its multitude of wires leading down to his thrashing submerged spine. But once I fully awakened and my mind became a little clearer I recognized the eyes, nose and jawline of the person I was gazing at, and noticed the thin wooden frame around the perimeter of the silver-backed glass. A man in a mirror—three guesses, first two don't count.

Drake had obviously put the mirror there just so I could see what they'd done to me. It wasn't enough for me to know I'd been reduced down to a disembodied head and spinal column—he wanted me to *see* it with my own eyes.

It's impossible to describe the series of emotions that washed over my damaged psyche at that moment. For Christ's sake, what are you supposed to think and feel when you can look down and count the number of vertebrae in your spine? Maybe shock, horror, sadness, denial, self-pity, fear, or insanity? Yep, I had all of those emotions, but as I said, it was when I started to get mad—no, make that furious—about what they'd done to me, that was the emotional life preserver I desperately latched on to. It wasn't much, but my wrath was all I had left. Either that, or take the big plunge and go straight out of my freakin' mind.

I was left alone for a long time, silently staring at what was left of my decimated body, my anger building and building until I was sure steam would start leaking from my ears. I couldn't even scream. I tried, you can be sure of that, tried and tried, but no sound was coming out. I didn't have any vocal cords left, or lungs to push air up past them to make sound. All I could do was open and close my mouth, raging in silence.

I soon realized it wasn't my voice I missed most, or any of the rest of my body. It was the beating of my heart. Normally we don't even hear it, or put any thought toward the job it performs—until it's gone, that is. I was still being supplied with sufficient blood to keep my brain alive and functional, but somehow it wasn't the same thing. Although I could hear the similar sounding *thump-swish* noise of the heart/lung bypass machine, the blood flowing through me was no longer mine, and no word of a lie, I could tell the difference.

Stop getting so fucking philosophical. These bastards have cut away your whole damned body, why the fuck are you so worried about your heart? Get over it.

I suppose that was good advice. Made sense, and jolted my mind back on track. Right now, I'd probably trade ten good hearts for one meaty fist and a powerful arm to take a wicked haymaker at both Drake and Dr. Marshall. That would be sweet, but it was a stupid, irrational thought. Not the last, I was sure. I was losing it, big time, and I knew it. There just wasn't much I could do to stop it. Then again, maybe sanity was overrated. What good would it do me in my present condition? I'd be far better off nutty as a fruitcake, lost in a delusional sense of reality that had me strolling down an imaginary white sandy beach with some dark-skinned beauty on my arm. Wouldn't I?

I spent a minute thinking about the dream beach, but my illusion was shattered when I heard Drake call my name from somewhere behind me.

"Looking good, Mike," he said, walking around and removing the mirror from in front of me.

The tank that held my spine was situated on a low table near the floor, and I had to crane my neck to look up at him. The muscle-bound head of security stared down at me for a full minute without speaking, then bent down to my eye level, leaning in so close our noses were actually touching. His breath stank of stale whiskey, but from the slightly glassy look in his drunken eyes, I was sure I had more to worry about from Drake than just his bad breath. He had the look of a hungry predator about him, and there was no doubt I was definitely easy prey.

"How you feeling, little man? You cold? I should get you a sweater . . . oh, sorry. Sweater wouldn't do you much good, would it? Perhaps a nice warm hat?"

Drake burst out laughing, spraying my face with spittle. I hated him more than anyone else in the world at that moment—even Dr. Marshall, who was most responsible for what had happened to me. At least the doctor was driven by his mad obsession to help his only son. Drake acted the way he did out of sheer viciousness. He was a wickedly evil, pretentious bastard and I vowed to myself that I'd hang on, somehow find the courage and strength to live long enough to see him die.

"Dr. Marshall wants to talk to you. Said he'd be along in a few minutes." Drake leaned down to whisper in my ear, "What should we do while we're waiting?"

He stepped back a few feet, pretending to ponder it for a moment, and then started to undo his pants.

You wouldn't DARE!

Of course he would. Seconds later, he had his manhood in his hand and was stroking it hard.

"I've had my eye on you right from the start," Drake said in a lusty growl. "I like 'em feisty like you, Mike. Now you be good, or ol' Drake's gonna have to hurt you real bad. Understand?"

Perfectly. I opened my mouth up as wide as I possibly could—an open invitation for him. *Drive it home, big boy, see what it gets you!*

God, I hoped he'd be stupid enough to do it. If he stuck that filthy thing in my mouth, there was nothing on earth that would stop me from taking a chomp. He could threaten me with pain, endless suffering, and even death, but I didn't give two shits about any of that. If he stuck it in, he was gonna lose it. Guaranteed!

Do it, Drake. Do it!

Something in my eyes must have given my intentions away, because I saw him hesitate, think things through, then decide maybe his present course of action wasn't exactly the smartest. I swear I saw a flicker of fear race across his face and when his penis started to soften in his hand I knew I'd gotten the better of him.

"You're not worth the bother," Drake said, trying to backpedal and cover his tracks.

He was far too macho to ever admit I'd managed to

scare him. Instead he zipped up his pants and walked out of the room without saying another word.

He sulked back a few minutes later with Dr. Marshall, who seemed to be walking around much better now than I remembered. Made me wonder how long I'd been floating around in recuperation land this time and I actually tried to ask, forgetting I couldn't speak. The doctor saw my lips moving and walked over.

"Save your strength, Mr. Fox," he said. "I've tried to master reading lips, so I could communicate better with Andrew, but I just don't seem to have the knack for it. Besides, I've come to tell you some great news."

I highly doubted that, but what could I do but wait for him to spill the beans?

"I've gone over all the test data at least twenty times, Michael. Everything looks exactly as I'd predicted and hoped. We're ready to go ahead and do the transplant. Yours that is, not Andrew's. I still need to study the results of your transplant into the flesh suit before I commit to doing Andrew."

This was his good news? That I was headed back for more surgery? Admittedly, I sure as hell didn't want to remain in the pitiful helpless condition I was in now, but the thought of being sewn up inside that hideous patchwork body I'd seen clumsily dancing in the second tank was too much to contemplate rationally. I mean, how could I possibly exist within a body made up of thirteen different people? Michael Fox: from street bum to Frankenstein, in four easy steps. What a nightmare.

I started to panic, helpless to do anything but squirm around and shout silent obscenities, but I had to do something. I couldn't just sit idly by and be turned into a walking freakshow without at least trying to fight. Not that it did me any good. As soon as Dr. Marshall saw me getting agitated and dangerously thrashing around, he filled yet another of his seemingly endless large syringes and injected it into one of the tubes flowing in and out of my neck. I felt the drug's effect immediately, and was powerless to fight against it. My eyes were closing before he even withdrew the needle.

"Don't worry, Mr. Fox," I heard Dr. Marshall say from what seemed like ten miles away. "You won't need to suffer in this bodiless state much longer. I'll have you fixed up in no time at all. You'll feel much better the next time you open your eyes. Like a new man, in fact. Literally, a . . . whole . . . new . . . man."

PART FOUR

THE MONSTER

CHAPTER TWENTY-SEVEN

For a while I disappeared. Gonzo. I lay perfectly still, strapped down unnecessarily tight in a bed, in a room, in a hospital, in a world I had no knowledge existed. I was far beyond any sort of rational thought, confused and disoriented for several eternities, as time laughed and passed me by.

The first thing I remember noticing were the lights.

I've done a lot of strange things in the past, but for the life of me, I couldn't figure out when (or why, for that matter) I'd decided to become an astronaut. Didn't they have fairly rigid standards about the people applying for that type of work? Not to be self-depreciating, but come on—*me?* Surely NASA could do better than that. One moment I was in a cold dark place (the shuttle's cockpit?) with my eyes closed, then the next someone pushed the blastoff button and I opened my eyes to a galaxy of exploding planets, fiery comets, and shooting stars—an unending supernova of bright lights and awesome colors that were truly awesome sights to behold.

Were there really rainbows in outer space?

I was tripping, of course, the blinding light show taking place only in my mind, my brain saturated with

enough pain medication, it was probably draining out
of my ears onto the pillow. For months I was a full
card-carrying member of Star Command, only touching back down to Earth long enough to refuel my meds.
Good thing too, because gravity hurt like hell. I was in
such extreme agony it hurt too much to waste energy
screaming. It felt like my body had been crushed to
pulp in an industrial metal press.

Later—much later—the stone-faced nurses told me
that I'd wake up screaming, "Send me back. Send me
back to the fucking moon." And with one push of a syringe they'd do just that—bless their cold little hearts.

Houston, we have a problem.

No doubt.

CHAPTER TWENTY-EIGHT

Drugs are wonderful things sometimes, having the power and strength to mask, in fact *alter* reality for an indefinite period of time. But all things pass—whether good or bad—and eventually so did my journeys to the stars. I'd be lying through my tightly clenched teeth if I didn't admit I missed them.

Being a juiced-up astronaut was far better than being a monster. And there was no doubt in my mind that's what I'd become—a pieced-together nightmare of thirteen mutilated men. Perhaps I was being overly harsh with that assessment; after all, having a body again had to be a step up from the liquid-filled glass tank I'd been calling home, but no matter how hard I tried to get my head around this, I couldn't change the way I felt. I should be dead. No ifs, ands, or buts about it. Everything about my continued existence was just *wrong*.

But damn it, I wasn't dead.

So where did that leave me? Well, in pain, for one thing. Son of a bitch I was hurting. They hadn't taken me off all my pain meds, even the nurses weren't *that* cruel. I was still on a shitload of them, but they'd begun what they said was my tapering-off stage. Apparently the powers that be wanted me coherent enough that I could get started on my next phase of torture. It was called rehab.

"Get the hell up," the nurse said, her tone sharp, confrontational. She was a chubby, sour-faced old dame with her gray hair cinched up in an ubertight bun. She looked a bit like the secretary downstairs. Had the same miserable disposition, anyway. I'd never seen her before and those were the first words out of her mouth as she walked in my room. No good morning, no how ya feeling today, no nothin'. A real sweetheart, this one was, I could already tell. Where did Dr. Marshall find these people?

"I *am* up," I said. "Been awake for an hour already for Christ's sake, waiting in agony for you to bring me my meds. Where's my regular nurse?"

She ignored me, of course. They all did. I could rant and rave, scream, cry, or bark like a dog and none of them seemed to give a shit. Most of the time I just kept my mouth shut. These weren't my vocal chords I was speaking with, and my voice still scared the hell out of me every time I opened my mouth. It wasn't necessarily a bad voice, nothing freaky like Pee-wee Herman or overly irritating like Arnold Horshack from that old '70s television sitcom, *Welcome Back Kotter*, but it was higher pitched than the voice I'd gotten used to and it freaked me out too much when I started thinking about whose voice I might have.

"I didn't say, *wake* up." The old nurse was bending over, squinting to read my chart on the clipboard at the foot of my bed. "I said *get* up! There's a difference. Better clean out your ears and start listening or you and I are gonna butt heads, you hear?"

"What are you talkin' about?" I asked. "Who the hell are you?"

"Call me Junie. I'm your resurrectionist."

"My wha—"

"Your physiotherapist, dumbass, but resurrectionist somehow seems more appropriate, for most parts of you anyway."

"Fuck you," I said. Every inch of my body ached and my head felt like shit. I wasn't in the mood to play word games and be the brunt of this old bitch's warped sense of humor. "Give me my meds and get out of my room!"

She stared at me for a long time, stared hard and mean as a snake. I was pretty sure it had been a long time since anyone had told her to fuck off, and I could tell she didn't like it much.

"You're still not listening," she said. "I told you to get up and I meant it. It's time to start your rehab. You've lain around long enough. Doc Marshall expects results, I hope you know. He did his part; time for you to do yours. On your feet, boy."

Now I was really pissed off. I'd been torn apart and sewn back together with discarded spare parts, been strapped to this ungodly hard bed for who knows how many bloody months, and my patchwork body hurt me so bad right now I had to fight hard not to scream. Who was this stupid old bat to just walk in here and command me to stand up? My resurrectionist—ha! Screw that.

"I'm not sure what cemetery they dug you up from, lady, and I really don't care, but someone should've clued you in to the fact I can't just leap to my feet. Stand up? Hell, you may as well ask me to float upside down and dance the jitterbug on the ceiling. I can barely move, asshole!"

"Nonsense," Junie said, having none of it. "Stop being such a crybaby. This may be the first time you remember seeing me, but I've been monitoring you for months. While you were recuperating in a semi-coma, Dr. Marshall had me hook you up to his fantastic machines to continually stimulate your new muscles and stretch out your ligaments and tendons. While you slept, your new body parts have been getting to know each other. We've rigorously worked your arms, legs, neck, back, hell . . . even your fingers and toes. So don't get all huffy and tell me you can't move. I've damn well watched you and *know* you can. Have you even tried? Or have you been too busy feeling sorry for yourself?"

"Of course, I've tried," I lied. "I can't do it. I get the shakes and a lot of leg cramps that make me move. They damn near kill me, but it's nothin' that I can control. Besides, I'm hurtin' way too much right now for this bullshit. Give me my meds and an hour to let them kick in and I promise I'll try anything you want. Not now, though. No way."

The old physiotherapist shot a look of pure hatred toward me, then shook her head in disgust. "You're pitiful, Mike, but the whining stops today. Right now. You want your pain medication? Here, come an' get 'em for yourself."

She walked over and placed the familiar plastic container containing my multicolored happy pills on the roll-away wooden meal tray, positioning it against the side wall of my room, about seven feet to my right. Then she turned to leave.

"You can't be serious," I said. Junie didn't answer me. She was already out the door and gone.

It took a full fifteen minutes before I finally accepted this wasn't some sort of weird trick and she really wasn't coming back. Junie the resurrectionist was gone and my pain meds weren't doing me a lot of good sitting halfway to the door.

Son of a bitch. Now what am I gonna do?

I stared at the plastic cup holding my pills—close,

sure, but they may as well have been on the other side
of the planet. My eyes wandered to the emergency call
button attached to a long white cord beside my bed. All
I had to do was push that little red button on the end
and one of my regular nurses would come running.
Surely they'd give me my pills. But first I had to get a
hold of it, and in my condition that was impossible. Or
was it? I had a sneaky feeling trying to use my new
arms would hurt like a bastard, but what alternative did
I have? I had to at least try. Either that or just lay here
and suffer.

Okay then, finger first.

No real reason for it, but I made up my mind to try
wiggling my index finger on my right hand, then work
my way up to trying to move the whole arm. Seemed as
good a plan as any. If crazy old Junie was telling the
truth about them working my muscles while I'd been
napping, this should be a piece of cake.

My finger moved; wiggling on command like it was
nervous. Trouble was, it was the wrong finger. I'd wanted
the index, and the one wiggling was my middle finger.
Not too bad—just one digit off. I concentrated harder
and really focused on moving my index finger. The
middle finger danced again.

Fuck!

Either I wasn't trying hard enough, or somewhere
along the line I wasn't hardwired up quite right. That
seemed possible. More than possible—inevitable, really.
With all the millions of nerve connections and neural
pathways inside a human body, it only stood to reason
some mistakes would be made when Dr. Marshall stitched
me back together. The question was, how many? How
many mistakes and bad connections made up my new
bastardized nervous system? With the kind of luck I'd
had lately, I didn't even want to think about it.

Back to the fingers.

I tried to bend them all this time, not be so picky. Clench up my hand into a fist and—

Hey, it worked!

I could open them too. Maybe it would just take a while to fine-tune things and get my dexterity back. I spent a minute playing with my new hand, smiling happily, a boy again with a macabre new fleshy toy. It hurt a bit, a stinging jab in my knuckles every time I bent my fingers, but it wasn't as bad as I'd imagined. In a way it felt good. That might sound ridiculous but it's true. After months of living in a bodiless state, it was nice to *feel* again. Feel anything, even pain.

Before I realized I was doing it, my right arm was sliding across the sheet and I was making a grab for the call button. It took several tries to grab and keep hold of the small plastic object, but I finally managed. My entire arm was tingling, a hot funky pins-and-needles feeling like when your arm falls asleep.

I started to feel a cramp coming on, the ache starting in my fingers and getting ready to spread up my arm. I concentrated as hard as I could and felt elated as my thumb acted like a good boy and started clicking the red call button just like I'd wanted it to. A buzzer started ringing outside my room, somewhere down the hall, presumably at the nurses' station.

I let my arm flop to the bed and relaxed. I'd actually done it, and damned if I wasn't feeling proud of myself. I'd used another man's arm, hand, and fingers to do my bidding. Might not seem like much, but to me it was an incredible achievement. Surely someone would be along to answer the buzzer and see what I needed. I just had to kick back and wait. I kept my eyes on the pill cup, anticipation bringing a light sheen of sweat to my brow. A mouthful of saliva, as well. Once a junkie, always a junkie.

Nobody came.

Not right away. Not a few minutes later. Not ever.

The buzzer rang for several minutes and then went silent. That got my hopes up, but no soft-soled shoes came to my door. No nurse, pretty or otherwise, came smiling into my room to hand me my pills. Instinctively, I knew I was on my own, just as Junie had said, but I refused to accept it. Getting out of bed to walk across the room wasn't something I even wanted to think about, much less do. Just moving my arm ten inches across a smooth flat sheet had caused my hand to cramp. What would happen to my legs if I were stupid enough to try supporting my weight on the cold hard floor?

Ten more minutes passed before I closed my eyes, gritted my teeth and slid my right leg off the side of the bed. It moved slowly and sluggishly and I couldn't really feel my foot. Everything felt numb below my knee. As soon as my knee cleared the edge of the mattress, my foot fell limply off the side of the bed and firecrackers of pain shot through my knee and up my thigh.

"God *dammit*!" I screamed, loud enough that I'm sure the entire floor heard me.

I could just picture the nurses sitting with old Junie, having a good laugh at my expense, and I vowed right then and there I wasn't going to cry out anymore. Bitches! I hated them all—everyone in this psychotic place. I wasn't gonna give them the satisfaction.

Somehow I managed to get my left leg off the bed too and shimmy my butt over to the edge. There was no way I could sit up. No way in hell.

But I did.

My desire, my craving—my *need*—for the pain medication was so great I was willing to try jumping through hoops if that was what it would take. My body was on fire; every muscle, every bone, every joint hurt. My eyelids fluttered and I came close to passing out, but I refused to let that happen. Instead I pushed hard with arms that felt like fifty-pound lead weights, and found myself standing on my feet. Tears were streaming down my face from the pain, but I was pumped up now—the joy of being out of that damn bed overwhelming, an adrenaline boost for my weary body.

I still couldn't feel anything below my right knee, but I took a small shuffling step onto it anyway. I had no choice—my body had started to sway and if I hadn't stepped forward to balance myself I would have been sprawled face-first onto the floor. White-hot pain blazed in my knee again and I nearly went down. I swayed, biting the side of my cheek, fighting to stay upright. I knew if I tumbled to the floor I was there to stay. The pain subsided and I moved on to another step.

The physical pain was horrible, but maybe worst was the disoriented feeling of moving around in a borrowed body. These weren't my arms. These weren't my legs. These weren't my feet. On and on the list went. Name it, and chances were that body part wasn't mine and deep down on some cellular level I think they knew it. More crazy talk, I know, but that's how it felt to me—like the flesh, muscles, and bones that made me whole resented me for using them. None of my patchwork parts worked quite the way they were supposed to. Every movement was slower, a half-second lagging behind what it should be as if my new body knew I was an imposter and was determined to fight me every inch of the way. It was a creepy, alien feeling that sent shivers down my spine, making me want to scream.

But I desperately needed the meds so I pressed on, robot-stepping across the floor for what felt like days until I finally—*FINALLY*—stood beside the meal tray carrying my multicolored salvation. With sweat pouring down my face and my hands shaking so badly I could hardly hold the cup, I dry swallowed the entire batch of pills in one gulp and let the plastic cup fall to the floor.

I'll be damned. I actually made it.

I smiled, savoring the moment. Then my eyes rolled up into my head, the world started to go black, and I went down hard.

CHAPTER TWENTY-NINE

Rehab went on for eight grueling weeks and Junie the sadistic old physiotherapist was with me every pain-filled step of the way. To tell you the truth, the old cow actually grew on me a little. She was cold and ruthless, and she bent, stretched, twisted, and basically worked me over every day until I could hardly stand, but she was as straight a shooter as I had met in my whole time here at the castle.

Junie never lied to me, not once. She hated bullshit, always telling me exactly what we were going to do and how we were doing it. I liked that about her. Don't get me wrong—I didn't like *her*—she pulled no punches and was probably the crankiest old bitch in the entire medical profession but as long as I worked hard, she treated me fairly. Unlike the rest of the goons around here, she was genuinely trying to help me get some semblance of a life back, and for that I appreciated her effort.

My new body held up remarkably well, all things considered. It was something I worried about a lot. At night I'd dream all these freaky worst-case scenarios about my stitches popping loose while Junie put me through my paces and blood splashing the walls as my arm or leg fell off. The nightmares were somewhat comical to think about during the day, but they scared the shit out of me while they were happening. I'd wake up screaming and crying and reaching down to hold my leg in place to stop the bleeding. Crazy stuff, I'll admit, but what else was new? My entire life had become one big crazy dream.

On the Monday morning that marked the start of my ninth week of rehab, Junie walked into my room doing something that shocked me, something I didn't know she was capable of.

She was crying.

Not wailing like a schoolgirl, nothing as dramatic as that, but there were tears running down her cheeks and I could tell from her red-flushed face she'd been trying to get a grip on her emotions for a while already. Maybe she was human, after all. Doubtful, but maybe.

"What's the matter?" I asked.

"Nothing. Mind your own business, and put that damn plate down. You've been eating like a horse for weeks now. Rate you're going at, you'll be a fat pig in no time. That what you want?"

She was changing the subject, hiding something from me. Mind you, it was the truth—I had been eating a lot lately, and yes, I was gaining weight, but I was still a far cry from being fat. It was Junie who had urged me to eat more, to help get my strength back quicker. So why would she bitch about it now? Simple: she wouldn't.

She wiped her tears away with a casual swish of her hand, then left no room for debate that the subject was closed, launching into another of her famous Hollywood military-inspired tirades.

"Come on, Fox, get your lazy butt in gear. We gotta get you on that treadmill. We've already lost ten minutes while you were filling your face instead of stretching. Now get to it, mister. Move it!"

"Yes, *sir*," I mocked her, but still jumped up and got ready to follow her out the door. Joking around was fine, disobeying direct orders wasn't. "Ready when you are."

Junie scowled, shook her head, and headed for the door. I stepped in behind her, goose-stepping in her tracks, feeling good this morning. My good mood only lasted until Junie pulled open the door and I saw Dr. Marshall and Drake standing patiently out in the hall.

Drake was bigger than ever. Huge bulging muscles and an impenetrable, menacing stare. I hadn't seen him in several months and by the looks of it he'd spent a good portion of that time in the weight room. He didn't look particularly happy to see me.

Nathan Marshall looked fit and trim, leaning against the door jamb, with a wild, feral look in his eyes. His handsome face was calm, but from the set of his jaw I could tell he was clenching his teeth, maybe angry about something. I hoped it wasn't me. Drake scared me, sure, an animal like that would scare anybody, but it was Dr. Marshall that worried me. He looked royally pissed and I couldn't stop myself from thinking he was here to take me back to the operating room again.

Anything but that! Kill me if you want, but no more operations. Not when I'm just starting to feel human again.

Seeing them outside the door caught Junie by surprise too. She didn't seem happy to see them either.

"What are you doing here?" she asked. "Just yesterday, you told me I had another full week."

Dr. Marshall smiled and stood up straight. "Well, as you're aware, certain *other* recent developments have forced me to rethink my plans. I'm tired of waiting around, getting reports that this fool"—meaning me— "keeps improving and getting near full recovery of his new body, while—"

He stopped right there, but he'd said more than enough. Obviously things hadn't gone well with

Andrew's transplant into the other flesh suit, but what had happened? Was Andrew back swimming in his glass container? Was he dead? This probably wasn't the best time to ask but my mouth had a way of doing things on its own sometimes, independent of my brain. Before I could stop myself, I went ahead and let my curiosity get the better of me.

"What happened to Andrew? Is he okay?" I asked.

If I thought Dr. Marshall had been clenching his teeth before, he was really clamping down now, grinding his teeth together to prevent himself from screaming. His face turned beet red in seconds. Now, I've seen anger on a man's face before, many times, but this look went way past that. Dr. Marshall gazed at me with pure, murderous hatred.

Uh-oh, now I've done it!

Drake stepped forward and kneed me hard in the groin, sending me to the floor in a hurry. My insides felt like they'd been set on fire. I lay there coughing and gagging, massaging my balls. I would have screamed but I was having too much trouble breathing. By the time the pain eased off and I managed to climb to my knees, Dr. Marshall was gone. Drake was still there, looming like the Grim Reaper in my doorway, watching me with only mild interest, as if I mattered as much as a flea on a hound dog. God, how I wanted to kill him.

"Have him ready tomorrow morning, Junie," he said, then walked away.

Junie looked at me with pity, or as close to pity as her sour face could ever muster, then headed for the door.

"Wait," I said, still on my knees. "Have me ready for what? What the hell is going on? What happened to Andrew?"

For a moment she paused, and I thought she was going to tell me. Instead, she started to cry again, and ran out the door. I heard the key rattle and the door lock, and then listened to Junie sob as she retreated down the carpeted hallway. Soon everything was quiet. Too quiet. It was as if the entire facility was collectively holding its breath, either in mourning for whatever had happened to Andrew or in silent fear of his father's wrath. I couldn't speak for everyone, but there was no question which one of those was keeping me silent.

CHAPTER THIRTY

Constantly staring at the back of a locked door wasn't a whole lot of fun. I couldn't help it, though, having convinced myself that Drake or Dr. Marshall was going to reappear suddenly, charging through the door to nab me if I let my guard down too long. Not only was it nerve-racking, it made for a bloody long day and an even longer night.

No one showed up, of course. Not Drake, not Marshall, hell, not even Junie. Just me and my overactive, paranoia-refined-to-an-art imagination. By morning, I was mentally and physically exhausted. I'd slept off and on for four or five hours, repeatedly waking up with an anxious start, thinking I heard the door opening.

To distract myself—either that or go totally loony and start ramming my head against the door—I decided to kill some time by exercising. Tired or not, anything seemed better than just sitting, waiting for something bad to happen. Most of the things Junie had been making me concentrate on in rehab could be done just as easily here in my room as down at the gym so I slid the bed to the side a few feet to give myself some elbow room and went to it. Nothing major, just bending, stretching, some push-ups and jumping jacks but twice as many as my usual routine and I was soon wheezing and panting like an old, overburdened farm mule. I was sweaty and smelling decidedly ripe, so I peeled off my soiled T-shirt and was heading across the room to find a new one when I noticed my body in the full-size dressing mirror hung on the wall. I mean *really* noticed it, for the first time since my transplant into this flesh suit.

Stopped me dead in my tracks.

Until now, I'd made a habit of *not* noticing—other than a few unavoidable peeks while bathing and dressing, but never taking in the full picture—quite content to ignore the stark reality reflected in the silver glass. For sanity's sake, the old adage "out of sight, out of mind" had become my new motto. Words to live by, but with my fears renewed that I might be revisiting the operating room again, suddenly I was curious to examine myself to see how bad I truly looked. Stripping naked, tossing my pants, socks and undies onto the floor beside the sweaty T-shirt, I slowly turned around and around, struggling to stifle the scream building in my throat.

It was worse than I'd thought. A lot worse.

Oh my God! What have I become?

A single cold word slithered to mind, describing my new body perfectly.

Abomination!

I'd known right from day one I was going to be ugly and god-awful to look at naked, but what surprised me—no, shocked me—most was how *un*human I looked. Ugly I could live with, but this pasty-skinned, sewn-together, wretched creature in the glass was worse than anything I'd imagined.

What was wrong with my skin? It just didn't look right. They hadn't used the same type of people for the donor parts, so some areas of my body were smooth and youthful looking while others—especially my legs—were old and wrinkled and covered with dense, matted hair. My left arm was covered in bright colorful tattoos but they ended at my shoulder, cut off mid picture. Something was wrong with my back, too. They'd forgotten something—fat, muscles, whatever—because the skin had been stretched so thin over my spine as to be almost translucent. I could see the vertebrae in my back pivoting on their disks every time I twisted to look over my shoulder.

Worse by far were my scars. Dr. Marshall had obviously sewn me together with function in mind, not fashion, alignment of parts far more important than aesthetics. As it had to be, I suppose, but surely he could have given some thought toward what I'd end up looking like and at least tried to minimize the scarring.

Oh my God!

I was unable to tear my eyes away from the stranger I saw crying in the mirror.

The scars were thick, puffy, dark red, and everywhere on my body. Twenty thousand stitches; maybe more. I looked like a pieced together mannequin covered in huge, blood-engorged leeches—bigger; tapeworms maybe—placed end to end to form living ropes around my body. The ropes of scar tissue intersected with other scars, and the end result was a patchwork quilt of meat—a jigsaw puzzle of flesh tossed together with no more care or concern for me as a human being than an angry child has for an old broken toy.

I sat down on the edge of the bed, and cried. At least my tears were my own and I let them pour out in rivers as I cursed Dr. Marshall with every ounce of hatred I could drum up within me. Marshall was a brilliant surgeon and I was convinced he could have significantly improved my appearance. He just hadn't wanted to.

No, this was *exactly* how he wanted me to look. I hated him for that more than anything else he'd done to me.

A key rattled in the lock on my door and five seconds later Junie came walking into my room without bothering to knock. Had it been Dr. Marshall, I'm pretty sure I would have went after his throat with my teeth, even if that meant going through Drake to get at him, but seeing Junie and the sad expression on her face as she gazed at my pitiful nakedness, I just lowered my head and started crying again.

"Help me," I sobbed, slumping to my knees on the floor. "Please help me get away from here, Junie. Escape or suicide, I don't care which. He's taken everything from me, *everything*, and I can't do this anymore. I just *can't*!"

Junie stood rooted to the floor just inside the doorway, silent for the longest time, but then she closed the door and moved over beside me. In the quietest of whispers she said, "I'll try."

That was it. Nothing more. Not even a reassuring smile when I looked up at her. It was back to business as usual and she was hustling me into my clothes and ordering me to get my ass in gear. Maybe I hadn't heard her right, or worse yet, she might not have said anything at all. Wouldn't surprise me a bit if my mind and ears were playing tricks on me but regardless, whether it had really happened or not, a tiny seed of hope had been planted within me. I wasn't ready to jump for joy, but it was enough to get me off the ground and moving again. For now, that would have to do.

"So what happens now?" I asked once I was fully dressed and in control of my emotions again.

"Drake will be along soon to bring you to the video conference room. He wanted me to make sure you were ready."

"Video conference room? So I'm not going back for

more surgery?" Junie shook her head no, scolding me with her eyes for jumping to silly conclusions. I was relieved but still confused. "What's Marshall up to, then?"

"Documentation, of course. No one has even attempted, much less succeeded, in doing what Dr. Marshall has done with you. You might not see it the way he does, of course, but the truth is you're a medical miracle."

"So he wants to parade me around like a freak on a leash for the cameras and let the world pat him on the back for being so brilliant. I can hear it now. Come see the pathetic little Jigsaw Man. Fuck that! That maniac needs to be locked up, not admired. He's murdering and mutilating people, Junie. Destroying people, mentally and physically, just to get his academic rocks off. And for that, what, they're gonna give him a fuckin' award?"

"Of course not. The videos are for his own personal records. He can't show you or the videos to the medical community. Nothing he does here would ever be approved or authorized by the boards. He's way off the charts when it comes to ethics, but his results are second to none. That's all he cares about."

"But what about you? He's a lunatic, Junie. You know he is. How can you work for him?"

"I don't have any choice, Mike."

"Oh bullshit! Everyone has a choice. You're here for the money. I'll bet he's paying you an enormous—"

"He's hardly paying me anything," Junie interrupted.

That stopped my rant in a hurry.

"He lets me live here free and I get fed, of course, but my paycheck's only eight hundred dollars a month."

"Then why are you here?" I asked, truly confused. "Surely a good nurse like you could earn triple that in a real hospital."

Junie closed her eyes, taking several deep breaths

before answering. "I have a son that lives in Jamestown with my ex-husband. He's . . . he's in a wheelchair and Dr. Marshall promised—"

"You don't have to say it, Junie. Sorry I asked. After everything you've seen, do you believe him?"

Junie started to cry.

"No, not really, but I just kept hoping if I did what I was told he'd help me. Part of me knows he's insane, but the other part knows he can do what he says. He *could* help my son if he wanted to. For his sake, it's so damn hard to walk away."

"I can understand that. Honest. Before I came here I was ready to kill myself to help my daughter. Desperation is a powerful thing, but it's also a tool that psychos like Dr. Marshall use against good people. He went off the deep end a hell of a long time ago, Junie, and somebody has to stop him or he's going to keep torturing and killing innocent people. We have to do something. Help me."

"I don't know, Mike. I . . . I don't want to talk about this anymore. Just get ready, okay?"

I wasn't letting her off the hook that easy. No way! "Don't want to talk about it? You kidding me? You work for a goddamned killer and just because he's rich and smart and tells you lies you want to hear, it makes things okay? Look around, Junie. You can't keep turning a blind eye. Have you seen the poor bastards in the blood bank up on the fourth floor, for Christ's sake? Would you like your son up there? He's better off in his goddamned chair!"

Junie never said a word. She couldn't I don't think, not without bursting into hysterics, and for a tough old bird like her, that was really saying something. It told me I was getting through to her, perhaps finally finding the ally I needed around her to make something happen. What, I had no idea, but *something*.

Then Drake poked his big shiny head around the doorframe and started barking orders at both of us. I didn't bother turning to look at him, I was concentrating on Junie, and I saw the lights go out in her eyes when she heard Drake's cruel voice. The hope and courage inside her withered away, died right in front of my eyes and I knew without her having to tell me that I was on my own. She sympathized with me, I'm sure of that, but in many ways she was just as much a victim here as I was. Her love and hope for her son, along with her fear of Dr. Marshall and his walking muscle, Drake, was too great for her to risk trying anything stupid. I couldn't blame her. Who was I to ask her to risk her life and family for me? Nobody. Absolutely nobody. I kissed her on her cold, wrinkled cheek, and without even acknowledging Drake I walked right past him and out the door.

He laughed at my pitiful show of defiance, but never said anything. I took that as a minor victory and headed for the video conference room with my head held high.

CHAPTER THIRTY-ONE

I felt a little like a movie star. There were so many video cameras running, halogen stands basking me in bright light, digital microphones recording every sound, and security staff as would-be photographers and videographers scurrying around following my every move that I couldn't help but feel special. Stupid, I know. I was well aware I was nothing more than a trained seal, barking and balancing a rubber ball on my nose whenever Dr. Marshall dangled a juicy fish under it. Not that I had any choice. Every time I complained or didn't immediately do as instructed, Drake would smile and casually open his jacket to show me the gun handle protruding out of the waistband of his pants. That was a fish I had no desire to taste, so I shut up and did as I was told.

It was no big deal. Like Junie had said, all Dr. Marshall wanted was video and photographic proof that my transplantation had been successful. I spent about two hours walking, sitting, jumping, kneeling, jogging on the spot, and doing many of the same exercises I'd been working on with Junie for weeks. They also had me catching and kicking balls of various sizes, and doing things like writing my name or tying my shoelaces to show I had decent dexterity in my hands and feet.

It was tiring and tedious, but no big hardship. After a break for lunch, I got a little upset—well, a lot upset, I guess—when Dr. Marshall suggested I remove my clothes and run through the same set of movements. He wanted the videos to clearly showcase where he'd joined my various body parts together. I told him to go fuck himself, that he could stick it up his ass if he thought I wanted him recording me naked. Five minutes, a nasty bump on my head, and one short pep talk from Drake later on how no one cared what *I* wanted, and I was stripped down to nothing and parading around the room like a good little seal again. It was humiliating and I'd never felt so self-conscious in my life. I was officially the freak I'd imagined myself as—the hideous Jigsaw Man on full display for one and all to laugh and point fingers at. It was awful.

Eventually, a few minutes shy of three o'clock in the afternoon, they gave me my clothes back and let me return to my room. Junie brought me an early supper but I wasn't up to eating anything. She tried to make conversation, trying to make me feel better and snap out of my funk, but I was in a sour mood and told her to get out and leave me alone. I just wanted to go to bed and forget today had ever happened. I was asleep in minutes.

CHAPTER THIRTY-TWO

"You speaking to me today?" a voice whispered.

I bolted upright, surprised to see Junie standing at the foot of my bed, holding an armful of clothes. My heart was trip-hammering inside of my chest. I hadn't heard her unlock the door or walk in, which was unusual seeing as I was on constant high alert around here. Must have been more tired than I'd thought, dead to the world, the video shoot taking a lot more out of me than my normal workouts down in the gym.

"Jesus, Junie. You damn near gave me a heart attack."

"You're not that lucky," she said, a half smile trying to form on her face, but she couldn't hold it and I instantly knew something was upsetting her.

"What's wrong?" I asked.

"Nothing. Well, I don't know. Something's not right. Drake told me to get you up and dressed. They want to do some more videotaping today with you outside and I'm not sure why."

"Who knows?" I said. "Doesn't sound like that big a deal. *Jesus*, you don't think he'll make me strip naked outside, do you?"

"No way, at least I hope not. It's too cold out for that."

Cold outside?

Wait a minute. Suddenly I realized that I had no idea what month it was, never mind the date. How long had I been here? It was September when I'd arrived, but how long had passed by while I was zoned out from the various surgeries or drugged out of my mind recuperating?

"What's the date, Junie?" I asked, more desperation in my voice than I'd intended.

With a little trepidation, she answered, "October the twentieth." Anticipating where I was going with that line of thought, she said, "You've been here just over thirteen months."

Thirteen months! Has it been that long?

Well, considering I'd probably spent at least half of those months either out cold or in la-la-land, I had no trouble believing that. I walked over to the window and took a good look outside—something I hadn't thought to do in who knows how bloody long. I was expecting to see dark storm clouds obscuring the sky and the ground below covered in a deep blanket of snow, but the sun was shining down on a grassy field. Beyond the field I could see a forest, and sure enough, I could see the leaves on the trees had put on their fall colors and many had already dropped off the branches.

"Doesn't look *that* bad," I said.

"Don't let the sun fool you," Junie said. "Windy today, cold enough to blow right through you and freeze your bones solid."

The trees did seem to be getting whipped around pretty good, especially the branches farthest up, which were performing a strangely hypnotic lean-to-the-left dance with the wind. Every few seconds, as if on cue, they'd straighten up but then immediately be blown back onto the dance floor.

"Make sure you wear a coat," Junie said.

"I don't have one."

"Sure you do. The coat you showed up in last year has

been sitting in a locker down in storage. I have it right here. Couldn't find any of your other clothes, maybe they got burned, but I found some other things that'll help keep you warm. The boots might be a little big."

Junie dumped the clothes she'd been carrying at my feet and the sight of my old blue bomber jacket put a smile on my face. It was old and ragged, and probably should have been burned with the rest of my stuff, but I bent down and picked it up with almost reverent care. My wife had bought me this coat for our last Christmas and a tear slid out of my eye as I realized it was the only piece of property I owned in the whole world. My legs weren't mine. My heart wasn't even mine. But this rotten old bomber jacket chock-full of as many memories as it had holes was, and that made me feel good. Really good.

"Thanks, Junie," I said. "This coat means a lot to me. More than you'd think, looking at it."

"Good. Get dressed, then. Drake's going to come searching for us again if we don't hurry."

I dressed quickly, excited to be going outside. Not entirely sure why, but I'd spent so long locked up in this hellhole that the thought of fresh air—regardless how cold it might be—thrilled me and urged me on. I wasn't allowed to just run out the front doors wild and free, of course. Junie and I were escorted by a big burly guard named Jackson, who took me out a side entrance I'd never seen before, marching me out to where Drake and the cameras were waiting.

Camera, I should say.

Gone were the bright lights, the camera crews, and the digital microphones. Gone were all the people from yesterday's shoot, too, most notably absent being Dr. Marshall. That wasn't a good sign. There was only Drake, looking pissed off and cold standing with a camcorder that looked like a child's toy in his huge paw. The look on his face knocked the smile from mine and

I finally noticed how cold it was outside the climate-controlled world of the castle.

It was freakin' freezing!

Jacket or no jacket, the wind stole my breath, cutting right through me just like Junie had warned. I'd lived through several icy winters on the street—nights so cold tears froze solid on the way down your cheeks—so you'd think I'd be used to bad weather, but damn, you stayed inside for a year and you soon forgot how nasty the elements could be.

"Get your ass over here, asshole," Drake screamed.

I didn't feel much like a movie star today.

I hunched my shoulders, trying to keep the wind off my neck as best I could, and trudged out to where Drake stood on the grass. Wasting no time, he started barking at me to do some exercises. He didn't care what I did as long as I kept moving and gave him something to film. This was stupid and research-wise not much good for anything, but I was glad to get moving, the physical exertion feeling great and warming me up nicely. I was starting to enjoy myself again, at least until I glanced over at Junie standing with Jackson beside the door into the castle. Why was she there and not inside, out of the cold? She looked sad, and the closer I looked, the more I was convinced she was crying.

For me? Why would she be crying? Unless—
Oh-oh!

I smelled trouble. Colossal trouble.

"Okay, that's enough of this crap," Drake shouted, bringing me to a halt and confirming my fears. "Come get this camera, Junie, and take it to Dr. Marshall's office. He's expecting it."

Junie walked out to meet us, but she wouldn't look me in the eye. I was right, she *was* crying. She took the camcorder from Drake and stood ramrod still, not sure what to do next. Drake had the answer.

"Get out of here, Junie. You're not needed anymore."

Junie turned to go, tears flowing freely down her cheeks now, but before she left she grabbed me and gave me a big motherly hug. Drake got quite a kick out of this and bent over laughing at her show of affection.

"Look, Jackson," Drake said to the guard, "Michael has himself a girlfriend. Isn't that sweet?"

I might have told Drake to go stuff himself but I was too busy listening to Junie. Under cover of Drake's laughter, she put her mouth to my ear and quietly whispered two words.

She said, "Left pocket."

That was it, and Drake was dragging her off me, pointing her in the direction of the door. She looked back over her shoulder and I gave her the tiniest nod, letting her know I understood. Then she was gone, leaving me out in the cold with Drake and Jackson. I knew what was coming before it was even said. I was dumb but sure wasn't stupid. Game, set, and match. Dr. Marshall was finally finished playing with me.

"It's over, Mike," Drake said. "You're of no use to us anymore. Dr. Marshall has done all he can with you, and now that we have the photo and video evidence to show how successful your transplants have been, the time has come for us to part ways."

"You're letting me go?" I asked. I knew it wasn't happening but what else could I say?

Drake just smiled.

"No, Mike. I think you're smarter than that so I'll just give it to you straight. Jackson is going to take you for a walk in the woods. We have a small cemetery in there, an unofficial one, naturally, that we used before the incinerator was installed. We could burn you, sure, but I kinda like the idea of the worms and maggots getting a hold of you. Cremation seems too good for a skinny little troublemaking prick like you."

I didn't say anything for a minute—partly because I didn't want to give him the satisfaction, but mostly because I was scared. I don't care what you see in the movies, no one is brave enough to joke around and be callous in the face of death. No one I knew, anyway. Certainly not me. I did get one crack in, though, and it made me feel better.

"Don't have the balls to do it yourself, huh?"

Drake laughed at that too. He was enjoying himself a lot today. Bastard. "Whatever you say, Mike. I'll admit I've enjoyed having you around. You've been a good laugh and a refreshing change from most of the doctor's patients, but you've also been a royal pain in the ass. When it comes right down to it, my friend, you're just not worth my time. Face it . . . you're a bum, Mike. A good-for-nothing, expendable bum."

I wanted to tell him what I thought of him, tell him how he was a psycho pervert steroid monkey or something equally colorful, but no words came out. Silence. My mouth was dry and my tongue felt swollen to three times its normal size—the bitter bile-flavored taste of fear nearly gagging me as I looked into his big stupid grinning face.

Say something!

I hesitated too long and the moment passed.

"Get this piece of shit out of my sight, Jackson." Drake said, turning away, dismissing me as if I'd never existed. That was how much my life was worth: nothing. Not even a glance back.

CHAPTER THIRTY-THREE

After Drake disappeared into the building, Jackson poked me violently in the ribs twice with the barrel of a shiny silver gun. The first was to get my attention but I'm sure the next was to make it crystal clear that this was his show now. "You heard the man," he said, his voice gruff and scratchy like steel wool, filled with self-importance. "Get your ass movin' or I can make this rough on you."

Rough on me? He was going to put a bullet in my head; how could it get any rougher? Another jab from the gun stung my ribs like a hornet and gave me a clue.

"Hold on a sec," I tried. "You can't do this, man. It's crazy! Drake's asking you to commit—"

Without warning, Jackson sucker punched me in the mouth, snapping my head back painfully and shutting me up in a hurry. I dropped to my knees but Jackson dragged me to my feet a moment later, shoving me forward. "Head for the woods and keep your fuckin' mouth shut. Whining all day won't do you any good, so save it. Go."

I went.

I'd seen Jackson around for months now but I'd never really talked to him or had any dealings with him other than to have him stand guard outside my room, or follow me around the gymnasium during my rehab. Sure, I recognized him—tall and muscular with dark curly hair, one of those bodybuilder types that seemed to have no neck—but knowing who someone was wasn't the same as *knowing* him. 'Course, I didn't really need to know him to understand he was a bastard chiseled from the same tree as his boss. Drake and Jackson were like two moldy peas in the same rotten pod. Bottom line: there was no way I was going to talk my way out of this. Someone was going to die at the end of this little stroll and if I didn't want that person to be me, I had to stop pissing off the guard and come up with a plan.

I put my hand into my left jacket pocket, slowly, casually, so Jackson would think I was just trying to stay warm. I'd wanted to do this since the moment Junie whispered in my ear, but two things had held me back. I didn't want to go frantically digging in my pocket and have Jackson realize I had something hidden in there. He'd just take it away from me and then where would I be? The other reason I'd been delaying this was simpler—I was afraid to find out what was inside. I was walking toward my death here, and so far I'd managed to keep my cool solely braced with the knowledge I had something in my pocket that would ultimately save me.

In my wildest racing thoughts, I was picturing a short-barreled gun with a full clip of hollow-point bullets ready to fly. Already, I was visualizing pulling it out, spinning around lightning fast and blasting Jackson four or five times, rapid-fire, like Clint Eastwood in his Dirty Harry days. The trouble was, I wasn't sure it was a gun, wasn't even sure it was a weapon in my pocket. Junie might have stuck a bottle of aspirin, or a pack of mint chewing gum in there—it could be anything—but she'd never said it was a weapon. No, but that was what my desperation-fueled brain sure was hoping for.

So with those conflicting thoughts bouncing around my brain, I reached into the left pocket and my hand closed around—

I had no idea what it was. Certainly not a gun, that was for sure. My heart felt like it stopped beating for several seconds, my blood running cold within my veins as my fingers numbly explored the contours of the item in my pocket.

What the hell is it?

It felt like a rectangular piece of plastic or wood, maybe five inches long, the corners rounded a little bit. It had a familiar feel, but what was it? I almost broke into a run then, almost bolted for the trees, panic higher on my list of priorities than common sense. I probably would have—definitely would have—risking the inevitable bullet in my back had it not been for the hard little button I found on the object with my thumb. I calmed down a bit, realizing what it was Junie had given me.

A knife.

Not just any knife—a switchblade—the little button under my thumb the trigger that would activate the hidden blade. In my relief I nearly pushed the button, which would have buggered everything up nicely. Just to make sure I didn't accidentally do it, I took my hand back out of my pocket and tried to think of some way I could get the jump on my would-be executioner and use the knife with enough force and accuracy to disable Jackson before he could use his gun. No matter how many scenarios I flashed through, all of them ended with me getting my brains blown out. After all, I had to turn around, pull out the knife, push the trigger, lunge in real close, and try killing Jackson with one stab of the blade. All he had to do was shoot me the second he detected any funny business. I'd probably get turned around okay, but the second Jackson saw me pull the knife he'd fire without thinking twice. There was no way I would get close enough to take him out, but even with the odds heavily stacked against me, I had to at least try.

We were approaching the edge of the forest and Jackson grunted and used his gun to prod me toward a narrow path that led into the trees. The path presumably would lead us to the makeshift graveyard Drake mentioned, but I could see along the path for quite a ways and there was no sign of anything except a hard dirt trail half-covered in fallen leaves. That was good; at least I had a little time on my hands to figure out what I was going to do. I took a few deep breaths and tried my best to calm down.

We walked on. One curve of the trail led to the next, taking us deeper and deeper into the forest but never leading to a graveyard. It was quiet in here, creepy quiet, not peaceful quiet, as if the trees and animals all held their breaths as Jackson and I walked by. Maybe the forest knew death walked hand in hand with us, the Reaper still deciding which of us to claim.

Think, Mike. Think.

"Move it, jerk-off," Jackson said, prodding me with his gun again because I was moving too slow.

Maybe that was it. If I couldn't close the gap between us without getting shot, maybe I could get him to do it for me. Every time I slowed down a little, Jackson would smack me with the gun to get me moving again. I experimented with it, slightly slowing up my pace. Sure enough, *jab*, Jackson dug me in my kidneys and swore at me to move my ass. If I could time it just right, be waiting for him to move close so he could hit me, I might be able to spin around, deflect his gun away, and drive my knife home.

It wasn't a perfect plan, and it probably wouldn't work but I had to admit it wasn't a bad plan either; the best I was going to get, anyway.

Do it then. Don't wait.

Adrenaline pumped through my veins, making me primed and ready to make my stand, but I'd always been a bit of a coward and fear made me hold off. I wasn't ready to die yet. Maybe a better chance would present itself around the next corner.

Dammit Mike! Do it now before it's—

"That's far enough, scumbag," Jackson said.

"What?" I stupidly asked. I looked around for signs of a graveyard but there was nothing in sight. The path looked the same as it always had, maybe even a bit narrower than a lot of the trail. "But what about the graveyard? Drake said there was a—"

"Forget the graveyard, Mike. This is far enough. I'm tired of walking and I'll be damned if I'm gonna freeze my ass off out here digging a hole for a freak like you."

I turned to face Jackson, scared and frustrated I'd wasted my best chance to win this fight, but there was also a part of me getting pissed off. Who did these people think they were?

"So, you're going to plug me and then what, just leave me here to rot?"

Jackson smiled, raised his gun to point it at the center of my chest, and said, "Yeah, that sounds about right. Any famous last words?"

This was really going to happen. Jackson was going to shoot me dead, his finger already tightening on the trigger. The time for delaying was over. One in a million chance or not, I had to act, and I had to act now, go for the knife and to hell with the consequences. I was a dead man whether I moved or not.

"No last words, Jackson," I said. "I'd like to show you something cool, though."

Even while I was saying it, I knew it was a pretty lame plan, but I reached for the knife anyway. Jackson was standing at least ten feet from me so how was I

supposed to close the gap without getting shot? Maybe
I could throw the knife? Maybe I could—

Holy shit!

I saw her before Jackson did, and it shocked the hell
out of me. If nothing else, my bumbling plan to draw
out my switchblade had distracted Jackson enough that
he was looking down at my hand to see what I was pulling from my pocket. He never registered the presence
of a third person in the forest until it was too late.

Junie!

Where she came from or how she snuck up on both
of us so quietly I'll never know, but when she attacked
she attacked hard. I thought she was carrying a baseball
bat but it was only a broken tree branch. By the time
Jackson realized what was going on, Junie was already
swinging. She was a small woman, but she walloped
Jackson so hard across the chest and neck he flew eight
feet backward, smashing against the trunk of a nearby
tree and slumping to the ground with a groan. Junie
moved in for another swing and I shook off my disbelief she was here rescuing me long enough to pull out
my knife, trigger the spring that released the shiny
steel blade out to its full length, and go help her.

Jackson was down and probably broken up inside, but
he was far from out. Junie raised the branch above her
head to strike again, but Jackson shot her point blank in
the belly, a red exit wound the size of a silver dollar
spraying out above her right kidney. The sound of the
shot was deafening, a thunderclap close enough to nearly
knock me off my feet. I didn't fall, though, didn't panic;
I kept running, closing the gap.

Junie fell off to Jackson's right, screaming only once
before hitting the ground. Jackson was watching her
fall, enjoying the moment from the look on his face,
but that look changed in a hurry when he saw me launch
into the air, diving on top of him. He tried to swing his

gun up to shoot me, too, but I was faster than him, my reflexes acting in survival mode now. I landed on him full force, using my entire weight to drive home the blade to the left of Jackson's sternum. He screamed but the force of my body had driven the air from his lungs and what came out sounded more like a car tire going flat than a cry of pain. There was surprisingly little blood but I knew I'd done some big-time damage. I was no fool, though. I'd seen enough cheesy horror movies to know that once you get someone down, you never give them the chance to get back up. So I drove the blade back into Jackson's chest a second time, and a third, and a tenth. I don't know for sure how many times I stabbed the guard or at what point he was dead, but by the time I rolled off him his chest was destroyed and there was no worry of a B movie sneak attack once my back was turned.

Junie!

I had to help her.

Please let her be all right, I prayed, but in my heart I knew that wasn't going to be the case. She hadn't moved from where I'd seen her fall. I dropped to the ground, scooping Junie into my arms and used my hand to help turn her face toward me. Her eyes were unfocused and distant, but with a heroic effort she managed to gather herself and look up at me.

"Why, Junie?" I asked, tears in my eyes, overcome by the magnitude of her sacrifice. "Why take a bullet for me? We barely knew each other."

She was fading fast, blood bubbling from the corners of her mouth, as well as from the grievous wound in her abdomen. "Because they've hurt you enough," Junie whispered. "I couldn't live knowing—"

That was it; the lights suddenly went out in her eyes and Junie went limp, dead in my arms without the strength to finish her sentence. She'd said all she needed to, though, and I pulled her closer to me and held her tight as I wept for her, her crippled son, and her senseless death. If I could have traded places with her on the bed of forest leaves I would have gladly.

In a heartbeat.

I closed my eyes and prayed for the world to go away.

CHAPTER THIRTY-FOUR

Surprise, surprise, my prayers went unanswered. When next I opened my eyes the world was still there, cold and rotten as ever, and I had two dead bodies lying at my feet to prove it.

I took a deep breath to steady my frayed nerves, then climbed shakily to my feet. I spent a couple of minutes covering Junie up with leaves and saying good-bye. She deserved a better grave and burial than that, but time was of the essence and the shroud of foliage was the best I could do with no shovel or tools. Jackson, I left to rot where he lay, just as he'd planned on doing with me. Let the birds pick out his eyes and the rest of the forest animals and bugs have their way with him for all I cared. I had to get moving. I wanted to put as much distance between me and this spot as I could before anyone figured out Jackson wasn't coming back.

I made it about a hundred feet farther down the forest path, just around the next bend, when I finally found Drake's cemetery.

My God!

The path didn't widen out a lot, maybe twenty feet at its widest, but there were grave markers everywhere, little white wooden crosses stuck all over the path and covering the forest floor to my left and right. I didn't bother to count, but there had to be sixty or seventy of them, easy—maybe as many as a hundred.

I hadn't expected to see anything like this. Why would Drake mark the graves? Dumping bodies was one thing, the animals and the elements clean up the mess in no time, but to mark the graves seemed like a silly idea to me. What if the police ever found this place? Drake would be sunk, Dr. Marshall too. I couldn't believe he'd allowed this. Unless, of course, they were both arrogant and brazenly stupid enough to think they were so far above the law they could do whatever they wanted and consequences be damned. That was it—had to be. There was no other answer for this evil place. And that's what it was—evil—a shrine to Nathan Marshall's God complex, a mockery of the poor souls unceremoniously buried here to appease Drake's deranged superego.

These were the men and women from before the basement incinerator, Drake had said. How many more had died since, their collective ashes dumped in the woods for the wind to scatter. Probably more than this—a lot more.

My God . . . all those people!

The full scope of Dr. Marshall's madness hit me then. I'd known he was completely off his rocker, and Drake was no better, but I'd never known just how nasty and cruel they truly were. This cemetery made me sick to my stomach. It also royally pissed me off.

Somebody had to stop these bastards.

Somebody with nothing to lose, a person who believed that retribution was far more important than their own personal safety.

Somebody like me.

That sounded good. It was just the thing the hero in every big-budget action movie would say. Trouble was, this was my life, not a movie, and I sure as hell wasn't anybody's hero. Far from it. But then again, it *was* true that I had nothing to lose. And somebody *did* have to put a stop to Dr. Marshall and his crazy boyfriend, Drake.

Ah, man, how did it ever come to this?

Deep down I knew I'd already made up my mind. I was just trying to avoid it for another few seconds. Freedom was finally within my grasp, but I couldn't just walk away. I knew I couldn't. My conscience, having always been a right stubborn bugger, wouldn't allow it. Too many people had suffered here. Too many people called to me from their nameless graves, tormented souls who whispered the word *revenge* in my ear. They deserved retribution—all of them, but especially Junie. How could I walk away from her?

Fuck it. Marshall and Drake are going down!

I had no idea what I was possibly going to do, or if I had it in me to pull something like this off, but as I turned and started walking back toward the castle, I felt good about my decision. I was scared, hell, who wouldn't be, but in a good way that made me feel alive for the first time in years. Today I had a chance to be more than just an expendable bum or a patched-together sideshow freak. Today I could be the great equalizer, the hammer of justice—a hero for the dead and downtrodden everywhere. That was taking it *way* too far, crazy talk, but I needed to believe in myself again—really believe—something I hadn't done since before the car accident that destroyed my family.

Back where Junie and Jackson had died, I stopped to see if the security guard had anything on him that might be useful. I grabbed his gun, of course, happy to see it still had nearly a full clip of bullets. I also found a small black penlight and a Bic disposable lighter, but the thing that shocked me and made me shake with an equal mix of fury and fear was a white, wooden cross tucked into his jacket pocket.

Another grave marker.

Mine!

I put the flashlight and lighter into my pocket along with Junie's switchblade, but the cross had a ten-inch vertical shaft and it was too big to fit. I considered just throwing it away but it had a point on one end that could maybe be used as a weapon. I stuffed it inside my jacket and decided to take the damn thing with me. The gun I kept in my hand and at the ready. Believe it or not, I already had the beginnings of a plan forming in the back of my mind. I didn't force it, just letting it simmer for a few minutes as I kicked some leaves over Jackson's body. People would be coming to search for him soon and covering him up might give me a few extra minutes before my best weapon—the element of surprise—was gone forever. In the meantime, I had to get my ass moving.

I took off at a run back down the forest trail. Well, it was more of a fast limp but it was the best I could do. I had to make it back to the outer edge of the forest before Drake sent the reinforcements to look for me. He would too; I had no illusions about that. Surely he'd have heard the shot that had killed Junie. My ears were still ringing from the gun blast. Drake would presume that shot had been Jackson shooting me, but if the guard didn't show up at the castle to give Drake the gruesome details, he'd know I'd somehow turned the tables on Jackson and immediately send out the guards.

How much time did I have? Junie had been killed about ten minutes ago. It was about a thirty minute long and winding walk out to this part of the woods, so I had another twenty minutes before Drake even started to worry. Say, another ten or fifteen minutes after that before Drake went bat shit and started screaming. A few more minutes to rally the troops and then I'd be public enemy number one around here again. All in all, that gave me about thirty-five minutes, which was loads of time to get to the edge of the forest and find somewhere to hide. I hurried anyway, not wanting to take any chances.

I made it back to where the path exited onto the field beside the castle without seeing anyone. Good, luck was still on my side. Not wanting to be seen by anyone who might be watching from out of possibly a hundred windows on this side of the building, I stayed back from the opening and set off on a course through the woods that would allow me to stay hidden when the guards arrived, but also stay close enough that I could keep an eye on what was going on. I walked a safe distance off the path, dropped to the ground, then wormed my way toward the edge of the forest on my belly. Just shy of the tree line, I scooped leaves over my legs and back, lay as still as I could and waited for whatever came next.

It felt great to lie down and rest. I was exhausted and just about every square inch of my abused body was aching, screaming out for my daily dose of painkillers. That thought made me think about Junie and how she'd never be bringing me—or anyone else—any more pills to make them feel better. A few tears ran down my cheeks, tough guy that I was, and as I lay there crying I started to have second thoughts about this wild vigilante crusade I was about to undertake. I mean, who the hell was I to take on Drake and his entire security staff? I'd killed Jackson in self-defense, but would I really have the guts to kill again just for the sake of justice? If the answer to that was no, I'd better turn tail and get the hell out of Dodge.

Drake walked out of the castle, his eyes scanning the

forest and seemingly looking directly at me. I knew he couldn't see me from where he stood, and was probably watching the mouth of the forest path for signs of Jackson's return. He kept glancing down at his wrist, checking his watch, then shaking his head. Even from this distance I could see how agitated the chief of security was, pacing back and forth and working himself into a slowly simmering rage. Another few minutes and just as I'd called it, Drake was screaming into his walkie-talkie and looking like he was ready to breathe fire.

Good on you, you bastard. Hope you have a heart seizure right in front of me.

Five minutes later, seven security guards were zipping up their jackets against the cold and loading identical guns to the one I was holding, while Drake barked orders at them. I couldn't hear what was being said, but it didn't take a genius to figure it out. They were being informed about Jackson and told to find me as fast as they could. All of them were in big trouble if I made it out of the forest and found my way to a police station. There was no way Drake was about to let that happen. I'm sure he even gave the guards some sort of incentive—cash or time off, *something*—for whoever put the first bullet in my head. By the time Drake sent his men after me, they were running like a pack of mindless bloodhounds trained to follow the scent of raw meat.

I'd expected as much, but Drake surprised me by pulling out his gun and running off into the forest after his men. Either he didn't trust them to get the job done right, or he had worked himself into such a frenzy he wanted to make the kill himself. Whatever the reason, it was an unexpected bonus for me. I'd worried how I was going to get past Drake and into the building if he had just stood there and waited for his men to return.

Now, there was no one to stop me from slipping out of the woods and getting inside. There was always the chance more guards were waiting inside the building, but my gut told me all of them were in the trees with Drake, all anxious to be the one to make their deranged boss happy.

I waited until I couldn't see or hear any of them anymore, then jumped to my feet and started jogging across the field to the castle. My body ached too much to run, but I covered the distance fairly quickly and without incident. If everything went as I figured, I should have at least an hour, maybe as many as three or four. They'd find Junie and Jackson's bodies easy enough, probably within twenty minutes if they ran the whole way, but after that they'd have no idea where I went.

I was counting on them searching farther into the forest, thinking I was running through the trees in a blind panic to get as far away as possible. There was no way they'd think I'd doubled back to pull a one-man Rambo on them—not even Drake would think me capable of that. So they'd be forced to split up and search the woods, maybe form a line fifty yards apart and look for me that way. That could take a long time. The best part was, for every step they took deeper into the woods, they'd eventually have to take every one of those steps again to get back here once the search was called off.

With my back pressed against the brick wall, I moved to the end of one side of the building and checked around the back to see if the coast was clear. It was, and I dashed around the corner, breathing a small sigh of relief to be out of the line of sight of anyone that might return from the forest path. There were several windows and one door that I could have tried to enter the castle, but I'd already spotted the place I wanted to go and made my way over to the small basement window a third of the way along the wall.

I dropped to my knees and took a second trying to peek inside but it was dark in the basement and there was nothing to see. I took that as a good sign no one was down there, so without hesitating I broke the pane of glass with the handle of Jackson's gun. The glass shattered easily and with less noise than I'd expected, but I had to waste several minutes clearing glass away and making sure I got rid of any shards left sticking up in the frame. The last thing I wanted to do was slice my wrists or neck open trying to clumsily crawl through a half-broken window.

I spun around, slipping in the window feet first and slithered backward until I was hanging off the inside wall with only a four-foot drop down to the floor. This was the point of no return and truthfully I wasn't sure I should let go.

In for a penny, I thought, having to rely on clichés to find some courage within me. What was that other one Dr. Marshall had teased me with? *Out of the frying pan, into the fire.* Shit, I'd gone way beyond that. This wasn't into the fire—this was going straight to Hell.

I took a deep breath, and dropped to the floor.

CHAPTER THIRTY-FIVE

Let's face it, any way you sliced it I made a woefully pitiful James Bond. I'd also misplaced my jazzed up Aston Martin sports car, my Rolex watch that doubled as a laser torch, and my attaché case filled with all my other neat superspy gizmos; so with only my brain and what limited brawn I could summon from this decrepit monster suit I called a body, I was forced to keep my plan simple. I had neither the time, skill, ambition, nor the luck required to pull off anything too complicated.

With those thoughts in mind, I pulled out the small penlight I'd recently taken off Jackson and set to work. The beam of light was surprisingly bright for such a small flashlight, easily illuminating the path ahead.

"Nothin' but the best for Drake's boys," I muttered, using even the little things to fuel my anger into what I hoped would give me the required adrenaline boost to carry my abused body through whatever tasks lay ahead.

I started looking for the furnace. It was cold outside, but comfortable in here, so obviously Dr. Marshall's medical facility had an adequate heating system. With a place this size, I was sure there had to be an immense furnace tucked away somewhere down here. Within minutes, I'd found it. The rusty metal furnace was massive, as I'd pictured it in my head, but there was one problem. A *big* problem. It was an oil furnace.

Shit! An old place like this, I should have known.

I could try tipping the oil reservoir over, or disconnecting the lines to spill the sticky black fuel over the basement floor, but all that would do was allow me to start a fire. I had the Bic lighter in my pocket, and a fire would do a lot of damage, sure, but not enough. Knowing Dr. Marshall, this place surely had a state-of-the-art fire control system with water sprinklers everywhere. All I'd end up doing was making a mess of the basement and tipping off Drake that I was back inside the castle. Not good enough. I was after *grand*-scale destruction here.

Think, Mike.

It was while wandering around trying to come up with a plan B that I found the second furnace. This one was smaller, newer, and in much better shape, but it was still an oil furnace, which left me in the same boat as before. It got me thinking, though. A place this size probably needed several furnaces, right? If there were two, chances were there might be three—or five—right? Were they all oil furnaces, or would they have newer, more modern types to complement the old? Maybe. Maybe not. Worth checking out, anyway.

I found the third furnace hiding in plain sight right in the middle of the basement under a set of cobweb-strewn wooden stairs leading up to the main floor. This one was quite tall, but considerably smaller than the last two. A bird named hope started beating its tiny wings in my chest and I held my breath as I moved in for a closer look. This furnace was relatively shiny, looked fairly new, and there was no bulky oil reservoir anywhere to be found. I'll be damned—this one operated on natural gas.

Yes!

Make a big bang. That was my master plan. Crude, lacking imagination, and had only taken seconds to dream up, but like it or lump it, that was it. It would either work, or it wouldn't.

Walking around the three sides I had access to, at first I couldn't see where the incoming gas line was. This sucker was getting its fuel from somewhere, but where? Then I looked up. The gas line, black and as new as the furnace itself, snaked down from the ground floor attached to the bottom side of the staircase and entered into the top of the furnace way above my reach. Not good. Discouraged but far from defeated, I started looking for the pilot light. It had to have one of them, and usually they were near the floor.

It was, but hidden behind a removable metal panel that took me a few seconds to find, and many more to figure out how to open. Once I ripped the panel free, I knelt down and peered in at a tiny flame and a series of open tubes that ran into the heart of the furnace. I'm no expert on gas furnaces, but I understood the general principal. Gas fills these chambers, is ignited by the pilot light; then a fan kicks in to blow the heat up through the vents into the building.

Obviously, I had to get rid of the pilot light. I didn't want any gas getting ignited around here until I was good and ready. No need to complicate things, so I just leaned my head in and blew the flame out. It was harder to extinguish than a birthday candle but required the same basic task—two big puffs and it was out.

Okay, now what?

A tiny amount of gas would leak out now, but nowhere near enough to cause the big bang I had in mind. No, for that, I'd have to cause a free flow of gas straight out of the main pipe. Remove the regulator to open the gas line wide and let it flood the basement for as long as

possible before someone figured out what I was doing.
Then I'd pull the Bic lighter from my pocket and kiss
all our asses good-bye in a shower of fire and exploding
bricks.

If only I had a pipe wrench.

But I didn't. I had a gun, a flashlight, a switchblade, a
lighter, and a wooden cross, but no tools that would
help me play amateur gas fitter. So I used my boots instead, standing up and kicking the pipe where the regulator controlled the amount of gas flowing into the
ignition chambers. Five kicks later my foot and leg
were killing me, and hardly any damage had been done.
I'd bent the pipe a bit and smashed off the top half of
the regulator, but the gas flow was still contained. Or
was it? You can't smell natural gas, but they add something in with it that you can smell to help detect leaks.
Whatever it was, I could smell it now, easily, and when
I bent back down and placed my hand on the fitting, I
was pleased to find a decent gush of gas pressure pushing my hand away.

All right! Now we're getting somewhere.

I gave the regulator one more hard kick, and planned
more, but it hurt too much. *Way* too much! Maybe I'd
busted something—a toe or two—in my first series of
kicks? Maybe I was just falling apart and this body
couldn't stand up to the physical pounding I'd been
forcing it to endure? Either way, I was done beating on
the regulator.

I rechecked the flow of gas exiting the furnace pipe
and was pleased with my efforts. The gas wasn't
free-flowing out of the supply line like I'd envisioned,
but it was pumping out a hell of a lot more than I'd
thought possible without the use of proper tools. I
wanted to get away from the pungent, chemically tainted
smell of the spreading gas vapor, so I hobbled away
down the center aisle and eventually sat down on the

floor against something white and made of metal, basking for a moment in my small but potentially major accomplishment.

All I have to do now is wait for—

Then I shone my flashlight behind me to see what I was leaning up against, and my simple plan instantly went up in smoke, morphing into something considerably grander in a matter of a few heartbeats.

Oh my!

I stood up to get a better look, shining my light around and marveling at how large this thing was up close. I couldn't believe I hadn't thought of this in the first place, but it goes to show how brilliant of a planner I was in the fine art of sabotage.

The oxygen tank.

Two of them, actually. Side by side. The huge, floor-to-ceiling cylindrical white metal oxygen tanks I'd been backed up against by Drake and his goons on the day they let me out of the gore-filled incinerator. The same tanks that Drake had prevented his over-zealous cohort from shooting me against because—

BOOM! I thought with a smile.

Big BOOM!

Now *this* had potential. The spreading natural gas could mix and be superenhanced by the oxygen and I should be able to make a monumental mess down here. Would it be enough? It would make a huge bang and destroy the basement, probably collapse some of the building too, but was that enough? I was starting to think clearer than before—not just looking at this through revenge-colored glasses—and if I was going to do this right, I wanted to leave nothing but a big flaming hole in the ground. It wasn't enough to just put Nathan Marshall out of business for a while. It wasn't even enough to get lucky and kill him. I needed to destroy everything here—*everything*—not leaving behind anything or anyone that might be able to put together the pieces of this horrific puzzle and start up shop again. That was going to be a bit trickier.

But not impossible.

I ran the flashlight beam up and across the ceiling, tracing the dozens of pipes that spider-webbed out from the top of the twin oxygen tanks. They spread out all over the basement—much farther than my light could shine—but I knew they all turned up, eventually, into the ceiling, snaking their way through the floors and walls to every operating room, every recovery room, every patient room, and every test laboratory in the castle.

Oh my! I thought for the second time in less than a minute, a brief vision of a huge mushroom cloud of fire and smoke playing before my mind's eye.

The vision might be a tad exaggerated, but it gave me a warm fuzzy feeling in the pit of my stomach and propelled me into action. I had a lot of work to do before Drake and his boys came home from their hike in the woods. I wanted to be ready for them.

First things first, I needed to get these tanks pumping pure oxygen into the basement to mix with the natural gas that was already spreading. Luckily, I wouldn't have to resort to busting my toes again to accomplish this. Both tanks had hookups where a hose could be connected to fill them from tanker trucks outside. The hose was interchangeable and right now it was connected to the tank on my right. It ran along the floor toward the back wall, but I couldn't see where it exited the building. Didn't matter; I had no intention of messing with it. Maybe if I was lucky, it would be connected to a supply truck and I could blow that up too. Regardless, if my plan worked as hoped, the gas inside this tank would soon be spreading around the upper floors.

For now, I was concerned with the other tank. I headed for the supply hookup on the left-side tank, and it was only a matter of turning a shut-off directional valve the right way and *WHOOSH*, the oxygen was blowing steadily out the hole where the hose wasn't connected. Couldn't have been easier, but I corralled my joy, knowing I still had things to do that wouldn't be accomplished quite so quickly and definitely not as easily.

As fast as I could go, I headed for the stairs.

CHAPTER THIRTY-SIX

When I opened the basement door, the light of the first-floor hallway nearly blinded me. The overhead fluorescents seemed brighter than normal, but I'm sure that wasn't true. It was just the realization that my plan, which required a certain amount of stealth, had a few more holes in it than I'd wishfully thought. Stealth wasn't going to have much to do with it. What I needed more than anything was a big handful of pure dumb-ass luck.

With another deep breath, I stepped out into the carpeted hallway and shut the basement door. I don't think I've ever felt so exposed in my life, but there was nothing to be done about it so I pushed the bad thoughts from my mind and went to work.

There was nothing on the first floor that interested me, and I was sure I'd run into Dr. Marshall or one of his secretaries if I hung around down here too long, so I made for the staircase at the end of the hallway, paused briefly to listen for voices inside, then quietly slipped inside. I felt much better in here, out of the area most trafficked, and took a second to calm myself before heading up to the second floor.

The hallway was deserted when I peaked my nose

though the barely opened door but I had no idea if there were going to be people in the operating rooms and labs. I'm sure there would be, in fact, but I couldn't do anything about them. If they saw me, so what? Most of the doctors, scientists, and orderlies around here were used to seeing my face and probably wouldn't bat an eye. That was what I was hoping for, anyway.

Moving down the hall, I soon came to the first operating room—the one where Dr. Marshall had taken my arms—and was pleased to see it was empty. The lights were off but the window blinds were half open, giving me more than enough light to see what I was doing. As quickly as I could I went around and turned on every gas valve I could find. I was extra pleased to see that not only were there several oxygen valves, but there was a row of stand-up portable tanks on the far wall labeled ETHER CYCLOPROPANE and ETHYLENE. I didn't know what they were—maybe the gases used as anesthetics?—but there was a flammable symbol on the side of each one, which was good enough for me. I pulled off the plastic tubes connected to them and cranked their valves wide open. Instead of standing around admiring my handiwork, I moved on.

The next half hour went by in a blur. There were two more operating rooms on the second floor and seven fully equipped laboratories. I moved as fast as I could, progressively limping worse as my foot and leg started hurting badly. I sucked up the pain, though, and kept moving. Room to room, lab to lab, each new door I walked through threatened to be my last. No one stopped me. No one screamed. No one put a bullet through my head.

Things were looking up.

As luck would have it, I managed to hit all three operating theaters and six of the labs. There were scientists working in the other lab, and although I wasn't

worried about them getting a look at me, I didn't think
they'd approve of me walking in and cranking all the
gas valves on in front of them. Best to count my bless-
ings I'd hit nearly all of the rooms, and just move along.
The third floor beckoned.

In the stairwell heading upstairs I met a tall redheaded
orderly named Jack O'Hare who'd sometimes helped
Junie during my rehab. He'd been decent to me the few
times I'd spoken to him and he just nodded to me, un-
concerned, and kept on descending the stairs. I held my
breath until I made it into the third-floor hall, then
exhaled loudly, surprised I'd actually made it this far
without being caught. I got over it, fast, thoughts of
Junie bringing the anger out in me again, and I was
more determined than ever to do this job right. These
fuckers were gonna pay!

The third floor was the quietest of all. Moving down
the hall, room to room, it was like tiptoeing through a
funeral home. The carpet was so plush I couldn't even
hear my footsteps as I walked along. It was starting to
creep me out. At every door, I expected to run into
Drake, or one of his guards, and no matter how many
empty rooms I entered, the feeling wouldn't go away.
My nerves were pretty much shot, I think. Getting
close, anyway.

*Get a hold of yourself, man. Get this done, and then you
can fall apart. Not now, Mike. Not now.*

Sounded good to me, but it didn't stop my rented
heart from hammering inside my rented chest or my
rented fingers from shaking each time I reached for
another doorknob.

Still, I managed, equal parts fear and rage keeping
me moving, driving me past the steadily growing pain
in my leg and the ever present doubt in my mind. I hit
every patient room I could get into. Some were locked—
maybe they were the ones with people in them—but

most were easy pickings. Twenty-five minutes later, gas was flowing all over the third floor and my plan was nearly complete.

Not quite, though.

No, there was something else I needed to do. Something I was dreading but important enough that I knew I couldn't chicken out and shy away from. I'd made a promise to someone here once—someone who'd suffered just as much as I had, maybe more—and if it was the last thing I ever did, I vowed I'd see that promise through. With a heavy heart, and a pit the size of a bowling ball trying to rise into my throat, I headed back for the stairwell. I needed to go up to the fourth floor for a few minutes.

I needed to visit the Bleeders' room.

CHAPTER THIRTY-SEVEN

I was in the hall outside the Bleeders' room, with no-where to hide, when a sour-faced nurse I didn't recog-nize exited the room. She was carrying a tray heaped with plastic blood bags that had surely just been har-vested from the group of cruelly vivisected men strapped to the beds inside.

"What are *you* doing up here?" the nurse said in a tone that made me want to beat the life out of her with my bare hands. Who the hell was she to treat these men like this, robbing them not just of their life juices, but of their dignity—hell, their *humanity*—as well? I kept my cool, though. No sense blowing things now, not when I was so close to success.

"Mr. Drake told me to deliver a message to one of the guys in there. Said he'd be up soon to talk to him personally. I'm supposed to wait here."

Pretty crappy cover story, I know. What possible message would the chief of security want delivered up here, and even if he did, why would Drake pick me to do it? In my winter coat and boots, no less. I was counting on the fact that this nurse—whoever she was—wouldn't really give a shit what I was doing. She had work to do and probably wanted to get it done and over with so she could go home. Thankfully, I was right.

"Well, hurry up then," she said, already dismissing me and moving away. "Don't you stir them up, or trust me it'll be your ass, not mine."

With that rather empty threat, she wandered off toward the front of the building. I slipped inside the Bleeders' room before she thought things through and turned back to ask me anything else. So far I'd been lucky—major league lucky—but I knew it wouldn't last forever. Time was running out.

Just give me another half hour, I prayed to the ceiling tiles, then looked around the sterile white room into a hellish scene I remembered all too well.

There were ten of them now—four on one side of the room, six on the other. Ten limbless sacks of meat that had once been decent men but had now been reduced to kegs of blood for Dr. Marshall to tap anytime he needed. It was diabolical—there was no other word for it—and it made me sick to my stomach to look at them. I couldn't suppress my shudder when I realized I knew most of these guys. His flaming red hair drew my eyes to Red Beard first, and then old Lucas, too, in the bed right next to him near the back window. Charlie, the confused guy whose shouts had led to my capture the first time, was still here, blankly staring at the ceiling along with at least four other men whose faces I recognized but whose names I couldn't remember.

Shit!

This wasn't a homecoming, or, for that matter, a friendly reunion, and I'd actually been hoping to walk into a room full of strangers. That would have been easier for me. Familiar faces only made things harder and pissed me off more. These same poor bastards had been lying here all this time, day after day, week after week, month after month, doing nothing but getting slowly bled dry and hoping to die.

I was here to answer their prayers.

I didn't want to do it—hell, I wasn't even sure I *could* do it—but I was here to try. These men had suffered enough and although I'd only promised Lucas I'd help him along to a better place, I felt I owed this same act of kindness to all of them. What other choice did I have? I couldn't save anyone, or make things better, but I could damn well put a stop to their endless misery and guarantee they wouldn't somehow live through the coming explosion. That was the last thing any of them would want. Death and, well, me were the only friends these guys had left.

Lucas must have heard me come in, because he turned his head and looked my way. I raised my hand and waved, moving toward him, but my smile froze half-formed, when I noticed the look of fear on the old man's face. He looked like he was about to scream. Didn't he know who I was? Or maybe his mind had finally shut down from the constant abuse.

This place wears a man down after a while. Wears him until he snaps.

I could still remember the day he'd said those words. Seemed like yesterday, and certainly nothing had changed around here to make me think his assessment wasn't bang on. I stopped walking and held my hands out in front of me. Hopefully he'd understand I wasn't here to hurt him.

"Don't be scared, Lucas, it's just me, Mike."

At the sound of my voice, Red Beard opened his eyes and looked at me from the next bed over. His eyes opened really wide and I was scared he, too, might be considering screaming. His mouth dropped open and several long seconds passed before he said, "Mike? Is that really you?"

Lucas's head snapped toward Red Beard and some of the worry left his wrinkled brow. "You see him too, Red?"

"'Course I see him," Red Beard's deep voice boomed in the quiet room. "He's standing right in front of us, ain't he?"

"You two okay?" I asked, not knowing what else to say as I walked up to stand at the feet of their beds.

Lucas flinched again at the sound of my voice, but he followed it with a nervous laugh that answered my question better than any words could have.

"Jesus, Mike, I thought you were a freakin' ghost. No foolin'. Red and I thought you were dead a long time ago and then you just show up out of nowhere, walking in like you're—"

Then he stopped, dead, the color draining from his already pale face. Both Lucas and Red were eying me up head to toe, a bit of fear creeping back into their eyes, and I knew right away what was going through their minds. Last time they'd seen me, I'd been getting wheeled out of this room strapped to a leather gurney, and I'd had the same number of arms and legs as they had—none! Now here I was standing in front of them a whole man again. No wonder they were freaked out. I would have been too.

I really didn't have the time or energy to go through the entire story and, in the end, it didn't make a hell of a lot of difference *how* I'd walked in here; the important part was *what* I'd walked in to do.

"Listen, guys, it's a long story and I just don't want to get into it. The short, no frills version is that Dr. Marshall is still up to his old tricks and he pieced me back together again using a lot of different people's body parts. I've been through hell and back so don't go thinking I'm luckier than you guys just because I'm standing. Trust me, I'm not."

The room was silent for thirty seconds as they chewed on what I'd just told them. They looked at each other a few times, puzzled expressions on their faces, but both seemed to buy it without any more questions. For that small mercy, I was grateful.

"Why *are* you here, Mike?" Lucas finally asked.

"Yeah, what's up?" Red chimed in.

Now how was I supposed to answer those questions? How do you tell your friends you've come to murder them? Damned if I knew. Instead of answering, I turned and went to the empty bed directly across from them. I paused for a moment, still fighting my inner demons as to whether I should be doing this, but in my heart I knew a mercy killing was the proper thing—the decent thing—to do.

I bent down and picked up the thin white pillow.

"Pillow fight?" Red asked, laughing hard at his joke. "I have a feeling you'll win that one, buddy."

Ignoring Red Beard, I turned and looked at Lucas, stared straight into his eyes, and in that instant knew he understood exactly what I'd come here to do. If he'd screamed, or showed me any trace of fear, I might have backed out and tossed the pillow away, but only one emotion was shining clearly in his eyes—hope.

"Bless you, lad," Lucas whispered.

It was barely audible, but those three small words gave me the strength I needed to see this awful task through. Even Red Beard had caught on, and was nodding his head, smiling at me as tears started to run down his once jolly cheeks.

"Do it, Mike. Please," Red Beard begged.

I looked at them both, nodded my head, and then went right to work before my nerve deserted me.

For no reason at all, I chose to do Charlie first. I knew he was basically comatose back when I'd been sleeping here and was probably worse now, so I figured he'd be as good a place to start as any. I'd already decided I would be leaving Lucas and Red Beard until last. These other guys were three-quarters dead already and just needed a little push to send them on their way. Putting the pillow over my friends was going to be a whole different ball game, so like the coward that I was, I would avoid it as long as possible.

Charlie never moved. Didn't struggle at all when the pillow covered his gaunt face. I wasn't even sure I was accomplishing anything until I noticed his skinny chest had stopped expanding and contracting. He'd died silently, in less than a minute, and tears sprung to my eyes as I realized I'd just murdered another human being. Jackson I'd killed in self-defense, and that hadn't bothered me in the least, but Charlie's death was my first murder. The first of many on this day but I forced myself not to think about it, tried to shut it out of my mind and just flick the switch over to autopilot. I hated myself, sure, but I truly believed I was doing these guys a favor—one they'd do for me if our roles were reversed. Still, murder was murder, no matter how hard I tried to justify it. But there was no turning back now. With shaking hands, I moved to the next bed.

Thirty minutes later, seven more men were dead. Some I knew, some I didn't, but all of them went to their great reward silently and without a fuss. Well, almost all of them. One man—his name was Glen, or maybe Ben—fought me a little, twisting and wiggling weakly beneath my hands, but it was his body reacting more so than his mind. I'd looked into his eyes before placing the pillow over his face, and I knew the lights were out upstairs.

Eight down. Two to go.

Ah, man! Here we go.

The entire time I'd been playing God with a pillow, I'd intentionally avoided looking at Red Beard and Lucas. I wasn't ashamed of what I was doing, and I wasn't afraid I'd lose my nerve, I just didn't want to see the look of anticipation on their tired faces. I didn't have to look to know they would be smiling, crying, and practically salivating at the prospect of escaping this rotten plane of existence for a chance at a better one. Unfortunately, I couldn't avoid Lucas and Red Beard any longer. Holding the pillow in front of me like a shield, I walked over to them and looked up.

It wasn't as bad as I'd expected. Sure, they looked excited and happy to see their suffering come to an end, but they also looked scared, not sure what—if anything—waited in the afterlife. It was a sobering thought, one that hit me equally hard as I expected to be joining my friends in death shortly myself. Would we recognize each other if we met up on the other side? Not my concern. Hopefully Heaven had a nice place waiting for Lucas and Red, but I was surely headed straight to Hell for the things I'd done today and I doubted I'd see either one of them again.

Stop stalling, Mike. Do what you gotta do.

"It's okay, Mike," Lucas said in a soft voice, seeing my trepidation at approaching any closer. "We've been dead for a long time already, our bodies just won't let go. None of this is your fault, lad. I know it's a lot to ask, but you gotta help us."

I silently nodded my head. What he was saying was true, but I still couldn't find the strength to make my legs take a step closer. Lucas had more to say.

"I never told you this before, but my wife, Charlotte, she died eight years ago from the cancer and I just know she's waiting for me on the other side of death's door. Help me open the door, Mike. I don't have the hands to do it myself and I miss her. I miss her so *damn* much!"

Lucas started to cry then, and I couldn't bear to see

him suffer for one more minute. Before I chickened out, I walked over and kissed him on the forehead.

"Kiss her once for me," I said, my own tears running freely now.

"Thank you, Mike," he said, "I will."

Then I put the pillow on his smiling face and pressed down with all my might. It hurt so much inside but I smiled, too, thinking the whole time about Lucas walking through that door, seeing his wife's beautiful face and running to throw his arms around her. Maybe that would never happen, but it was nice to think about and, for Lucas's sake, I sure hoped it would. Either way, Dr. Marshall would never hurt him again and I guess that was good enough. The rest was out of my hands.

Red Beard had been quiet for a long time, but he spoke to me now. "I think he's gone, Mike."

I checked to see that Lucas's chest had stopped moving, and it was still, but I held on to the pillow another minute before I took it off his face. I'd failed him last time and I wanted to make damn sure I'd done the job right this time. No worries, Lucas was gone and had died with a smile on his face.

"You got anyone waiting on the other side for you, Red?" I asked, hoping for the best.

"Not really. My parents, I guess. Be nice to see them again. Maybe a few old firemen buddies. Who knows? How about you?"

"My wife and little boy. Car accident. I don't know much about this stuff, Red, but if there *is* a Heaven, and they'll consider letting a fool like me in, I'm looking forward to seeing them soon too. It's crazy to think about, but it helps, you know?"

Red Beard nodded, tears flowing down his cheeks almost as much as mine. "Let's do this, Mike. I'm ready."

I walked over beside him, kissed him on the forehead too, and was about to put the pillow on his smiling face when I saw his eyes open wide in surprise. There was fear in those eyes as well. When I turned to follow his gaze, I understood why.

Drake was standing in the doorway.

Too long, Mike. You took too long.

The head of security looked astonished to see me. He was still sweaty and breathing hard from his search in the forest, and finding me standing here in the castle had him at a temporary loss for words. He got over it, though, quickly.

"Are you out of your fucking mind, Mike?"

I didn't say anything.

"You somehow get the jump on Jackson, and instead of hightailing it away from here, you decide to come back to say good-bye to your friends?"

Then he took a few steps into the room and a closer look at the men lying in their beds, then down at the pillow still clasped tightly in my hands, and he started laughing. Laughing hard, the thought of me killing the Bleeders somehow hilarious to him.

"You *are* crazy. I knew it. Hot damn! This is one for the record books. We're out running around in the damn forest, and here you are playing Kiss-the-Pillow with your old buddies. Dr. Marshall's gonna love this."

"How'd you find me?" I asked, stalling for time.

"Nurse Harper," he answered. "She mentioned someone delivering a message up here for me and I knew it was bullshit. Tell you the truth, though, I thought it was one of my guards slacking off. I came up here to rip him a new asshole for not helping us look for you. I damn near fainted when I saw you standing there. You're full of surprises; I'll give you that. It's almost a shame to kill someone like you, but I gotta—"

"Leave him alone, Drake, you bastard!" Red Beard shouted, his voice seemingly far too loud and powerful to have come from such a small, wasted body.

Drake laughed again. "Fuck you, Torso Boy. Shut your mouth or I'll cut your eyes out next."

To add legitimacy to his threat, Drake withdrew a short-bladed, nasty-looking knife and drew circles in the air in Red Beard's direction. My friend groaned, closed his eyes and started praying in whispers, which pleased Drake immensely. With Red Beard put back in his place, the hulking guard turned his attention to me, pointing the knife in my direction and licking his lips. He started walking toward me.

"Be a good boy, Mike, and I'll make this quick and painless for you. I'm too tired to keep fucking around with an irritating turd like you. Your choice. Either way, you're going down."

Don't be so sure of that, big boy.

Drake had a sharp knife, but I had Jackson's gun.

With no time to spare, I tossed the pillow and dug in my jacket pocket. As quickly as I could, I pulled out the shiny silver gun, more than happy to pump some bullets into this big mouthy cocksucker, fill him with enough lead to make him magnetic, then spit in his face as he dropped at my feet. Wishful thinking.

Drake was damn quick for a brute, and by the time I transferred the gun to my shooting hand and tried to pull the trigger, he was already in my face. He grabbed my left wrist in his right hand, making sure he pointed the gun away, and then started squeezing. My skinny wrist bones were like matchsticks in his vicelike grip and I screamed as something in my lower arm went *SNAP!* Fire engulfed my hand for a moment, and then everything went numb. My fingers spasmed and the gun fell to the floor between us. Drake kicked it away, across the room, smiling at me like a hungry carnivore.

"Good effort, Mike, just not good enough," Drake said, keeping a hold of my shattered wrist as he thrust his knife toward my belly.

Instinctively, I twisted my body to the right to avoid his deadly blow and Drake's knife tore a long gash in my jacket, scratching me along my left ribcage, drawing blood but not incapacitating me. I swung my right fist as hard as I could at Drake's throat, hoping to catch him in the Adam's apple but he saw the punch coming and ducked. My fist connected solidly with his chin, but I didn't have enough strength to do much damage. Drake shook it off easily, his arrogant smile still in place, and came at me with the knife again.

I tried a second time to twist away, this time to the left, but Drake wasn't being fooled again. He anticipated my move and drove the short-bladed knife into my right side, below the ribcage. The knife sticking out of me, Drake finally let go of my wrist and let me drop to my knees on the floor.

Time stood still for a moment.

I held my breath, waiting to die.

Drake was triumphantly standing over me, laughing, and I could just make out Red Beard crying on the other side of the room, but I wasn't paying much attention to either one of them. All I could think about was one crystal clear thought.

Why doesn't it hurt?

A knife in the belly is supposed to hurt, right? Death by stabbing is supposed to be a horrible, painful thing, right? Then why wasn't it?

I couldn't feel anything. In fact, the first cut across my ribs hurt more. Maybe adrenaline and my hatred for Drake were blocking the pain, but even if that were true, they wouldn't do much to stop the blood.

And there was no blood.

I looked down, saw the knife sticking out of the ripped hole its entry had made in my coat, and wondered what was happening. I doubled over so I could yank the knife out of me with my right hand without Drake seeing me, and was shocked to see a round rubber disk come out stuck on the end of the knife. The short blade had speared it almost dead center, but not penetrating enough that it was sticking out the backside.

Son of a bitch! Puckman!

It was the crazy Mexican's silly puck. The one I'd stolen all those months ago, hoping to bean him in the kisser with it before the train ran me over. It had been sitting in my coat pocket all this time, forgotten and of no use to anyone—except to save my life!

Or just prolong it.

I was still in big trouble here. Before I lost the only chance I was likely to get, I faked a pain-filled groan and collapsed even further to the ground, hiding my uninjured belly from Drake's view and using my left forearm to pry the puck off the knife blade. The numbness was going away and my wrist was starting to hurt like a bitch, but that only helped make my groans all the more realistic. Drake was still laughing at me when I looked up into his ugly face. He was really enjoying my death, getting off on my pain and suffering.

That was when I shoved the knife up into his groin, rammed it into his balls as hard as I could. Then I twisted it, first to the left, then the right, then back to the left again, just for the hell of it. Blood was pouring down onto my hand by this time, and Drake wasn't laughing anymore. No, he was screaming like a girl, high-pitched and really, really loud.

Perfect!

Let the bastard scream. It was sweet music to my ears and something I'd waited an awfully long time to hear. Part of me wished Drake's suffering could last for hours, days, weeks maybe, and everyone in this room was still alive to see it, but that wasn't going to happen. The big man dropped to his knees beside me, a look of sheer disbelief on his face. He tried to speak, but I wasn't in the mood to listen to anymore of his bullshit so I drove the knife deep into his chest. I think I lucked out and stuck it in his heart first try. Blood gushed out of his nose and mouth, his eyes rolled back in his head, and he toppled over backward never to move again.

Just like that, big bad Drake was dead.

CHAPTER THIRTY-EIGHT

Part of me wanted to jump to my feet and dance a jig over Drake's dead body. In my humble opinion, the world was far better off without the sick perverted fuck. I wanted to get up and kick the muscle-headed ignoramus about a hundred times, then kiss him on the lips just to thank him for the sheer pleasure his death had given me. I was giddy with joy, for sure, but another part of me was too hurt, too exhausted, too damn bone weary to bother doing any of those silly macho things. So I just sat there quietly on the floor, covered in sticky blood, not sure what to do next. I might have been in shock.

My mind went away for a while.

Someplace quiet.

Next thing I knew, I was standing at the foot of Red Beard's bed, looking down at my friend without the slightest clue how I'd gotten there. One quick glance behind me confirmed Drake was still lying in a rather large red puddle—which was a relief because for a second I thought I might have hallucinated the entire confrontation with Dr. Marshall's security chief.

"You okay, Mike?" Red asked, his big puppy dog eyes red from crying.

I was covered in Drake's blood, and my wrist, ribs and knee hurt like hell, but for the most part I was doing all right. Better than Drake, that was for sure.

"Yeah, Red, I'm fine. How about you?"

Red just nodded, a small smile touching the corners of his mouth. "You had me worried there. Thought you were in over your head with Drake, but damned if you didn't give him what he deserved. Good for you, buddy. Couldn't have happened to a bigger asshole, you ask me. Hope he's already burning in Hell."

"You and me both," I said, unzipping my soiled coat and tossing it on the floor.

My coat had taken the brunt of Drake's bleeding, and, fond memories aside, it was a sloppy mess and I wasn't keeping the damn thing on another second. I spent a few minutes wiping my hands off on Red's bedsheet, more to prepare for what was coming next than any real need to clean my hands. I also tore a strip off the sheet to wrap around my damaged left wrist, using my teeth to help cinch the knot tight. Again, I suppose I was stalling, but I was starting to feel really good about all this. My plan was holding up. Killing Drake was surely a good sign things were meant to work out. I'd help Red move on, then blow this charnel house as close to Heaven as all the spreading gas would get me once it ignited.

"Okay," I said, walking over and grabbing another pillow, "Let's finish this thing. You ready?"

I wasn't expecting Red to be happy about what was going to happen, but I never expected him to look at me with such fear. The first time I'd approached with the pillow he hadn't looked like this. What had changed?

"What's the matter, man? I thought you wanted this?"

"You've got my . . . my . . ." Red began, but then he started to shake, what was left of his body trembling beneath his thin blanket. He wasn't looking into my eyes; wasn't looking at my face at all, but lower, at my left arm. I looked down, saw what was giving him such grief and nearly screamed. There on my bicep was a tattoo of a bright red fireman's helmet, with a yellow ladder and an axe crisscrossing in front of it. The words N.F. STATION #5 were boldly written below.

Holy shit!

"Is that *mine*?" Red asked me, his strong voice breaking on the last word.

How was I supposed to answer? What could I say to justify and explain why I was wearing his fucking arm?

How could I have been such an idiot not to have noticed this before? Sure, I remembered him showing all of us how proud he'd been of this tattoo, but I'd been so busy whining about how ugly my patched-together body looked, I'd never made the connection. I hadn't stopped to wonder if I knew any of the donors or what might happen if they ever found out I'd received their stolen body parts. I hadn't been the one to take their limbs from them, but standing in front of Red Beard, I couldn't help but feel like a thief. Worse, actually, because not only was I wearing an arm that didn't belong to me, I was holding a pillow with it, about to murder him using the strength of his own flesh.

"I'm sorry, Red," I said, knowing I had to say something to make him understand. "I didn't have a say in any of this, same as you. It's Dr. Marshall that caused all this suffering. It's his fault. He put me to sleep and I woke up looking like this. Please don't hate me."

Red Beard didn't say anything for a long time, but he was looking into my eyes again. His trembling slowly subsided, but tears were still streaming out of his swollen eyes. "I don't hate you, Mike. Christ, no, you know that. I just can't take it anymore. I've hit the wall and I wanna go away. Heaven or Hell or just a big black hole in the ground, I don't much care. Just get me out of here, okay? Please."

I nodded, not trusting myself to speak right now. Grabbing the pillow, I moved to the side of his bed and numbly prepared to commit murder again.

"Promise me something, Mike?" Red Beard asked as I was lowering the pillow.

"I'll get him, Red," I said, knowing what he needed to hear. "Count on it, my friend. Nathan Marshall will be dead within an hour."

I didn't have total faith in what I was saying, but every word came straight from my heart and I vowed to do everything in my power to make it reality—or die trying. Red Beard nodded and smiled. I smiled back, then placed the pillow down on his face before he could see me break down in tears.

CHAPTER THIRTY-NINE

Red Beard was gone and his death weighed heavily on my mind. The pillow I'd used was still resting on his face, a poor man's shroud if ever there was one. I'd been too distraught—and I'll admit it, afraid—to remove the pillow and look at him. I didn't want to see if he'd been suffering in his last few moments. I wanted to believe he was smiling under there, just like Lucas had been, but damned if I was going to find out. No way.

My head was spinning. I had to fight to keep my thoughts moving in the right direction. If I stopped to think too hard about what I'd just done I'd go mad, probably lie down on the floor between Lucas and Red and be done with it. I still had a job to do, though, and more importantly, a promise to keep.

Before leaving the Bleeders' room I gathered up my growing arsenal of weapons and supplies. I now had two guns: Drake's and Jackson's; two knives: Drake's buck knife and Junie's switchblade; a Bic lighter; and the wooden grave marker.

Problem was, I couldn't carry it all. The knives could slip into my pant pockets, no problem, but with my injured wrist I could only carry one of the guns. I could stuff one down the front of my pants but with my luck

I'd probably blow my dick off. No, one gun was surely all I'd need. Drake's gun still had a full clip, so I grabbed it and left Jackson's on one of the spare beds. I almost left the wooden cross behind, but on a whim I stuck it down the front of my shirt.

Last but not least, I made sure I cranked on all the oxygen gas valves—one stationed at the head of every bed in the room—before saying good-bye to Lucas and Red and heading out into the fourth-floor hallway.

Thankfully, it was deserted, but I knew I'd really have to be on my toes now. If Drake had come back to the castle, no doubt the rest of his boys were back, too, and none of them would let me walk on by like the nurse and the orderly had done earlier. If I was spotted again I was in big, big trouble.

Mind you, so was whoever spotted me because I was armed and determined to go down fighting. I didn't give a damn whether I got my throat cut in a fight or was gunned down in a standoff, but I desperately needed to get somewhere that I could ignite the gas before I let them take me down.

And I knew just the place.

I headed for the front stairwell.

My guess was all of the remaining security team would be congregating down in Drake's office on the ground floor. They'd be waiting to see what Drake wanted to do next. They weren't stupid and would soon start trying to reach their leader on the walkie-talkies, but they'd stand around talking amongst themselves for ten or fifteen minutes, at least, before anyone started to get antsy. Then they'd spread out and start looking for him, which didn't bother me because I wasn't going anywhere near Drake's security office, or for that matter, anywhere in the labs, operating theaters, or patient rooms where the guards might eventually start searching. No, I was going to the one place I didn't think they'd bother looking—the tower room above the fourth-floor stairwell at the front of the building.

Andrew's room.

It had been Drake's room when I first came here, but now that Dr. Marshall no longer needed his wheelchair, I'm pretty sure Andrew had been moved up there on a permanent basis. Maybe they'd all slept in the tower together. One big happy family. Regardless, if Andrew was alive I knew that's where he'd be. Partly I wanted to find him out of curiosity; I'll admit that. I wanted to know what had happened to him. I needed to see if Dr. Marshall's son was dead and gone or if he was wearing a flesh suit the same as me—only his would be Bill Smith's upgraded model with a hell of a lot less scars on it. The main reason, though, was I knew the tower room had several oxygen hookups and its small confined space would be a perfect spot to spark the first explosion.

I considered trying to hunt down Dr. Marshall first and pull an incredibly satisfying Rambo on him, fulfilling my promise to Red Beard as well as getting the face-to-face revenge I so richly deserved, but I was smart enough to know it was a bad idea. I had no idea where Dr. Marshall might be, and any attempt to locate him would probably get me killed—either by the insane doctor himself, or by one of his guards—before I could ignite the spreading gases. That was a risk I wasn't willing to take.

Besides, it was pointless. If Dr. Marshall was still in the building when the explosion went off—and I was 99 percent sure he was—he was going to get what was coming to him, whether I was standing there to see it happen or not. Sure, I'd have loved to see the look on his face knowing I'd gotten the last laugh on the rich psycho, but knowing without a doubt he was going to die along with his cruel staff members and his unethical medical secrets was good enough for me.

As soon as I opened the door leading into the front stairwell I heard voices. Two people, their voices muffled, neither one sounding happy. They were clearly arguing, but I couldn't make out what about. I prepared to duck back into the fourth-floor hallway, but no footsteps were coming up the stairs and I figured I could slip into the tower room before anyone spotted me.

Quiet as a mouse, I climbed the last staircase, and was halfway around the corner when I realized the voices I was hearing were getting louder, clearer.

Someone's in the tower room.

Andrew? Who else?

This wasn't good. Definitely not part of the plan. I inched up the stairs, hearing the voices clear enough now that I recognized one of them as Dr. Marshall's. My heart shot into my throat, fear trying to strangle me, but I fought it hard, swallowing the anxiety down with the soothing realization that I'd be getting my chance at personal revenge after all. The other voice sounded familiar but I couldn't place it yet. My gun at the ready, I took another few steps up and peered over the riser to see who Dr. Marshall was arguing with.

It was Andrew, but not the Andrew Marshall I remembered meeting. He was no longer a disembodied man trapped in a glass tank, but like me, his body had been made whole again. He sat upright, strapped into a silver high-backed wheelchair equipped with a head brace, near the skillfully restored stained glass window I'd tried to take a header out of on my last visit to this room.

Although Andrew was fully dressed, wearing a dark blue wool sweater and baggy jeans, I knew he was transplanted into Bill Smith's flesh suit, which accounted for his familiar voice. It was Bill's voice I was hearing. Andrew had inherited his benefactor's vocal chords along with the rest of his body. I hadn't known Bill for long, but it was kind of creepy hearing his voice. Made me wonder again whose voice I was speaking with.

Doesn't matter, don't get sidetracked. Just run up there with your gun blasting.

I was full of good ideas today, but that wasn't one of them. I wasn't sold on the notion of shooting Dr. Marshall. A bullet was too clean of a way for him to go out. I was also worried about the shot being heard all over the building and Drake's guards coming on the run. Besides, I wanted to hear what they were shouting about, so I stayed put, listening in on their argument.

"You're a fool," Dr. Marshall said to his son. "An *ungrateful* fool. I've spent my life trying to help you walk and you want to quit on me now when we're this close to success?"

"Success?" Andrew yelled back. "You call *this* success? Look at me, father. You cut my real body away piece by piece until there was nothin' left, then you try sewing me up inside another man's dead body, but guess what, Dad, I still can't walk."

"I know that, Andrew. And I transplanted you into another man's *living* body, not dead. There's a big difference."

"Not to me, there isn't."

"The problem was you were in the submersion tank for too long. The infection spread to your spine and shut down a lot of your neuropathways, basically leaving you a quadriplegic in your new body. Don't worry, though, we aren't out of options yet, son. All we have to do is take a few steps back. We'll get another flesh suit for you, only this time what we do is leave the spinal column of the donor intact and just transplant your head onto the healthy neck. I can do it, son, I swear I can!"

"Oh Christ! What's next after that, Dad? You gonna

just scoop my brain out and dump it into another stranger?"

"I won't have to, Andrew. This time it'll work. You have to trust me."

"No way. Never again. I don't want to live like this anymore, Dad. *Please*. I can't handle being cut apart again. You have to stop this insanity."

"Never! I'm going to make you walk again, Andrew. One day, you'll thank me."

"No, Dad. I won't. You treat me like a lab animal and expect me to worship your genius like the other sheep around here. I hate you for what you've done. You can't make me go through that again. I'd rather die."

"Don't be so naïve. Of course I can make you, and I will. Who's going to stop me?"

From my hiding place on the stairs, I knew that was my cue. If ever there was a time for me to play the action hero, this was definitely it. In the movies, this was where any good secret agent worth his salt steps out into the open and confidently says, "I will." Unfortunately, this wasn't the movies. I had no intention of being so civil and—let's face it—stupid enough to give away the element of surprise I was going to need.

For all my big talk about finding Dr. Marshall and getting my face-to-face revenge, I would have preferred to have found this room empty and gone about my plan of blowing up the castle quietly, without complications. That obviously wasn't going to happen, but if I was forced into confronting Marshall, I could at least do it on my own terms, hopefully sneaking up and taking him out before he knew I was there. I was too banged up and exhausted for another fight.

Just shoot him, then, my conscience suggested again, but I dismissed the notion a second time. It would be a cowardly thing to do—which I had no problem with at all—but I couldn't risk having Drake's security team hearing the shot. No, the gun was out, which left me with only two options. Drake's knife was sticky, literally painted red with his blood, but so too was Junie's blade that I'd killed Jackson with. I really didn't have any desire to touch either one again but I had to so I went for Drake's. I'd have to push the blade release button on Junie's and in this cramped stairwell I was fairly sure Dr. Marshall would hear the sound of the blade sliding out. Maybe not, but it wasn't worth the risk.

I laid the gun down on the top stair, grabbed the buck knife in my right hand, and as quietly as I could, started creeping toward Dr. Marshall's exposed back. I only made it five feet before he turned and spotted me. Noise hadn't given me away; it was Andrew. He'd been facing me as I stepped clear of the stairwell and let's just say his poker face needed work. Andrew's eyes shot wide open and damned if he didn't keep staring at me until his father had turned around to see what was distracting him.

Thanks, Andrew. Just the help I needed.

When Dr. Marshall saw me, he didn't seem nearly as shocked as his son. He actually looked happy, smiling a big toothy out-of-his-freaking-mind grin that scared the bejesus out of me. Fear wasn't an option right now, so I threw caution to the wind and charged Dr. Marshall in a wild offensive attack before he had a chance to defend himself. I think my boldness surprised him, his smile faltering as I rapidly closed the gap, bloody buck knife held out in front of me like a medieval knight's jousting lance.

Dr. Marshall spun around, searching for a weapon, but there was nothing within arm's reach. I'd have taken him right then, quick and easy, if my left knee had held up for a few more strides. With victory and revenge literally five feet away, my knee gave out and I dropped face-first to the carpet at Dr. Marshall's feet. I hit hard, stars dancing in front of my eyes as my chin bounced off the floor. My knee was throbbing horribly, too, but I had worse problems than pain. I had to shake it off and get to my feet—fast.

Dr. Marshall had other ideas.

While I was sprawled on the floor, he stomped on my hand, savagely grinding his heel down until I screamed and released the knife. He kicked the blade under the neatly made bed off to our left. Then he started kicking me in the ribs, arms, and legs—anywhere he could get a swing at—really laying the boots to me. I curled into a ball and tried to protect my head.

Knowing being defensive would only get me killed, I uncurled and launched myself at his legs, grabbing them and tugging him off balance. He tumbled to the floor, landing with a satisfying *thump*, but he didn't miss a beat and was back on top of me in seconds, flailing away at my head and chest with his fists. I landed a few good licks of my own, but he was stronger than me and had me pinned to the floor. My mind wasn't too clear, what with the beating I was taking, but I was lucid enough to know I needed to get my hands on one of my other weapons if I wanted to win this fight. Trouble was, the gun was sitting on the top stair, out of the equation. The switchblade was within reach, in my right pant pocket, but with Dr. Marshall straddling my lap, it was impossible for me to get at it.

Dr. Marshall smacked me once more in the face, crushing my nose, nearly knocking me out cold. It didn't hurt that much, but by the time I shook the cobwebs from my head, he'd wrapped his long powerful fingers around my neck and was trying to strangle me. The surgeon's fingers were strong, digging into my flesh and tightening like ten baby boa constrictors. I tried to punch him in the face, but I didn't have much fight left

in my battered body and my punch barely fazed him.
He started smiling again, thinking he had me and there
was nothing I could do about it.

Wrong, asshole!

As my vision started to blur and my lungs screamed
for oxygen, I slipped my right hand inside my shirt and
grabbed hold of the last hope I had of surviving this
fight. My fingers tightened around the shaft of the
wooden cross, the marker that had been meant to adorn
my grave. Right sentiment—wrong body!

I pulled the cross free, my fist wrapped around the
top bar with the sharpened shaft protruding out between my second and third fingers, looking nasty, like
something Abraham Van Helsing might use on a vam-
pire hunt. I drove the makeshift weapon up at Dr. Marshall's body with every ounce of strength I had left. He
saw it coming but couldn't get out of the way. The crude
wooden blade caught him in the throat, under his chin,
and all ten inches of the shaft slid up through the roof
of his mouth and into his brain, jarring to a stop when
the tip scraped the roof of his skull and my bloody
knuckles slammed into the bottom of his jaw.

Dr. Marshall went rigid for a moment, his fingers
clawing into my throat even tighter than before, but
then his body relaxed and his fingers went limp. I
tugged the cross out of his ruined throat and a torrent
of blood poured out of the wound down onto me, a
crimson rain mixed with chunks of gray matter that
looked like oatmeal cookie dough. Dr. Marshall fell off
me, tipping over backward, dead long before he hit the
floor.

I should have felt jubilant, whooping it up, celebrat-
ing my grand victory over the man who'd ruined my
life, but I didn't. Emotionally, I didn't feel anything.
Spent, maybe. Empty. I lay on the bloody floor, covered
in gore, hurting like hell, and having a hard time catching

my breath. There was still work to do and I should be getting at it, but man, I was tired. All I could think of was how nice it would be to close my eyes and take a nap—a quick power nap to recharge the batteries and forget about all my problems for fifteen minutes.

Yeah, right. Who are you trying to kid?

If I closed my eyes now I knew the game was over. I'd never get up again. The next sight I'd see was the barrel of one of the security guard's guns as he kicked me awake before putting a bullet in my head. I hadn't come this far to quit now. Mind you, maybe with Drake and Dr. Marshall now both dead, I didn't really need to blow up the castle. I'd killed the two men most responsible for the crimes committed here, so maybe I could just crawl over to the stairs, pick up my gun, jam it in my mouth and call it a life. Not a bad idea.

The easy road wasn't in the cards for me, though. There would be files, and lab reports, and journals, and videotapes, and who knew what other proof around here that would show that what Nathan Marshall had been working on actually worked. He was out of his mind, insane with his obsession to help his son, but those things aside—he *was* a brilliant man. There was no denying his crazy Frankenstein experiments were a whopping success. I couldn't bite a bullet and leave all that documentation lying around for some other scientist to discover. The police would turn it all over to someone higher up the ladder, and eventually the government scientists would swarm this place like ants to a honey jar. That was unacceptable.

Sure, Dr. Marshall's work had the potential to help a lot of people but it wouldn't work out that way. Someone with power would corrupt things, maybe see the potential to create soldiers that could be continually re-fitted with new bodies after their current ones broke down or were damaged. They wouldn't need to retrain troops—all they had to do was take the experienced soldier's head and give him a nice new strong body to fight another day with. Maybe none of that would ever happen and I was just being paranoid, but the thought of an army of super soldiers scared me, and the vision of warehouses full of readily available flesh suits dancing in their watery tanks chilled me to the bone.

No way. Bring this place to the ground, Mike. Don't leave nothin' but a big smoking hole.

My mind made up, I tried to sit up and get moving. Bad idea. My knee, wrist, ribs, nose, and body hurt so bad I didn't think there was any way I could ever get to my feet. For a heartbeat, I seriously worried that I might be too beaten and battered to carry out my plan, but I pushed those negative thoughts aside. It was crunch time.

Get up, man! If not for you, get your ass up and do this for Junie and for all the other innocent people who've died here while Marshall and Drake were playing God.

That got me moving, and although I felt like I'd gone fifteen rounds with Lennox Lewis, I gritted my teeth and stood up. My head spun again, and I nearly went down, but I took several deep breaths and managed to stay on my feet.

I ignored Andrew for the moment. He'd been sitting silently through everything that just happened, staring at me now like I was from outer space. I didn't know if he was relieved I'd killed his father or in massive shock, but before I dealt with him I had to crack open all the gas valves in the room while I still had the strength to do it.

Silently, I went back to work.

CHAPTER FORTY

The tower room was turning out to be a better place to start the chain of explosions than I'd originally thought. Not only were there four oxygen gas valve stations in the room, but there was also a row of six large stand-up oxygen tanks strapped together against the far wall. It looked like they were there strictly as a backup to the plumbed-in system, a fail-safe just in case the regular system wasn't working. There was also a portable ethylene cylinder hooked to the metal safety rail on the side of Andrew's bed. I cranked them all wide open, and then sat down on the bed to wait for the gases to saturate the room. When this place went up, it was going to be one mother of a boom.

Too bad I won't be around to see it.

With the work done, I couldn't ignore Andrew anymore. I didn't want to, anyway. I wanted to talk to him while we still had the chance. He was sitting in his chair with a funny look on his face, silently watching me with an accusing glare that made it hard for me to know where to start. Sure I was sorry he'd been forced to watch me kill his father, but I wasn't the least bit sorry about what I'd done. It would have been nice to do it cleaner, but it didn't change the fact that Nathan

Marshall had to die—that he *deserved* to die—and I'd do it again without hesitation. Hopefully I could explain my reasons to Andrew, but I wouldn't blame him if he hated me.

"Listen, Andrew, my name is Michael Fox and I just wanted you to know—"

"Are you going to blow this place up?" he asked.

His first question didn't have anything to do with his dad and that caught me off guard. "Ah, yeah. That's the plan, anyway. Look, I'm real sorry about—"

"Will it work?" he cut me off again. "I mean, you're using more than just the gas in this room, I hope. This is a big building."

I didn't know how to respond to the way Andrew was acting. Didn't he want to discuss his father's death? Maybe not. I decided just to play along. "I know it is. I've opened every gas valve I can find in the building, and not just the oxygen. I found a shitload of portable ethylene and ether tanks down on the second and third floors. Even better, before I started sneaking around, I caused a massive oxygen and natural gas leak in the basement. Gas has been free-flowing and mixing throughout the building for quite a while now. I can't guarantee it, but my guess it there won't be much left of this place once I'm done."

"Good," Andrew said, and shocked me by smiling.

For a moment I wondered if he might be as crazy as his old man, but I soon realized it was a genuine smile. He was honestly happy and relieved to hear what I'd been up to.

"You're okay with that?" I asked.

"Absolutely. Listen, Michael, if I could step out of this chair, I'd do the same thing."

That was good to hear. Now, for the hard question.

"And your father? I hope you understand—"

"He was an evil bastard that got what he deserved,"

Andrew said, his quiet tone layered with years of bitterness and deep-seated hatred for the man lying between
us on the blood-soaked floor. "I understand perfectly.
Don't get me wrong, there was a day I loved my father
dearly, thought he could do no wrong and was a saint
for trying so hard to help me. That was before I found
out how many people he was hurting on my behalf. I
begged him to stop, but he just wouldn't listen."

"It's a shame," I said, trying to find some words that
might allay his guilty feelings. "Your father was a brilliant man—"

"He was brilliant, sure, but his brilliance took a
detour into madness and crazy obsession somewhere
along the line, a downward spiral that eventually led
to this. I mean, look at us! That man lying on the floor
isn't my father anymore; hasn't been for a long time.
Not the father I loved and respected, anyway. It might
sound cold, but I'm glad he's dead. Somebody had to
stop him."

I dug into my pocket and showed Andrew the Bic
lighter I had, getting it ready for the big show.

"The job's only half done. We have to blow this place
off the face of the earth so no one else can walk in and
take over where your dad left off. I have no problem dying, but what about you, Andrew? I overheard you tell
your father you'd rather die than live like this. Did you
mean that?"

"Of course. I've wanted that for years now but I've
never been able to pull it off. I was either too sick or just
didn't have the body parts to hold a gun or pop a bottle
of pills."

Yeah, I know that feeling. Poor bugger.

"Good, 'cause I don't think there's any way I can get
you out of here. Drake's security team is going to start
looking around soon. We're relatively safe up here, I
think, but I couldn't get you out the door. Besides, I'm

too busted up to carry you, so I guess we'll just wait here together and take it easy. Sound okay?"

"Sounds fine, but why do *you* need to die? I agree you can't take me, I wouldn't go even if you could, but there's no need for you to stick around."

"Sure there is. Who's going to set off the explosion if I'm not here?"

"Well, me, obviously."

"You? But you're paralyzed."

"I'm paralyzed for the most part, but not everything. I can still wiggle my fingers, especially on my right hand. Here, look—"

Sure enough, he could move a few of his fingers on his left hand, and all of the ones on his right. I watched him wiggle his right thumb rapidly up and down and I couldn't believe it. It was almost as if fate, or some other higher power, had preordained that Andrew would need to use that digit for something important.

Like flicking the Bic.

I shouldn't have thought that. Shouldn't have even considered it. I'd never for a moment envisioned the possibility I might live through this day, but now that I had, my mind started racing, my heart pounding, and the short hair stood up on the back of my neck. A big shit-kicker grin was slowly creeping onto my face and I tried to kid myself it was only the oxygen-saturated air making me feel so giddy.

Maybe Andrew's right. If he can operate this lighter, I could slip down to the fourth-floor hallway, use the back stairs to get outside, and go hide in the woods. Get a front row seat to watch the fireworks!

Those were bad thoughts—silly thoughts—and I had to stop right now before they started making sense. There was no way I could leave Andrew up here to finish this. It was my job to do. My responsibility. Wasn't it?

Seeing the confusion on my face, Andrew pressed

the issue. "I can do it. I know I can. Here, let me show you I can hold it."

Curious, but all the time cursing myself for starting to get my hopes up, I handed Andrew the lighter, helping him get it into the correct position and seeing if he could hold on. He did. Easily.

"What did I tell ya?" Andrew said, probably more excited and happy than he'd been in twenty years.

I could tell he really wanted to do this—*needed* to, maybe.

"Are you sure you want to do this alone?" I asked. I already knew the answer, but needed to hear Andrew say it one more time before my conscience would allow me to leave.

"More than you'll ever know, Michael. I'm the reason my father became obsessed with transplantation and if it wasn't for me, none of this would exist. All those people died because of me."

"That's not true," I said. "Your father's to blame. Maybe Drake, too, but none of this was your fault."

Andrew sat quietly for a moment, a single tear sliding down his cheek. "I know that, I really do, but it still doesn't make me feel any better. There's no denying a lot of people would be alive today if I'd just died at birth. I can't do anything about that, but I can at least do this. My fault or not, I started this madness; it's only right I be the one that ends it. My life has to have had some purpose. Maybe this is it."

How could I possibly argue with that? Life had been cruel to Andrew. He'd been getting the short end of the stick his entire life. If being the one who triggered the explosion would give him a sense of satisfaction, closure, or perhaps atonement for all the suffering and death inflicted on his behalf, who was I to stand in his way?

I wheeled his chair over beside the cluster of emergency oxygen tanks. "Let the gas build up for as long as you can, okay? The longer, the better. Soon as you see a security guard's head pop out of this stairwell, let that thumb of yours work its magic. Don't worry about me. If I'm not out of here by then it's my own bloody fault. Understand?"

"Get moving, then," Andrew said, a contented smile on his face. "My trigger finger's getting mighty itchy."

I nodded, and headed for the stairs.

CHAPTER FORTY-ONE

I picked up the gun off the top stair and made my way down onto the fourth floor as quickly and quietly as I could. I was in big-time pain, hurting all over, but there was nothing I could do except clench my teeth and keep moving. Turning the bend in the hall I made my way toward the back stairs and was nearly at the exit when I heard the sound of heavy boots stamping on the other side of the door, getting closer.

Guards!

Had to be, which meant the search was on. Sound echoed in the stairwell, so I wasn't exactly sure if they were coming to this floor or were still down on level two or three. Didn't matter; if they were on the way up it meant I couldn't risk charging down the stairs to get outside. That would be suicide, and now that I'd been given the opportunity, I desperately wanted to live to see this hellhole crumble. As much as I wanted out of here, I needed to slow down and think. The front stairs would be just as bad of a choice, maybe worse, because Drake would have his men trained well and I was sure they'd post someone to man each stairwell, covering the exits. There had to be another way—a safer, un-guarded way—out of here.

My mind drew a blank. I couldn't think of a single thing to try and I was seriously considering returning to the tower room to see this through to the end alongside Andrew. Either that or take the mad dash down the back stairs and hope for the best. I had Drake's gun if need be, but I couldn't really picture myself doing a Lone Ranger sprint into a crowd of security guards, gun blazing, and consequences be damned. Just wasn't my style.

Limping back along the corridor, my heart nearly stopped when I heard shouting coming from just around the corner. I tensed up, brought my gun into what I thought was a respectable policeman's shooting stance, and waited. Ten grueling seconds went by but nothing happened. I lowered my weapon and peeked around the corner only to find the hallway empty. I was starting to relax when I heard the voice again, this time coming from inside the room on my right.

The Bleeders' room.

I approached the door, noticing that it was half open. I tried to recall if I'd left it that way when I exited the room but I couldn't remember. With my heart doing a drumroll within my chest, I shoved the door wide open and prepared to shoot anything that moved.

The room was empty. Well, empty of living, breathing, ready-to-kill-me people, at least. Dr. Marshall's blood bank looked just the way I'd left it—a sticky red mess and stinking of death. The phantom voice sounded again, but this time I realized where it was coming from and what was happening.

Drake's walkie-talkie.

The voices I kept hearing were the other security guards shouting for Drake and communicating amongst themselves via radio. I felt like a goof, wasting precious minutes and nearly giving myself a heart attack over nothing, but it wasn't a total loss. If I grabbed Drake's

radio and carried it with me, I'd have a better idea where
the guards were and where they might be searching next.
That kind of information might get me out of here alive
so I walked in and slipped the walkie-talkie out of the
leather case on Drake's belt.

*Maybe I can say something on the radio and send the
guards all running on a wild-goose chase toward the front of
the building. Then I can slip out—*

Something caught my attention and shut me up, mid-
thought. The curtains in the room were pulled open today and outside of the window I could see the woods off
in the distance across the grass-covered field. I wasn't
looking that far away, though. What caught my eye was
the mass of green ivy leaves visible on the left side of the
window.

The metal trellis!

The same ivy-covered trellis I'd used to climb out of
my guarded room and up here to the fourth floor so
long ago, back when I was just starting to figure out the
truth about Dr. Marshall and his little castle of horrors.
It ran all the way up the side of the building to this
window, and, more importantly, all the way down to the
ground. I could crank open the window, climb down
the trellis and make a dash for the woods. From the
chitchat still going back and forth on Drake's radio, the
guards were busy doing a sweep of the third floor and it
was doubtful anyone would be watching the outside
grounds. Sure, someone might look out a window and
spot me, but at least I'd be outside and have a chance.
Definitely the best option I was likely to get, so I stuffed
Drake's radio in the front of my pants and decided to
go for it.

When I cranked open the left-hand window, a freezing blast of air hit me in the face, stealing my breath.
Man, it was cold out today. I wouldn't make it very far
outside in this weather, not the way I was dressed.

I needed a coat.

Turning around, I glanced at my own old coat I'd discarded on the floor earlier, but it was ripped and torn and so covered in Drake's blood I dismissed it immediately. That left only Drake's big security bomber jacket. It was bloody, too, but not nearly as bad as my own. Better yet, it was practically brand-new, and was made for this kind of frigid weather. I hated the thought of touching Drake again, but it had to be done. Thirty seconds later, I'd manhandled Drake's considerable deadweight and managed to wiggle the coat off his arms. Wrapped up in my nice warm coat that had a large gold patch proclaiming me the new chief of security around here, I headed back to the window and started to climb out.

Getting onto the trellis was tricky, only having one good hand, but once I'd swung onto the metal ladder, climbing down wasn't a problem. I had no way of knowing if anyone would be watching the windows, so I just started hobbling as fast as I could toward the entrance to the wooded trail, hoping my luck would hold up for a few more minutes.

It was a strange feeling, moving toward the relative safety of the woods, seeing it get closer but with every painful step fully expecting to get a bullet in my back. I didn't dare turn around and look, but in my imagination I could clearly see the members of Drake's security team all lined up in the windows taking aim at the center of my back, waiting for the signal to let the bullets fly. I'd hear someone shout, *"FIRE!"* on the radio tucked in my pants and half a second later feel the sting of a dozen bullets rip through my body, the sharpshooters peppering me with lead even after I went down and sprawled face-first in the frozen grass.

I reached the wooded trail without incident.

As I'd done earlier to stay out of sight, I lay down on

the ground off to the side of the path and spent a few seconds camouflaging myself with a blanket of leaves before finally looking back in the direction of the castle. Everything looked quiet. No one was rushing out into the cold after me, and nothing that was being said on the radio indicated that I'd been spotted. Somewhat surprised, I congratulated myself on a clean getaway. All I had to do now was lay still and wait for the big bang.

Let 'er rip, Andrew. Blow her straight to hell!

This was exciting stuff. I could hardly wait to see the first fireball and I didn't want to miss any of the show so I kept my eyes riveted on Andrew's tower. When he sparked the lighter, that room would be the first to go.

Ten minutes passed and nothing happened.

Even the guards were staying silent on the radio and that was starting to worry me. What if they'd discovered my plan and were quickly and quietly going around shutting the gas valves and opening windows to air out the rooms? Or what if the guards had rushed the tower room and grabbed the lighter before Andrew could ignite the gas? Or Andrew had accidentally dropped the lighter onto the floor, and being paralyzed, couldn't move to pick it back up?

All of those scenarios were valid reasons for worry, and with every passing minute, the tension in me was cranked up a notch. Leaving Andrew alone might have been a big mistake.

Dammit! Should I go back?

Maybe.

Probably.

Yes.

Leaving my bed of leaves behind, I started back across the grassy field, not having a clue what I intended to do once I made it back to the castle. I could head for one of the basement windows and—

BOOM!

The tower room detonated, the sudden explosion catching me unprepared, a mighty crack of thunder smashing into my eardrums from what seemed like two feet away. It was a good thing I still had most of the field between the building and me, or I'd be a goner. Andrew's room was there one second, gone the next, and then the sky darkened and started to rain chunks of brick. Chunks of Andrew and a guard or two, as well, I'd imagine, but I tried not to think about that. I hit the deck, curling into a ball on the grass, protecting my head with my arms.

Seconds later, there was a huge explosion on the fourth floor, followed immediately by an overlapping series of minidetonations throughout the building. When the basement blew, it appeared that the entire four-story structure—foundation and all—lifted fifteen feet into the air, the superheated gases expanding and pushing upward in the same way volcanic eruptions occur. There was no lava flow from the basement, but fires raged and the thickest, blackest smoke I'd ever seen came pouring out to obscure the final explosions that tore Nathan Marshall's research facility apart at the seams.

I never saw the castle come back down to earth, but I sure heard it. There was a tremendous *growl* within the swirling smoke, then a volley of jarring *thuds* that shook the ground under me like an earthquake. I had my head buried and my eyes tightly shut, praying none of the thousands of pounds of concrete, brick, steel, plaster, and glass being torn apart and thrown skyward would land on me, crushing me in my moment of triumph.

I kept my eyes closed for a long time, feeling very much like Chicken Little as the sky fell all around me. Nothing touched me. Not a thing. When I opened my eyes, the billowing smoke was so thick over where the building had been, I couldn't tell how much damage I'd actually done. Had I demolished the entire structure, or did some of it still stand, untouched? As black and acrid-smelling as the smoke was, it had to be the oil furnace reservoirs that were burning. If that were the case, the fire might rage for a while yet. I sat up with my legs crossed at my ankles, and waited.

It gets awfully quiet after a large explosion. Too quiet. Once the fires and smoke died down a little, I could see that my hopes had been granted—there was nothing left of the castle except a large hole in the ground. I should have felt ecstatic, but in all honesty, what I felt most was empty. Everyone that I'd channeled my hatred, fear, and anger into for so long, as now gone. Dr. Marshall, Drake, the security team, whichever of the cruel doctors, nurses, and orderlies unlucky enough to have been on duty today—all gone in the destruction that had just ended. I felt like the sole survivor of a terrible plane crash, sitting here amid the debris scattered over a three-hundred-foot blast radius. It was a creepy feeling, alone among the charred pieces of the dead, so I tried thinking about me and what I should do next to get my mind focused on something different.

Bad idea.

My thoughts about the people who'd just been blown apart started me thinking about my own new body and how it was also made from pieces of the dead. From there, my thoughts swirled darker and darker, wondering where I was supposed to go from here. Where could a freak like me possibly fit in? And would I even be given a choice? When the authorities finally showed up, it wouldn't take long for them to realize I wasn't exactly an innocent bystander. One look at my body by a policeman or an ambulance attendant and the gig was up. I'd soon find myself hurried off—for my own protection, of course—to some hospital room, where they'd poke and prod me until someone with more power got wind of me and sent his own people to poke and prod me more thoroughly.

I had a bleak vision of my life becoming a never-ending series of tests and medical examinations, every doctor, scientist, and government official in the country vying for the right to keep me as their own personal oversized lab rat. It would happen, too, I wasn't just being paranoid this time. Nathan Marshall had been a brilliant man and his success with me was a huge leap forward in nerve regeneration and transplantation research. For science, finding me would be the equivalent of the Wright brothers getting their hands on a space shuttle. They wouldn't stop testing, scanning, questioning, examining, pushing, pulling and molesting every square inch of me—body and mind—until they uncovered all of Dr. Marshall's secrets. The same secrets I'd vowed to destroy along with the rest of this place.

Son of a bitch!

What had I done? Here I thought I'd had the last laugh on everyone, the bum who had defied the odds to defeat the mad scientist and destroy his research forever. Only now was I realizing I should have stayed in the building and went up in smoke along with everyone else.

Briefly, I considered taking off, disappearing before anyone showed up to investigate the explosions. No one knew I was here so all I had to do was slip away and never say a word to anyone. People who saw me would cringe at my scars but with the crowd I hung out with it wouldn't really matter much. Blue J would still be my friend, regardless of how hideous I looked.

It was a nice dream but I knew it couldn't happen. For one, someone would rat me out eventually and someone would come to check out the mysterious reports of the homeless Frankenstein monster. Even if that didn't happen, and people just left me alone, I was on several antirejection medications to keep my body from attacking all the foreign parts. They were expensive drugs that I'd have no way of getting my hands on. Without them, my body's immune system would start waging war in a hurry. If I went back to live with Blue J and Puckman, within a few weeks I'd start getting sick and I'd be dead before Christmas.

Stay here or take off? Either way I was screwed.

I had no idea what to do. No idea what I *could* do. Then I heard a noise coming from a long way off in the woods. It was a familiar sound that put a smile on my face and erased the nagging questions in my mind. I rose to my feet, instantly knowing what I had to do. Turning away for the smoking chaos I'd created, I started hobbling back toward the woods, hearing the sound again, only closer this time.

The lonely sound of an approaching train whistle.

PART FIVE

THE END

CHAPTER FORTY-TWO

Full circle.

For obvious reasons, those words were stuck in my head and I couldn't shake them. The idea of things always returning to where they'd begun was a total crock, but there was no denying the notion appealed to me. After all, if I was going to kill myself I had a perfectly good gun that would do the trick with one pull of the trigger. There was no reason for me to lug my battered, aching body through the woods on a freezing cold day just to achieve the same goal on a railroad track I might never find, much less find before the train passed me by.

But something inside of me wanted to try.

Swallowing Drake's gun would be quicker, easier, and far less messy, but that was part of the reason I didn't want to end my sad excuse of a life that way. The bullet would ruin my head and send my soul packing—if I still had a soul left—but it would leave the scientists my body intact to slice, dice and dissect at will and I wasn't going to let that happen. The train, although harder to get to and a potentially agonizing death if it didn't kill me on first impact, would at least leave nothing behind bigger than a bread box. I'd seen pictures of train wreck victims and, man oh man, most had to be scraped up off the tracks and put into little plastic freezer baggies. Let the government scientists try do their research on me that way. Good luck.

More importantly, when they identified my remains on the railway track, my daughter Arlene would still get her college fund from my life insurance policy. Good old dental records. At least my teeth were still my own. Arlene and Gloria would have no idea why I was out wandering in the woods so far from Buffalo, but neither would anyone else. No one knew I had ever been here, which was good. The insurance people could squawk but in the end they'd have to pay. That thought put a smile on my face.

I couldn't remember crossing any train tracks when Jackson had been marching me to my death along the wooded trail, and I'd walked a fair distance along it. My guess was Dr. Marshall and Drake had known where the tracks were and made the trail out to their macabre graveyard in the opposite direction. It wouldn't do to have the railroad crews passing by just as Drake was dumping a fresh body into a shallow grave. People tend to remember things like that. No, the tracks would be nowhere near the trail, so when the path veered to the right, I cut into the trees and headed left.

I was fairly confident I'd find the tracks, but not at all sure if I'd make it on time. Judging from its whistle, the train had seemed to be fairly close, but the way sound travels in the open woods, there was a better chance it might still be miles away.

I hurried as fast as I could manage, my knee throbbing in time with each step across the uneven, leaf-shrouded terrain. The trail far behind me now, my sense of direction was getting all screwed up. There was nothing to see but trees and bushes. No wonder people always got lost in the woods. Every bloody thing looked the same. For ten minutes I charged forward, one foot in front of the other, hoping I was headed in a reasonably straight line. Ahead of me, the land started to slope upward, and when I crested the hill the trees fell away and I suddenly found myself standing on large chunks of rock and gravel instead of frozen dirt.

The tracks were twelve feet in front of me.

Bingo!

Had the train passed already? That was the question. I walked out into the center of the tracks and looked both ways. Nothing. The track was straight as an arrow and clear for miles on my right. I was on a bit of a curve heading to my left, but I could still see for a long distance down the line. I considered going down on my knees and putting my ear to the track like I'd seen train robbers and Indians do countless times in the old Western movies, but my knee hurt too much to bend and I didn't know what to do once I got down there. Were you supposed to put your ear to the track and listen for the *chug-a-chug-a* sound of the approaching train wheels, or was the purpose to feel the silent vibrations along the steel rail?

Either way, it wasn't necessary. One look at the top of the rails told me everything I needed to know—the train hadn't passed yet. There was rust on them, which would have been scratched and buffed shiny had a couple of hundred steel wheels jostled and rolled over them recently.

As if to confirm my deduction, the train whistle blared again, louder this time, making me jump and twist my bad knee again. I fell to the ground between the tracks and tried getting back up but it hurt like a bugger and wasn't really worth the effort. I made it to a sitting position, straddling the one rail, and decided to stay there. I'd be less likely to be seen low to the ground like this, and the engineer wouldn't slam on the brakes to try stopping the train. I wanted him going full bore when we had our first kiss. It had to be less painful that way, and the damage to my body would be much greater. Especially the way I was sitting, one leg on either side of the rail.

The whistle had sounded off to my left, and just now I could see the front cowcatcher and the louvered steel radiator grille of the big diesel engine rumble into view. Despite the curve, I had a fairly unimpeded line of sight in that direction but it was still hard to tell how far away the train was, or how long I had until it was on top of me. All I could do was wait it out.

Do you really want to do it this way?

Good question. I was nervous and scared. There was no sense denying that. Far more scared than I'd been on the Carver Street tracks back in Buffalo. There was no reason why—I was more than ready to die, glad I might finally be helping Arlene, and more than a little excited about the possibility of seeing my wife and son again—but deliberately sitting in the path of a speeding locomotive takes a lot of balls and makes even the bravest of men rethink their plans.

Maybe I should just shoot myself now, let the train destroy my body when I'm already dead and gone.

Now that was tempting, but it might not work. I wasn't a big guy and I was seriously worried I'd fall between the tracks and the train would scoot right over the top without touching me. It might clip a leg or a foot off, but again, that would leave the scientists more of me than was acceptable. No, I'd come this far; I was determined to see it through to the end.

As far back as I can remember, even as a young boy, I'd always loved trains, and being run over by one wasn't as bad of a way to die as you might think. The aftermath is nasty, absolutely, but death would be instantaneous and relatively painless. One quick *SLAM*, and it's over. My body might be strewn over a mile of track, but my suffering would only last a second. That's not so bad. I could get through that.

The train was getting closer, smoking along the track, maybe two hundred yards away. I closed my eyes and tried to conjure up a picture of Jackie, thinking the sight of my wife would be the perfect way to end things, but I couldn't do it knowing the train was barreling down on me the way it was. I couldn't keep my eyes closed, some masochistic need forcing me to watch my death approaching.

One hundred and twenty yards to go.

So far there'd been no whistles or the shrill screech of brakes to indicate that anyone had spotted me. That was good. At the speed they were traveling, even if someone did see me sitting here, there wouldn't be enough track left between us to safely stop the train now. We'd passed the point of no return, as they say, which brought a smile to my face. I'd suffered a lot in the last four and a half years—from my family's tragic car accident, to my subsequent downward spiral that left my daughter hating me and me living on the streets, to my time in Hell here with Dr. Marshall and Drake— and it was all finally coming to an end. It should have ended back in Buffalo, back before I let Drake and the promise of easy wealth lure me into this crazy detour, but I wasn't even unhappy about that mistake.

If I'd killed myself as originally planned, Dr. Marshall and Drake would still be alive, carrying on their warped sense of scientific advancement for years—maybe decades—to come. Countless people would have suffered and died at their cruel hands, but that wouldn't happen now. I didn't consider myself a hero, no way, but I'd proven to myself I was more than the worthless expendable bum they'd thought I was. It was useless to think it now, but maybe my daughter would have been proud of me. It made me feel better to think so, anyway.

Good-bye, Arlene. Take care of yourself, sweetie.

Fifty yards, and still coming hard.

There wasn't much left to say. Not really. No words of wisdom or epic conclusions about life sprang into my head. My life didn't even flash in front of my eyes the way you always hear it does at times like this. That sucked. I'd been looking forward to that. I wasn't sure if this was the end of everything, or perhaps the beginning of the next phase in my existence. I'd never been big on religion, but in my heart of hearts I'd also never really given up hope God was out there somewhere, keeping an eye on me even if I wasn't worthy of his attention.

Thirty yards, and closing.

With death racing toward me on multiple steel wheels, and the wooden ties below me vibrating with the approaching thunder, I began to pray. If anyone was listening, I asked for only one thing. I wanted to hold my wife and son in my arms again, hold Jackie and little Daniel close and kiss them and try my best to apologize for the damage I'd done. I'd made a mess of Arlene's life but I'd outright destroyed theirs. They'd both deserved far better than me but perhaps I could make it up to them in the afterlife. For one chance at that, for a shot at redemption in their eyes, I'd sit here and face a thousand trains. Ten thousand. Love can be funny that way.

Ten yards away.

Five yards.

Two.

Turn the page for an advance look
at Gord Rollo's next terrifying novel . . .

CRIMSON

Coming in April 2009

IN THE BEGINNING . . .

The Genesis of a Small Town's Fear

Dunnville, Ontario—June 21, 1955

A tall, heavyset old man walks along a desolate country road by the cloud-filtered light of the summer moon. In his wake he leaves a dotted crimson trail dripping from the blood-smeared head of the axe casually slung over his left shoulder. He is oblivious to the cool north wind blowing the thin branches of the willow trees around him into a lashing frenzy. His feverish mind is a jumble of broken thoughts: *Get home, Jacob, before the police . . . that fucking bastard, Sanderson. How dare he try . . . get hold of yourself. You've gotta . . . the blood, oh how I love that sweet coppery taste . . .*

Jacob stops at the end of a narrow gravel driveway, not entirely sure where—or for that matter, who—he is, until he glances at the battered metal mailbox with the crudely painted HARRISON scrawled on both sides. *Ah yes . . .* he thinks, shambling over to smear a big red *X* over his family name with the sticky liquid covering his trembling hands.

Home sweet home . . .

Vivid images of his family flash helter-skelter through his confused mind, rapid-fire snapshots of recent days and years long past. Emma and Jacob smiling on their wedding day, her white dress badly wrinkled from sneaking out of the party for a quickie in the barn loft . . . Holding little Emily in his arms last year, joy etched on his face at having fathered such a beautiful child so late in life . . . His oldest son Josh spitting out a mouthful of thick, syrupy blood after Jacob smashed his face against the dining room wall, two front teeth still stuck in the otherwise smooth plaster surface . . . Proudly walking hand in hand with the two boys when they were little, heading to their favorite fishing hole in the woods . . . Christmas day five or six years ago and Jacob dressed in a red Santa hat, merrily dancing around the brightly lit tree . . . Plunging a fork into Jack's throat to shut up his youngest son and finally stop the whiny little bastard's screaming . . . Using his body to hold Emma down as he sawed through the wrist bones of her left arm with a rusty hacksaw . . .

These images and more swirling out of the dark abyss his consciousness has become. Part of him is sickened by these vivid memories, making him long for better days, but part of him also rejoices, reveling in the blood, torture, and pain. Death has come to the small Canadian town of Dunnville, and madness is Jacob's only companion now.

The shrill blare of a distant police siren brings Jacob out of his reverie. *The cops.* He knows they'll be coming for him soon, once they realize what he's done to Danny Sanderson back at the textile factory.

He turns from the mailbox to gaze toward the house at the end of the gravel drive. The Harrison farmhouse is a large two-story wooden box with a covered porch tacked on the side facing the road. There's a floodlight on the porch, but it's unlit. In fact, none of the lights in the house are burning, the visible windows as black as Jacob's murderous mood. Devoid of life now but not empty of occupants. Jacob's family is still there—most parts of them, anyway—keeping a quiet vigil along with the gathering flies, waiting patiently for his return.

"They're all . . ."

Dead, Jacob is about to say, a smile forming on his bloody lips, but before he can spit the word out, over the noise of the howling wind, he hears a sound from within his home.

A baby crying.

Emily?

He's forgotten about Emily. Sweet little Emily, who until recently has been the light of his life. How long has she been left alone, lying in darkness, in filth, amid the slowly rotting bits and pieces of the family she'd never know? Jacob doesn't know the answer to this question, and the weight of the shame that washes over him brings him to his knees. His mind is clear for the first time in months, crystal clear, but the dementia returns almost immediately, clamping down on him like a steel-toothed bear trap. A war rages within him, an internal battle between good and evil, sanity and oblivion, life and death.

Thirty seconds later, Jacob Harrison regains his feet and begins walking toward the porch. He's dragging the axe behind him, cleaving a thin groove in the gravel as he approaches the stairs. There is no emotion on his face, no pictures racing through his thoughts. He's a man on a mission now, his decision unalterable, knowing exactly what must be done.

Inside the house, Jacob heads straight for the child, homing in on the infant in the dark by her high-pitched squeals. He finds her underneath an end table in the living room, wrapped in a blood-, urine-, and feces-soaked bath towel, half-hidden by an old newspaper. Emily is disgustingly dirty and screaming loud enough to shatter glass, but she's unhurt. Jacob hurries her to the large country kitchen, where he gently places her in the sink and washes her soiled body with soapy warm water. After she is thoroughly clean, Jacob gets her a bottle filled with apple juice from the refrigerator. Emily, starving and dehydrated from neglect, greedily slurps it down. After the bottle is drained, Jacob finds her pacifier and soon little Emily is fast asleep in her father's powerful arms.

Jacob quietly searches for what he needs, careful not to make any noise that might wake the child. He finds the large metal pan on the floor in the walk-in pantry. He places Emily inside the deep pan, and then Jacob, without thought, without emotion, without remorse, carries the pan back into the kitchen, pops it in the oven, and cranks the temperature dial up to its highest setting.

Jacob then turns away from the kitchen and heads up the staircase to Jack and Josh's bedroom at the rear of the house. He retrieves a thick rope from the boys' closet, skillfully fashions a perfect hangman's noose, and slings the rope over an exposed rafter in the ceiling. He takes a moment to scribble a quick suicide note for the police, then gets up on Josh's bed to put his neck through the noose. Stone-faced and completely out of his mind, Jacob Harrison steps off the bed and into urban legend—his legacy of evil to influence the nightmares of the people of this small town for generations to come.

PRELUDE

Present Day

I was only a kid when it started, when we released the evil that would destroy our lives. Four of us—Tom, Peter, Johnny, and me, David. We set free a nightmare that warm Saturday in June of 1977, cursing our lives from that moment on.

We were only ten years old.

We lived in the small Canadian town of Dunnville, a rural Ontario farming community on the banks of the Grand River, near where its murky waters emptied into Lake Erie. The madness began on the day we released the creature, but everything was set in motion the day before, on Friday, the day Tom, Pete, and I met Johnny for the first time. He was the new kid in town, and fate saw to it that he became our grade five classmate.

Our whole class was shocked to find out Johnny and his mother had moved into the abandoned Harrison farmhouse on Logan Road. It was common knowledge to everyone in Dunnville that the farm was haunted. In 1955, twenty-two years earlier, Jacob Harrison had done something so vile, so terribly evil, no one would ever consider moving there. Everyone wanted it burned to the ground. So it sat empty, waiting for Johnny . . . and, eventually, the rest of us.

We were stupid enough to agree to go play at Johnny's house the next day, Saturday morning. We couldn't find a way of telling him about Old Man Harrison or the legacy of the house he was living in, so we didn't bother. Why should we have? Sure, Tom, Pete, and I were terrified of Old Man Harrison, but he was just a legend, a scary ghost story told around a roaring campfire. It was our buddy's place now, and nothing bad would happen to us there.

We were fools. The evil was waiting for us.

The line between imagination and reality is thin, my friend. Very thin indeed. Our tale begins at Johnny's farmhouse, on that Friday night in June of 1977, the night before we stepped over that line . . . and all hell broke loose.

BOOK ONE:

SCARED LITTLE BOYS

The Late Spring of 1977

CHAPTER ONE

Johnathan Page had a good life. He was poor, but had everything he needed. He'd dreaded moving out of the big city of Hamilton to come to a tiny town like Dunnville, but he already knew he loved it here. He'd met some decent friends, and no longer felt like an outsider, a nobody, like he had in the city. Here, he felt like he belonged.

Since arriving home from school, his mother had been lecturing him endlessly about how careful he should be. Mary Page was a huge woman with bleach-blonde hair who proudly admitted weighing two hundred and sixty pounds.

"You're not familiar with this place yet," she warned.

"I hear you, Ma," Johnny said. "I promise I'll be careful. Okay? I'm real tired. Think I'll hit the sheets."

Before his mother had a chance to drown him in her arms for her nightly kiss, Johnny hurried up the creaky old staircase, off to bed.

Mary exhaled deeply, wondering again if moving to this farm had been a good idea. Not that they had any choice—Johnny's father, George, had disappeared about eight years ago. Johnny had just turned two, and one rainy night George had failed to come home from work. The police didn't consider foul play, even though Mary stubbornly refused to believe George had simply walked out on her. Listening to Mrs. Page droning on about how good a wife she was convinced the police running away was exactly what he *had* done.

Mary and Johnny lived on as best they could with a quickly declining bank account. How was she going to look after her poor son without an income?

Her salvation had come in the form of a piece of paper. Mary's lawyer had been collecting the necessary paperwork for her to claim bankruptcy, when he'd found the deed to a house George had purchased before his disappearance. The Dunnville property had cost next to nothing, was fully paid, and Mary legally owned it. George had even rented the land to a local farmer, so suddenly Mary found herself with a new bank account with sixteen thousand dollars accrued from the land rental. She tried to sell the property and stay in Hamilton, but no matter how low she dropped the price nobody was interested. Eventually she packed up and brought her ten-year-old son to Dunnville to begin a new life.

Mary popped a dusty record onto an even dustier record player and settled into her favorite brown chair. She always promised herself that someday she'd get up and exercise a little, move to the rhythm of the big band music she loved, but she never worked up the energy to follow through with it. She did, however, imagine dancing to the music and losing weight. She'd get up and exercise for real soon—but not tonight. Tonight she'd just reach for a doughnut from the box on the table beside her, and chew along with the beat.

Upstairs in his bedroom, Johnny undressed in front of his window, the darkness outside turning the glass into a mirror. He was a good-looking kid with short-cropped blond hair and clear blue eyes. His tall, athletic body already showed signs of natural muscle. Still too young for vanity, he pulled on his pajamas and jumped into bed.

It made him happy that his mother seemed content here. He loved her very much; he just wished she'd cut him a little slack, stop being so overprotective. Johnny figured she secretly feared he'd abandon her like his father had. She'd never admit he left, but Johnny could see the truth reflected in her sad eyes. Personally, Johnny never hated his father for running out on them. He often wondered about his father and where he was now, but that was all.

Downstairs, he could hear the record player, but it didn't stop his eyelids from drooping. Even the scratching of the weeping willow's branches against his dirt-smeared window couldn't bring him back from the brink of sleep. In fact, the sound of the branches lulled him closer, the same way the endless roar of waves at a beach do for others. The record downstairs finished, and the old farmhouse on Logan Road returned to the quiet it had enjoyed for the past twenty-two years. One final soft brush from the willow's branches pulled him over the brink of consciousness into the dark chasm below.

The moment Johnny fell asleep, the wind abruptly stopped blowing. Having lost their partner, the willows along Logan Road swayed gently until they finally stood still, awaiting the next dance.

About seventy yards south from Johnny's bedroom window was an old, abandoned well. Twenty feet down into the murky, stagnant water lay a decomposing body. It had been there a long time and would be totally decomposed if not for the water staying cold during the summer and frozen in the winter.

At exactly the same time Johnny fell asleep and the

wind stopped blowing, the long-dead body at the bottom of the well slowly opened its eyes. From lifeless gray ovals, tiny pinholes of crimson began to form, which grew into bulging red orbs illuminating the dead man's face in the deep water's blackness. In that piercing red glow, it slowly examined itself to see how it had fared in its long and lonely sleep. Its skin was almost gone, but everything else seemed to have survived, the rest of its body thriving in its watery grave.

It felt incredibly strong as it flexed its massive chest muscles around an unbeating heart. It had somehow become bigger. Uncurled and standing, it would tower well over seven feet. Its hands had also changed. At the tip of each heavily muscled digit was a six-inch spear of bone that punctured through the end of the man's fingers. The spears were razor sharp, and as an experiment, the creature brutally sunk its index finger deep into its left knee. It sliced through the bone and tendons as easy as a wood sliver stabs into the tender flesh underneath a fingernail. The creature removed its finger with a sickening plop that echoed under the well's foul water. The kneecap was left with a gaping wound that spilled blue blood, threatening to cloud up the already murky water. The blood only flowed for a moment before the wound began to heal. Within seconds the knee looked as old and rotted as it had before.

Everything I had hoped is coming true, the creature thought.

If the creature had still possessed a full set of lips, it would have smiled. However, the smile would have quickly disappeared as it remembered it was still a prisoner of the well. Not for long, though, because someone must have moved into the farmhouse—otherwise it wouldn't have awakened tonight.

Its body was trapped in a watery grave, but that didn't

mean the creature couldn't find out what was going on. Up through the murky depths its mind's eye traveled, slithering along the cool grass, and immediately sensing two occupants within the house. It moved in for a closer look.

Mary Page awoke with a start, the phonograph player crackling with static. The record had ended and was skipping continually at the end of its groove. While putting the record away, an overpowering feeling that she was being watched came over her. She spun quickly to see if anyone was there, but moved too fast. Her hefty body wasn't used to sudden movements and she lost her balance, crashing down hard on the coffee table, pieces of wood flying everywhere. All thoughts of being watched forgotten, she picked herself up and hobbled off to bed.

Upstairs, Johnny slept on. He dreamed of his friends and the fun things they could do tomorrow. He also dreamed that an angel was outside his window protecting him and his mother. Again, he heard the scraping of the branches against his window. This time, however, the sound didn't soothe him into deeper sleep. The scratching sounded like long claws scraping against bone. In his dream, the angel morphed into a sickening beast with long talons for fingers, trying desperately to get into his room to tear him to shreds. What terrified him most about the dream was the creature's eyes. Johnny sat up to get a closer look, and when the creature made eye contact with him, its eyes glowed bloodred.

Outside his window, the creature's mind's eye dreamed along with Johnny and was finally satisfied. It slipped back toward the well where its decaying body waited.

You might be the one. I've been waiting a long time for

you, my friend. Don't worry about anything, Johnny. I'll take good care of you . . . and your friends.

The abomination reared back and howled with laughter, releasing great torrents of black water from its lungs. The well literally churned with evil laughter for a moment, but soon the monster settled down to wait for its new "friends."

Contented, the creature closed its fiery eyes and plunged back into restful blackness. The moment its eyes closed, the wind outside began to blow again, and the trees along Logan Road slowly resumed their dance.

CHAPTER TWO

David Winter reluctantly crawled out of bed at 6:34 A.M. and began getting dressed. He was feeling depressed. His large hazel eyes stared blankly into some far-off imaginary world, while he unconsciously fiddled his pudgy fingers through his tangled mop of dark curly hair. He was so preoccupied with other thoughts that he failed to notice the outfit he threw on didn't match. One white athletic sock had been lying next to a gray one, so he pulled them on. His blue sweatpants didn't coordinate with his orange pumpkin T-shirt either, but fashion was the last thing on his mind today.

David sat for a few minutes with his hands in his pockets and his mind in the clouds, delaying his trip to Johnny's for as long as possible. David truly believed Old Man Harrison would be waiting for him and his friends today. No matter how often he told himself he was being stupid, that Jacob Harrison had died over twenty years ago, the feelings of dread simply wouldn't go away. He finally made his way downstairs. Rice Krispies® didn't sound very appetizing and the thought of runny eggs was even worse, so he headed out the back door, deciding against breakfast.

The slam of the door closing startled Steven Winter out of a pleasant dream where he and Donna were rich and didn't need to work for a living. The booming noise brought him back to reality, and he jumped out of bed to see what had caused the racket. Out of his window, he could see his son wandering aimlessly in the backyard.

Steven and Donna worked on their three-hundred-acre tomato farm, left to Steven by his father ten years back. He was a big, powerful man with thinning dark brown hair, while Donna was his mirror opposite, a tiny wisp of a woman with long blonde hair flowing down to her waist. They toiled hard to eke out an existence from the soil, and the last thing either of them needed was a son startling them out of a restful sleep.

Donna entered the bedroom and surprised Steven when she wrapped her arms around his midsection. He had thought she was still curled up in bed.

"Whoa, big guy . . . it's only me," she said. "Didn't mean to sneak up on you; I just wanted to say good morning."

"Sorry, Donna, I didn't mean to jump. I just got a bit of a fright when the back door slammed. I've told that boy a thousand times not to bang it on his way out."

"David seems a little weird today, actually," Donna said. "I got up to go to the bathroom and saw him with this really sad look on his face, like he was scared or worried about something."

"I think I know something that might cheer him up."

Without another word to his wife, Steven quickly dressed and was outside talking to David in the backyard. From the bedroom window Donna watched their brief conversation, and noticed a big smile light up David's face. Moments later, David was racing out of sight and her husband was coming back upstairs.

"What did you say to get a smile like that?"

"I asked him if he'd help me out this afternoon. I told him it was time to crucify Rodney again."

Johnny Page woke with the shocking thought that he'd wet the bed. His legs and feet were wet and he could feel the embarrassing and unpleasant way his Captain America pajamas clung to his skinny legs. When he opened his eyes, he received an even bigger shock. He hadn't wet the bed after all. In fact, he wasn't even *in* bed. Johnny was outside in the backyard, his legs dangling into the old well.

He was soaked from the waist down, the cold water causing him to shiver uncontrollably, his legs literally numb as he dragged them out of the stinking black water. Waking up to discover he'd been sleepwalking was one thing, but to pull his legs out of the water and discover they were covered in huge, black, pulsating bloodsuckers—well, that was quite another.

Johnny began screaming, a high-pitched wail of shock and horror he couldn't contain. No wonder his legs were numb. Countless leeches had been feeding on his legs for who knew how long. The parts of his legs not covered were pale and pasty white.

Johnny began frantically picking and clawing at the slimy beasts, desperate to get them off. He'd heard stories that you could only get them off by burning them, but thankfully they detached from his legs easily, dropping into the filthy water with a sickening plop.

Mary Page thundered out the back door and charged over to him. Johnny removed the last of the leeches just before his mother reached the well. His relief was so great he did something he hadn't willingly done in over two years. He stumbled to his feet and gratefully hugged his mother, who'd come to the rescue with open arms.

"What the dickens is going on here?" she asked, noticing her son's pale, blood-smeared legs.

Johnny had many answers flash through his head. He desperately wanted to cry in his mother's arms and tell her how horrible it had been to wake up covered in leeches, but he couldn't. He knew how overprotective she was. She'd probably send him to his room and forbid him from playing with his new friends.

"Johnny, what's wrong? I wake up hearing you screaming loud enough to scare the devil, and then I find you soaking wet with blood on your legs."

"Nothing's wrong, Ma," he said. "I was dangling my feet in the well and I slipped and scraped my legs on the sides. Sorry. I just scared myself a little."

Johnny could see a fat juicy leech squirming on the ground a few inches from his mother's brightly painted big toenail. Johnny didn't want her to see the sucker and possibly make the connection with the blood on his legs. It wouldn't take a genius to find a few other leeches and notice the suction marks on his legs. Thankfully, just before the leech reached his mother's toe she wheeled away, dragging him toward the house.

"You'll be the death of me yet, boy. I told you yesterday about being careful, didn't I? You never listen to your old mom, even though all I ever do is try to take care of you. Maybe if your father were still here, you'd listen to him. He wouldn't put up with your silliness, I can assure you. There had better not be any trouble with those kids here today either, or I'll send them straight home and you to your bed. Understand?"

Johnny nodded, his solemn expression breaking into a grin the second his mother turned her great expansive rear toward him. Happy again, he quickly headed up the stairs and into the bath. He wanted to be ready when his friends arrived.

The creature at the bottom of the well was happy too. As the blood-bloated leeches drifted down through the murky water, it snatched them out of the darkness, stuffing its mouth. Its razor-sharp fangs easily sliced into the soft tender flesh of the leeches, sending gushes of blood into and down its rotting throat like it was eating ripe, juicy, orange slices.

Johnny's blood, it thought evilly, stuffing another bloodsucker into its already filled mouth. *You taste delicious. I can hardly wait to taste your friends.*

As the creature enjoyed its "breakfast," it sent its mind's eye into the house again. It was pleased to find out Johnny's friends were still coming over. It was even happier when it found out that Johnny, who was undressing to take his bath, was only now discovering that one repulsively fat leech had crawled up his shorts and attached itself to the bottom of his scrotum.

"Hurry up, Pete . . . Tom's here," shouted Ken Myers, peering up the stairs in hope of catching his younger brother's attention. "What's taking you so long?" he tried one last time, before returning to the living room disgusted to tell Tom what kind of an idiot he'd chosen for a friend. Deep down Ken loved his younger brother, but you'd have a hard time getting him to admit it.

"I'll be right down . . . keep your shirt on," Pete shouted over the railing, his mouth still full of peppermint toothpaste. He returned to the bathroom to rinse his mouth, then bolted for the staircase.

"Hold it, mister," said his father.

Mark Myers was a handsome man in his early forties, a single father who had raised his sons to listen. He had a steely voice that commanded respect. Lately, a touch of gray had started invading his dark curly locks, but this distinguished look only added to his authority. Skidding to a stop at the top of the stairway, Peter apprehensively walked back to his father's bedroom, but relief flooded through him when he found out his father only wanted him to go switch off the bathroom light.

"I've told you a thousand times to remember to turn off the lights, but you never listen. Everyone forgets from time to time, Pete, but you always do. You really want me to ground you over something so stupid? Promise you'll at least try and remember."

Pete promised he'd try, then hurried back to the bathroom. He paused to gaze at his reflection in the mirror, trying once more to wet down a stubborn cowlick at the back of his head. Pete had the same dark curly hair as his father, and could never keep his wild locks in check. No matter how much spit he put on it, the cowlick sprang right back up.

"Great," he muttered to his small freckled reflection. "Not only do I have to go to a haunted house today, I have to go there looking like Alfalfa." That thought brought a grin to his face, but his smile vanished as he thought about the Harrison farm. He really liked Johnny, but he wasn't sure he liked him enough to spend time there.

Pete didn't actually know the whole story of what had happened on Old Man Harrison's farm all those years ago. He'd heard the start countless times, but just as the story began to reach its gory conclusion, Pete would always get scared and leave. Jacob Harrison had done something ghastly to his family, but Pete didn't know what. He didn't want to know either. He was more into making people laugh than trying to scare anyone.

Another yell from his brother brought Pete back from his daydreams. He reluctantly accepted that all the spit in the world wasn't going to make his hair look any better, so he flipped the light switch and headed downstairs.

All this time, Tom Baker had sat on the couch watching Saturday morning cartoons. He normally laughed himself sick watching Bugs Bunny and the rest of the crew, but today he barely cracked a smile. He sat rigid and tense, managing to look far bigger and older than his age. He had dark brown hair too, the same as Pete's, but his was straight and fell down to his shoulders.

His thoughts were also centered on the Harrison farm, but they were different than Pete's. Pete had a naïve fear of the farm, whereas Tom had firsthand experience. He'd been there once on a stupid dare, and had suffered nightmares ever since.

Last year, Tom had joined up with a few older kids from his neighborhood, who'd formed a club called the Adventurers. The leader had been a tough eleven-year-old with slicked-back blond hair by the name of Boots. His real name was Lawrence, but pity the kid foolish enough to call him that. He was Central Public School's toughest kid, and he enjoyed his "bully" label to the fullest. He was big for his age, loved to start fights, and the boys in the Adventurers listened to him more than to their their parents or teachers.

Anyone wanting to join their club had to perform a dare, chosen by Boots. These dares usually involved shoplifting or drinking alcohol or some other stupid thing that showed your worth to the members. Tom had been asked to spend one hour inside the Harrison farmhouse all by himself. Most kids were terrified of the place, but spending an hour inside the old house didn't bother Tom in the least. He wasn't a coward like Pete, and didn't have the imagination of David, so he wasn't scared of ghosts.

He'd pretended to be scared as Boots and the boys in the club crowded around him and reminded him of what had supposedly happened there. If he seemed scared going into the house, he would look braver and stronger once it was over and he hadn't chickened out.

Once inside the house, which he'd entered through a broken window, Tom felt much better. He could still hear the guys in the club out front on the road making what they thought were scary noises. "Idiots," muttered Tom under his breath as he checked his watch that he had synchronized with one of the member's outside.

"One hour now, and not one second less or you're not in the club," Boots had warned with a big grin on his face.

"I'll give you an hour," Tom said to himself. "In fact, just to show them I'm not scared, I think I'll stay an extra fifteen minutes."

With his bravado fully pumped up, he decided he might as well look around since he had nothing better to do. In twenty minutes Tom Baker had accomplished two things. He'd completely searched the house and found out that he'd been right all along, there was nothing there. He had also hurt his left leg rather badly. He'd been searching the upstairs bedrooms when, staring at a ceiling strewn with cobwebs, he stepped on a dusty toy train that had been left on the floor.

If there was anything in this world that truly scared Tom, it was spiders. He despised them. As a small child he'd awakened to find his brother Roger's pet tarantula trying to crawl into his mouth, Roger above him, laughing his guts out. The trauma of that event had stayed with him. He knew the Harrison house had been vacant for many years and had expected to find spiderwebs here and there, but he hadn't anticipated anything like this. The upstairs of the house was swathed in webs.

The one thing Tom couldn't find anywhere were the spiders. Not that this was a particularly unpleasant thing. In fact, it was a blessing. If those webs had been filled with furry crawling nightmares, Tom would have probably hightailed it out of the house faster than if he'd come face-to-face with Jacob Harrison himself.

As he was staring up at one particularly nasty web, he'd stepped on the toy train, flying ass-over-teakettle onto his back, wrenching his knee in the process. He had slightly twisted his left ankle too, and the scream he let out greatly improved the mood of the boys outside who were beginning to get bored.

Hobbling downstairs on a sore ankle and puffed-up knee wasn't exactly his idea of a great afternoon, but he was still determined not to give in. He decided to pick a relatively clean room and sit down to read the paperback Western he'd brought with him. In a few minutes he was riding along the range with Billy the Kid and was so engrossed in his book he almost forgot where he was.

Then the scratching noises started.

Long, slow scratching noises, like sharp claws dragging across a hardwood floor, quickly threw Tom off his imaginary horse and back to reality.

"What the heck . . . ?" he began, but stopped. The house was again silent. "Get a hold of yourself, Tommy boy. You're starting to spook yourself like you promised you wouldn't. It's probably just a mouse."

He began reading some more, but the scratching started again. This time it was accompanied by a series of long, slow growls. No, more like deep breaths; like someone gasping for air. Tom bolted upright, causing needles of pain to shoot down his injured left leg. He could no longer ignore the noise and pretend it was a mouse. It sounded like a person, and the noise had come from the basement.

He hadn't checked the basement on his first search because the staircase leading into the cellar had crumbled away and was lying in a heap at the bottom.

An old tramp might have snuck into the deserted farmhouse during the storm a few nights ago. Probably stumbled in blind drunk and tumbled into the basement without noticing the staircase was gone. Tom knew he should help, but what if the person was dangerous?

Quitting and going home was very much on Tom's mind and he went as far as turning toward the window he'd entered. Just before deciding to exit, the noise came again, only this time the moan seemed weaker and more pain filled.

Who the heck is down there?

Tom had to hang from the second step down, the last one still intact, and then drop the rest of the way to the basement floor. The second his feet connected with the hard concrete floor, firecrackers of pain shot off in his left leg. The impact was excruciating. It was as if his knee had exploded inside and only his bruised and swelling skin was keeping it from leaking down his leg.

The scratching and the moaning cracked through Tom's wall of pain and he dragged himself into a sitting position to look around. There was no sign of whoever had been making all the noise. A deadly silence now filled the lower floor. For the life of him, he couldn't decide why. They obviously knew he was here. Even someone almost stone deaf would have been able to hear his scream when he'd hit the concrete. Maybe whoever was down here had passed out from their own injuries.

The only place where a body (which wasn't how Tom wanted to refer to it, since it brought up another idea as to why the moans had stopped), could be out of view was behind the furnace. It stood in the farthest corner, and in the shadows cast by the fading light, he could just make out a large shape and some movement.

"Well, at least the old bugger isn't dead yet," Tom said.

He attempted to stand up and go over to the furnace but only made it to his knees before falling back onto his rear end. He'd hurt himself worse than he wanted to admit and suddenly the idea of climbing up and out of the basement didn't seem that easy. With the way his leg was feeling, standing up was going to be hard enough.

A sudden movement distracted Tom from his thoughts. He spun around, thinking the person behind the furnace was trying to catch his attention. Well, his attention was certainly caught, because sitting beside the furnace was a spider—a large spider.

Its body was about the size of a man's fist and was covered in thick black-and-red bristles. Tom froze. It was as if quick-setting concrete now ran in his veins instead of blood. A scream rose in Tom's throat, but before it could squeeze its way out a leg stepped out from behind the furnace and crushed the spider into a mushy, convulsing pulp. Tom watched the spider's death spasms with glee and was about to thank the person behind the furnace when he noticed something odd. The leg grinding the dead spider into the ground didn't appear to have any pants on. The closer Tom looked, the more it appeared to be covered in thick black hair.

Black hair, like that of a . . . *SPIDER*.

The scratching noises started up again and this time Tom heard them for what they really were. They were the scratching and clawing of a colossal-sized spider trying to free itself from behind the furnace where it was tightly wedged. The human-sounding moans he'd heard upstairs turned to high-pitched laughter as he struggled to get to his feet. Tom knew he had to get out of this basement, and get out fast.

"You shouldn't have come here, Tommy," said the spider, having managed to scratch and claw half its bloated body clear of the furnace. "You've been a bad boy, Tommy, and you know what happens to bad boys, don't you?"

The hideous spider ground its hairy foot into the mushy remains of the dead spider again, just to emphasize its point. Tom got the message loud and clear and frantically began climbing out of the basement, oblivious to the volcano of white-hot pain that had once been his knee.

There were still small blocks of wood attached to the wall where the stairs had been anchored to reinforce each step. Now they functioned as his only means of escape. The king spider (a name his frightened mind had for some reason latched onto) would be on top of him before then. Such a thought brought all his early childhood fears racing back, spurring him onward.

He reached the wall and began to climb the wooden blocks as fast as his injured leg would allow. The doorway to the kitchen and freedom was only a few feet away but it seemed so far out of reach. Behind him, the scratching had stopped, and except for his own exertions, the basement was silent.

The joy of freedom was dashed in an instant as his injured left knee gave out on the last block. The damaged knee couldn't support his weight any longer and he crashed back to the basement floor in a fall that seemed to last forever.

It only took a moment for Tom to shake off the pain and spin around to see what had happened to the spider. It was sitting, silently staring at him from three feet away. The king spider was every arachnophobe's worst nightmare come true. Long black legs attached to a bloated red body that measured about a foot and a half across. Its spittle-drooling mandibles worked endlessly, revealing a sticky pink tunnel outlined with razor-sharp fangs. Everything about the spider's appearance was ghastly, but its eyes terrified Tom more than anything else. Six large rotating orbs the size of golf balls fixed unwaveringly upon Tom's own terror-stricken eyes. They all glowed red—the shade of freshly spilled blood. Each eye cast an ominous crimson beacon over the basement, which was quickly losing whatever meager sunlight it had been getting.

"You almost made it out, Tommy, my boy." Seeing the look of despair on Tom's face, the monster said mockingly, "What's the matter? Scared of a little spider? Well, you're not gonna like this very much, then."

The grotesque spider opened its mouth wide and Tom was sure it meant to bite him. It wasn't until he saw the first of the small spiders scampering out of the large spider's glistening throat that he realized he was wrong. One spider dropped wetly to the floor and soon others followed until hundreds of creepy crawlers were spilling out of the king's gullet in a stream of gooey blackness. All the little spiders' eyes glowed red, and Tom realized, just before he ran for the wall again, that these must be all the spiders from the rest of the house. No wonder he hadn't seen any upstairs—they had all been swallowed and stored away inside the rotting stomach of the king spider.

With an army of spiders on his tail, Tom tried to scale the wall again. Thousands of red eyes locked on him as the tiny horde clawed over each other in pursuit. His terror gave him the strength to overcome the pain in his leg. He leaped at the wall like an Olympic pole-vaulter and clung to a pair of blocks halfway up. The army of spiders wasn't far behind; they too hit the wall and started to climb. One horrifying glance was enough to propel Tom up and out of the cellar, and soon he was sprawled on the kitchen floor. Relief spread through him, but he wasn't safe yet. The spiders had also gained the kitchen; a swiftly moving river of black and red poured out of the basement doorway toward him.

That was the last thing Tom saw before he dove out

the same window he'd entered just over forty minutes earlier.

"You come back and see us anytime you want, Tommy, my boy . . . anytime at all," was all he heard as he raced around the side of the house and right past the members of the Adventurers club.

Boots and the gang had laughed themselves sick at how scared Tom had looked, unanimously voting not to let him into their club.

Somebody else had been laughing that day. Somebody with an active part in what had happened. Unknowingly, Tom had awoken the creature at the bottom of the well by simply stepping foot inside the house. Twenty minutes of wandering around in there and he'd certainly gained the creature's interest.

It had sent its underdeveloped mind's eye up into the house and had been furious to find out it was just some dumb kid on a dare. The creature needed rest as it was still in the process of transforming. It still basically resembled the human being it had once been. There was no way the creature could have gotten back to sleep with Tom in the house. The boy had to be forced into leaving.

The creature hadn't been completely transformed, but it could make its presence felt—it could play with little Tom's mind and make him see and hear things that weren't really there. With a big smile that had caused the last of its human upper lip to fall off, the creature had put its plan into action. It had learned Tom's worst fear by probing his subconscious and from there it had been easy to make Tom see the giant spider.

It will be a long time before that boy comes snooping around my house again, I'll bet, the creature had sneered. It had been pleased and contented with its developing powers. One more quick scan of the house to make sure it was empty and the creature had settled back down to sleep, and to change.

Back in his living room, Pete was trying to rouse Tom from the semitrance he'd fallen into.

"Hey, Tom . . . wake up, bonehead. You're going to make us late."

Startled, Tom snapped back to reality, looking glassy-eyed and perplexed.

"I thought I'd lost you there for a moment," said Pete with a grin. "Come on, let's get going, okay? We're supposed to meet up with David, remember?"

"Sure . . . I'm ready," replied Tom, unsteadily rising to his feet, still thinking about his last trip to the basement of the Harrison farmhouse.

He had later learned Boots and his buddies had slipped a little whiskey into a coke he'd drank before going into the house. He'd reassured himself it had been the alcohol that had caused him to hallucinate that day and see the spiders. Reassured as he was, he followed Pete very slowly and reluctantly out the door.

David Winter ran along Cedar Street with a wide grin on his face. All bad thoughts about today had vanished after his father told him it was time to crucify Rodney. Every year around this time, for as long as he could remember, he and his father had performed the crucifixion, and every year he enjoyed it more.

The act of crucifying Rodney wasn't as sinister as it sounded. Rodney was just a big stuffed scarecrow his dad had put together to scare away the birds from their tomatoes. Actually, the scarecrow didn't do much of anything since there weren't many crows in the area. There were lots of seagulls that flew in from the lake, but they were more interested in heading toward the Grand Island Bar-B-Q and getting French fries from the tourists than they were in the Winters' tomato fields. The only reason his father went to the trouble of putting up the scarecrow was that David enjoyed it so much. With his wild imagination, David would talk to the scarecrow all summer, and considered it his best friend.

The term "crucifying" had come from a botched attempt to intertwine religion with something David enjoyed—Steven had hoped that David might take more interest if he could associate religion with things he liked. The lesson never really worked out, but the "crucifixion" label had stuck.

"This gives me the perfect excuse to go home early today," David said, as he turned onto Logan Road.

His good mood diminished and his fears began to rise as he looked over at the Harrison farmhouse, until he noticed Tom and Pete laughing and running his way. Tom was covered in mud. His blue denim cutoff shorts were now black and most of his faded yellow T-shirt was the same.

"What happened to you, Tom?" asked David.

Pete was bent over, holding his stomach from laughing so much. "The goof was in a daze on the way over here. We get to the corner and he walks straight into the ditch. I made the turn and he didn't. It was the funniest thing I ever saw."

"Ha, ha, ha," mocked Tom, who was grinning in spite of himself. "I suppose you've never done anything stupid before?"

Pete gave him the "who, me?" shrug as they laughed and noticed Johnny bolting out of his front door to join them.

Seeing the look on Johnny's face as he skidded to a halt, Tom said, "Before you ask . . . I fell in the ditch. I had other things on my mind and I wasn't paying attention."

Pete piped in with one of his usual quick comebacks. "Yeah, Johnny, Tom was thinking about Becki Sullivan again, and he sort of lost his brain for a while."

Tom, who knew it was common knowledge he had a crush on Becki, and knew better than to try out-joking Pete, simply turned beet red and began chasing him around Johnny's lawn.

The wrestling match ended with Tom pinning Pete to the ground and making him take his last comment back. Pete did, and Tom rolled off him onto the grass. All four boys lay down to catch their breath. The common act of scrapping around in the grass had helped everyone relax and dispel most of David, Tom, and Pete's fear. This wasn't Jacob Harrison's farm—it was Johnny's. Nothing bad was going to happen to them here. This unspoken assurance seemed to pass between them and together they laughed away the rest of their doubts and fears.

Pete eventually asked, "Well, what are we going to do? I'm not gonna have to rough you guys up all day, am I?"

"You better hope not," said Tom.

Pete considered restarting the fight, but realized Tom was probably right. Instead, he turned to Johnny and said, "It's your house, kiddo; you make the call."

All eyes turned toward Johnny and for the first time he realized he had no idea what they would do. He had so much else on his mind this morning, it never occurred to him to make plans. An idea surfaced in his head that seemed to come from nowhere. One second his mind was completely blank—the next, he knew exactly what to do. It was very strange.

"I've got a great idea. There's something I want to show you, and I think you're really gonna like it."

He turned and led the small troop around the side

of the weather-beaten farmhouse and past the large willow tree that grew outside his bedroom window. Without really knowing why, Johnny led his new friends into the backyard. He was marching them straight out toward the deep, murky well.

COVENANT

WINNER OF THE BRAM STOKER AWARD!

The cliffs of Terrel's Peak are a deadly place, an evil place where terrible things happen. Like a series of mysterious teen suicides over the years, all on the same date. Or other deaths, usually reported as accidents. Could it be a coincidence? Or is there more to it?

Reporter Joe Kieran is determined to find the truth.

Kieran will uncover rumors and whispered legends—including the legend of the evil entity that lives and waits in the caves below Terrel's Peak....

JOHN EVERSON

ISBN 13: 978-0-8439-6018-1

GET FREE BOOKS!

You can have the best fiction delivered to your door for less than what you'd pay in a bookstore or online. Sign up for one of our book clubs today, and we'll send you *FREE* BOOKS* just for trying it out...**with no obligation to buy, ever!**

As a member of the Leisure Horror Book Club, you'll receive books by authors such as

RICHARD LAYMON, JACK KETCHUM, JOHN SKIPP, BRIAN KEENE and many more.

As a book club member you also receive the following special benefits:
- **30% off all orders!**
- **Exclusive access to special discounts!**
- **Convenient home delivery and 10 days to return any books you don't want to keep.**

Visit www.dorchesterpub.com or call 1-800-481-9191

There is no minimum number of books to buy, and you may cancel membership at any time.
*Please include $2.00 for shipping and handling.